WELL, I

The Yarns

Constable Bobby Wing
of
Skedaddle Gore, Maine

SANFORD EMERSON

Well, Hell
© 2022 by Sanford Emerson

Table of Contents

Dedication:
For Kathy and Kaitlyn
(Turnabout is fair play!)
Thanks for everything

Explanation

Let me just say right up front that I don't personally believe that *everything* in this book actually happened. I'm pretty sure that some of it *might* have happened, but I can't guarantee more than that. Well, actually, some of it *did* make the local papers along the way, so I guess those things probably did.

I'm not really the author of these stories, you see, so they're not my fault—well, *mostly* not my fault. I'm only doing this as a favor for a friend, but he said I could put my name on it because I did all the heavy lifting. These are *Bobby Wing's* yarns, and I just wrote them out because he asked me to. Each of them was recorded at a different time and sometimes in different places, so it will probably appear that Bobby repeats himself, which he often actually does—especially if he has somebody new in the audience. I *have* edited some of the language, tightened up the grammar as best I could and rearranged a few things to try to have the whole thing make a little more sense, if that's possible.

You may have seen parts of some of these stories in mystery anthologies published by Level Best Books in 2015 (*Red Dawn*), 2016 (*Windward*) and 2017 (*Busted*). Bobby got such a kick out of seeing them in print that he thought I should put a bunch of them into a book. With his permission I have also renamed some characters and locations because I guess a few people in the area were offended when they read the first versions. I apologize for that.

About the title: *"Well, Hell . . ."* is an expression Bobby uses about as often as a milk cow farts. I actually kind of like it because, depending on his tone of voice, rate of speech and emphasis on one word or the other, it can evoke a whole gamut of emotions. I'm sorry that I'm not a good enough writer to get his exact meaning across every time. You'll just have to imagine how it would sound in the moment, taking into account Bobby's probable state of mind and

3

sobriety at the time. He and I both hope that you enjoy this book. If you've got a problem with anything, though, talk to him.

Finally, please keep that in mind that *you are about to read a friggin' work of fiction!* Well, mostly . . .

Sanford Emerson
    Wilton, Maine

One: Deathtrap

I knew that I'd fallen and couldn't move. Oddly, that struck me as a little bit funny. It also struck me that I had to be wicked stove up inside to boot, which wasn't funny at all. I was pretty oblivious to anything else. I'd forgotten who or where I was and how I'd gotten there. The only two things I did know were that I had a splitting headache and I was looking—at very close range—into the eyes of someone who had obviously been dead for a *very* long time.

Mister man, I'm not ashamed to say that at that point I fainted dead away.

Well, Hell . . .

#

Fly Fleance, our dump guy up here in Skedaddle Gore, Maine, has always struck me as looking—and smelling—like somebody beat him to death a month or so ago and buried the body in a shallow grave, then had a change of heart after a couple of weeks and dug him up, pumped him full of old used motor oil, rubbed him all over with bearing grease to hold the loose bits together and permanently propped him up against his rusty old '53 Dodge Power Wagon next to the entrance to what is now called our "Transfer Station."

Back in the day most Maine towns had a dump, which was usually just a handy hillside where the townspeople could dispose of their trash. It was best if it was situated downwind of town and not too close in so that the smell wasn't too bad in the summer, but not so far out that folks couldn't get to it easy enough. Most Maine country boys—and a fair number of their sisters—learned to shoot at their local dump to help control the rats, which I personally think resulted in a bumper crop of wicked nasty sharpshooters, a handy asset over the course of American military history. Sometimes

towns used to spread a little dirt on the trash pile if the smell got
too bad, and once in a while the whole place would catch fire and
burn off—sometimes even accidentally—but that usually stunk up
the neighborhood pretty bad, so the practice was generally frowned
upon.

I'm told that up here in Skedaddle Gore, a nice little town of
about three hundred souls in the highlands of western Maine, the
Board of Assessors had a dilemma some thirty years ago—well
before my time—when the State of Maine was forced by the
bureaucracy in Washington, D.C., to do away with all the little town
dumps and, as they were known in the moneyed southern part of
the state, the "sanitary landfills"—a jeezley stupid hoity-toity name
for something if ever I heard one. Despite some consternation the
state was ordered to make everybody start sending all their trash
and garbage to a couple of big boggy fields somewhere way north of
Augusta, which were inconvenient and expensive to access but some
friggin' profitable for those former rumrunners who'd bought up all
the wild northern woodlands after the repeal of the Volstead Act and
then greased a few palms to get their relatives and cronies elected to
high enough office so they could tell us ordinary folks dumb ways to
do what used to be simple stuff.

For years the Gore's residents who didn't just burn their trash in
a barrel in the back yard took it over to the Fleance place out on the
Midden Road. The story goes that when the growing population of
farmers, woodsmen and Civil War draft dodgers decided to become
semi-organized, Fly's great-great-grandparents, who were frugal
Yankee types, started taking in their neighbor's trash. They reused
what they could and sold what they could of what was left.
Everything else they dumped in a ravine in their backyard. Over the
years that ravine got filled up and became a fair-sized hill.

After much comment and debate over the stupidity of the
government order—which is still pretty normal here to this

day—the Board of Assessors signed an agreement with Fly's mother to buy her land for an *official* town dump, which is what it was anyway. As part of the deal, they gave her son Fly, who was always a willing fellow, if quiet and a bit slow, a job for life watching over it. That way they solved two problems at once, which appealed to everyone's sense of practicality. The Gore wouldn't have to foreclose on a pile of trash for unpaid back taxes and the Fleances would keep their home, which also kept them out in the back country where they could stink up the place without offending the sensibilities of all the "sports" from away who came up for the hunting, fishing and "rusticating." As a bonus, Fly could always have his pick of the best junk, which is a surprisingly lucrative profession, as it turns out. But I'm getting ahead of myself.

Early on, out of sheer curiosity, I asked Fly what his real name was. He looked at me like he thought I was a dite numb and said, "Fly." After that I changed tack and asked why his parents had given him such a strange name, as I could imagine it had gotten him teased a lot in school. He said he couldn't recall getting teased a lot as he hadn't gone to school all that much. He did tell me that he *had* asked his mother once before she died why she'd named him like she had. He said that she told him that she couldn't remember and that he'd have to ask his father. That would have been difficult to accomplish, Fly advised me, since his father had up and disappeared suddenly about twenty years before. He took the ratty looking old pipe out of his mouth and showed it to me. "Pa used to smoke this," he said. "It's all he left us." He stuck it back between his teeth and sucked hard, producing an oily smelling cloud that would've gagged a maggot.

Now, the reason I led you through all of that history just now was to give you the background that leads up to the main part of my story, which will explain how I got to that point I was describing back at the very beginning. My name is Bobby Wing. Unlike most of my neighbors I wasn't born here—or at least in the Franklin

Memorial Hospital in Farmington, which is the seat of Franklin County. I *am* a Maine boy, though, born up in Bangor to a fine woman who, against her parents' wishes, took up with a Coast Guard sailor during her second year in nursing school. I was born nearly six months after they got married. By that time my grandparents had become pretty reconciled to the inevitable, although until the day he died my Grampy Mac always called me his "wee bastard whelp." I didn't mind because I wasn't real sure what he meant until Stevie Collins explained it all to me in the fourth grade. Mom would always wind up throwing something at Grampy whenever he said that. He'd duck and laugh and give me a quarter. I still miss him sometimes, especially around the holidays.

Anyway, my dad went career after he got married and did a couple of tours at the Coast Guard station in Rockland, which is smack in the middle of the Maine coast halfway between New Hampshire and New Brunswick, Canada. He eventually retired there and got a job as a guard just down the road at the Maine State Prison in Thomaston. He and Mom bought a place in town and Mom became the nurse at Georges Valley High School, before they closed it—not my fault, by the way.

I finished up high school there at Georges Valley and enlisted in the Coasties as soon as I could. Mom was against it, but Dad pointed out that he'd made a fair living over the years and, aside from a couple of overseas billets, he'd spent most of his career pretty close to his family. She finally threw up her hands and gave in. I signed up as a Machinery Technician initially. I'd always been handy, and I really liked working on car engines with my dad and in shop class, so it seemed a good fit. I switched over to being a Gunner's Mate after my first tour because they had a shortage of armorers, and at the time that rate offered a wicked generous reenlistment bonus, which looked some good to a newly married twenty-something. A lot of what I did in the Coasties was maritime law enforcement—think

SWAT on a speedboat. I even personally sank a couple of smuggler's cigarette boats. It's awesome what a Ma Deuce with armor piercing ammo can do to a boat's engine block!

After I retired from all that I moved into an old hunting camp here on the side of Skedaddle Mountain that was left to me by Master Chief Culinary Specialist Phillip "Filthy" Phillips, who was the best damn Culinary Specialist—us old timers called them "mess cooks"—in the whole friggin' Coast Guard. The man was so good that he got himself assigned as the head chef at the Coast Guard Academy in New London, Connecticut, and cooked for two U. S. Presidents. He even prepared High Tea (pinkies up!) once for the Queen of England. He did all this, believe it or not, while permanently three sheets to the wind. The two of us met at the Chief's Club in the Washington Navy Yard and quickly went from bar buddies to true brothers in arms. Eventually the booze caught up with Phil, though, and a couple of years before I retired he died of cirrhosis in a nursing home outside of Boston. I used to visit whenever I could. He could tell you some stories, mister man.

Sorry, I'm getting just a dite off track here. You might have noticed that I *do* tend to do that. I meant to say that while I was remodeling and improving Phil's old cabin the year after I retired, I took pains to go out and meet as many of the locals as I could. It didn't hurt that I wasn't really "from away" and I knew at least a little of the local language and "culcha," as we say. That's kind of important to folks around here. Besides, I like talking to people. I was a widower by that time and my mostly grown-up daughter was away trying to repeat her Granny's mistake with a golf pro from Florida, so I found myself at loose ends.

I joined the Skedaddle Gore Volunteer Fire Department not long after I moved into town. I'd met the chief, Marti Wallace, when she delivered the mail to my rural route box out by the road. We got to talking—because she does that a lot too, as I found out. She told me the department was just getting organized and she was looking for recruits. There was an old but still serviceable American LaFrance engine that Rangeley, the next town over, was willing to give us the loan of. It was going to be housed at our town garage, which is sort of diagonally across the road from my place. I figured out later that Marti must of seen all the tool and car parts catalogs I was getting in the mail and reasoned that I was probably a mechanic. I rode over to Rangeley with her and looked over Engine Five and fell ass over teakettle in love. She was the most beautiful junk of chromed-up, gold-leafed old fashioned heavy gauge steel I'd ever seen. I was hooked. I usually drive her as her tranny isn't synchromesh and most of the young kids on the department never learned to double-clutch, much less handle a stick shift. It's because of that, I think, that I got elected lieutenant by the membership and put in charge of the old lady's care and feeding, which suits me fine.

The fact that I liked helping out my neighbors—read that as "works cheap"—and had some law enforcement experience in the Coasties probably influenced the three-person Board of Assessors of Skedaddle Gore to come over after a bit to ask me if I'd be willing to accept the part-time offices of Constable, Fence Viewer, Deputy Fire Warden and Animal Control Officer. It seems that I'd let some of my history slip out one day when I was chatting up the checkout clerk at the IGA in Rangeley. She told her boss, who told a buddy who happened to be the Gore town clerk's husband. Then he told her about me and, lo and behold, it turned out our Board of Assessors needed someone to post legal notices, serve tax lien papers and generally be "the guy in town who does that sort of stuff."

The job only pays minimum wage and mileage but it isn't real taxing timewise and the extra income helps covers my tab down at Sally's Motel and Bar and Live Bait and Convenience Store. Jake Beaverstool, the First Assessor, explained that they just needed somebody in town to handle the "little things" that come up from time to time. You know, the minor annoyances that aren't important enough to call the sheriff or the state police, who usually arrive with a jeezley big commotion and get folks all worked up. The job sounded like it might be fun—at the time—so I said yes after thinking it over for all of about two minutes.

At that point the members of the board unlawfully assembled right there in my dooryard and illegally voted. You see, their meetings are supposed to be public, with agendas and all the paperwork and such that goes with that, but . . . sometimes . . . well . . . Anyway, they were quite clear—after I took the oath of office from Aggie Heikkenen, the Town Clerk, who'd illegally tagged along, of course—that they didn't want me carrying a badge or a gun and "for God's sake, no arresting people." That wouldn't be legal unless I went to the police academy in Vassalboro, which would be time consuming and expensive for the town. Luckily I haven't needed to arrest—or shoot—anybody so far, so that part's been working out.

They somehow neglected to tell me that all of my newly sworn-to offices had been vacant for years, even though they were required by the town's charter. I found that out—and the reason why—just ten minutes after the swearing-in ceremony when they gave me my first job to do. A "commission" they called it.

It seems the board had been getting complaints from some of the new people, the bunch from away who'd bought vacation condos and time shares in the past few years up at "The Mountain"—which is what we locals call the Skedaddle Ridge Ski Resort. These folks weren't aware of all the local traditions and ways of doing things. A couple of them were actually expensive lawyers from down in Massachusetts who thought it was their civic duty, even though they live here for only a few weeks out of the year, to point out that the town-owned house occupied by Fly Fleance had become dilapidated and—to them at least—constituted a "health and safety hazard to the general public." After some discussion, the board members reasoned that, since the flatlanders *were* taxpayers and, as such, are entitled to have their opinions—however misguided—taken seriously, an investigation into their concerns should be undertaken to cover the Gore's backside. Now that they had a sucker on the payroll, they could get *me* to do it cheap.

#

I arrived at the transfer station one early June morning a few days later before it was actually open for the day, although there's no gate and anyone can pretty much get in to use the trash and recycling dumpsters any time they want. Fly gets a little put out, though, if you interrupt his routine, which mainly consists of standing out by his truck, smoking that stinking old pipe of his and staring into your trunk or pickup bed to see if there's anything worth picking out later after you've gone.

The Fleance house in question hadn't changed at all since I'd come to live in town, but I'm told it used to have paint on it that Old Man Fleance applied, sort of haphazardly, a few years before he disappeared. It'd pretty much all worn off and the siding, what there was left of it, had weathered to that off-grey color that those house flipper people on the satellite TV are so friggin' fond of. I thought it actually *did* go pretty well with the ambiance of the rusty old logging chains that ran from a couple of big honkin' glacial boulders in the dooryard up to the eves of the west side of the house. They'd held it more or less upright for years against the winter gales that can really rip off The Mountain, let me tell you.

I went around to the door in the ell, which is a long shed off the kitchen that serves as a way to get from the kitchen to the two-holer in the barn when the dooryard is full of snow. It used to be a common feature of homes in New England before the advent of indoor plumbing, the concept of which hadn't reached Fly's place yet. Most people usually call at the side door first. The front door, facing the road, is traditionally used only twice in your lifetime—to carry your blushing bride in, if you can lift her, and your coffin out.

It was the only time I'd ever been inside the place. Fly was sitting on his bed, which was situated next to an old Princess Atlantic wood cook stove in the kitchen. He was drinking what I assumed was coffee and eating what appeared to be a mess of scrambled eggs and stuff out of an ancient cast iron spider that looked like it had never seen a scrubbing. At least he was dressed. Being as it was early summer it was some hot in there with that stove going, let me tell you.

I made my way to the kitchen table, which required navigating around a couple of boxes of what appeared to be old junks of electrical wire. The room was full of stacks and stacks of cardboard boxes, wooden crates and miscellaneous stuff which reached all the way to the ceiling. The only open space I could see was occupied by Fly's bed and the stove. There *were* what looked like two narrow paths, one to the hand pump slate sink by the back wall, which was piled with dishes that I suspected had never actually been washed, and another that headed out in the general direction of the front of the house. There was one of those old-fashioned porcelain steel roasting pans sitting on what I guessed was once the kitchen table. It was full of motor oil. In it was resting what I recognized as the disassembled pistons and crank from an old Harley Davidson knucklehead motorcycle engine. There was a goodly layer of dust on the top of the oil. There was no chair anywhere in sight to sit on, so I stood.

I explained to Fly what the Board of Assessors had asked me to do and asked if he minded me looking around. He shrugged and said "OK," after which he went back to his breakfast. He didn't get up or offer to escort me, so I figured I was on my own. I had to turn sideways to sneak between the piles of junk into the next room, which would probably be called the living room in most places.

The place smelled a lot like Fly himself—musty with a distinct underlying touch of something really rotten. I quickly decided to breathe through my mouth. It helped. Over to the side there was what looked to be a doorway into what was probably the front parlor at one time. I could just see the top jam over the stacks of boxes, but there was no path going that way. I continued toward the front hall, where I found the stairway to the second story. Covered in what appeared to be years' worth of accumulated cobwebs and dust, it looked passable enough if I picked my way through and was careful. Thankfully I'd thought to bring a flashlight, as the hallway was dark as the inside of a pocket and there was no light switch—or fixture, for that matter. Just as I reached the top of the stairs and stepped onto the landing, I realized that here was no power at all in the house.

#

I woke up in Room 319 of Franklin Memorial Hospital. You might guess that I was confused and pretty woozy, what with the bed spinning like it was. My head felt a little better now than the last time I remembered being awake, but my nose itched something wicked. I whacked myself in the forehead trying to scratch it because they had some sort of a board strapped to my left arm where there was a bunch of wires and tubes attached to some needles stuck in the back of my hand. For some unknown reason I couldn't move my right arm at all. I felt kind of silly when an alarm that sounded like a dump truck backing up went off and a young woman dressed in what appeared to be camouflage pajamas came bookin' it into the room. She was pretty, but wicked annoyed.

Well, Hell.

#

A week or so after that Marti Wallace came down and picked me up and took me home in her Jeep, along with a rented set of crutches—what with the casts on my left leg and right arm and all. The hospital folks gave me a follow-up appointment to go see a specialist and start physical therapy at the Togus V.A. Hospital near Augusta, along with a prescription for Tylenol mixed with something I couldn't pronounce. The first time I took a couple of those horse pills they knocked me for a loop, which put me off. Shipyard Summer Ale works just as well and is cheaper, too. Take my word for it.

Marti filled me in on the drive. She told me that Fly had heard the noise of me falling through the ceiling of his mother's old bedroom, but he wasn't too concerned until I'd been gone for an hour or so. He told Snort Benson, who'd brought his trash out later on that morning, that I'd suddenly vanished off the face of the earth. Snort, who can be a bit on the excitable side, called 911 on his cell phone and Franklin County dispatch center toned out the Fire Department and Northstar Ambulance and even sent over the high sheriff of Franklin County himself, who had been headed up to go politicking at a Rotary lunch at the Red Onion restaurant in Rangeley anyway.

The Fire Department had to tear a big hole in one of the front walls to get to me once they figured out where I was. There was a flurry of consternation when they realized that I had landed on top of the remains of Fly's father, who'd apparently never actually left home. He'd been lying there under his late wife's bed for all this time with a hunting knife buried to the hilt in his mummified chest. Marti told me that Fly was surprised to see him again. Interestingly enough, there was over two hundred and fifty thousand dollars' worth of 1970's and earlier U.S. and Canadian currency scattered all over the room. Imagine that. It seems that most of the late Mother Fleance's cloth mattress had rotted away, and my landing had sent the hidden family fortune flying every which way.

Well, Hell!

After the dust had literally settled, the Gore's insurance company decided that the damage that had been done during my rescue would be more expensive to repair than the place was actually worth. Accordingly, the Board of Assessors condemned the house and ordered its demolition, there being no objection at all from the Historical Society. Marti successfully proposed that the fire departments of several surrounding Franklin County communities could benefit from the training opportunity. So, after three weeks spent clearing out the detritus—during which time an additional fifty-seven thousand two hundred seventy-four dollars and ninety-five cents in cash and spare change strewed around the place was recovered as well as about eighty-five hundred dollars' worth of salable scrap—Engine Five (with Snort Benson at the controls, dammit!) and her sisters from the rest of Franklin County got a pisser workout and the citizenry got a gratifyingly showy demonstration of their tax dollars at work.

Nadine, the half-owner of Sally's Motel and Bar and Live Bait and Convenience Store, which is pretty much the social center of town and is where we hold our monthly fireman's meetings, arranged a sales promotion with the Shipyard Brewing Company down in Portland and did a land-office business rehydrating all the trainees—and a good portion of the spectators—after the fact. She was on cloud nine for a week.

The Probate Judge in Farmington eventually awarded Fly all the money found in the old family homestead. Honoring their deal with his mother, who was thought to be the probable perpetrator of her husband's long-ago demise—we trust in self-defense—the Board of Assessors moved a nice new manufactured home, which was paid for by the town's insurance company, onto the vacant lot once it was all cleaned up, with the stipulation that Fly couldn't use it for storage. It did take him a while to adjust to having electricity and modern plumbing, but eventually he even started to bathe on a semi-regular basis. One of the condo owners up on The Mountain was a retired financial advisor from New Yawk City who took Fly on as a client for free, at least in the beginning. Last summer he got his old Power Wagon truck professionally restored. He's some proud of her. She *is* slick.

I healed up with the help of my neighbors and the Veteran's Administration. Say what you will, but they treated me real well. Workman's Comp paid my other medical bills, after some protest. Woody Bernstein, the lawyer down to Farmington who handled the inheritance of my cabin, straightened them out some quick. For my investigating time the Board of Assessors eventually paid me twenty-seven dollars and fifty-four cents, less withholding, which wasn't too bad considering I was unconscious for most of it.

Two: Devious Doings

Frenchy Plourde always had a reputation as a wicked dink, so it was no real surprise that he had a nasty, pissed-off expression on what was left of his face that January morning when I found him frozen to the floor of his cabin. Most of his 300 or so neighbors up here in Skedaddle Gore, Maine, weren't too upset when they heard of his passing, as they'd all of them borne the brunt of his lewd, crude and rude behavior for years. The majority of those I talked to, though, thought it was just damn sad the way Frenchy's mangy, three-legged dog was found curled up next to his master's body. Before he too froze to death, poor starving Sumbitch had gnawed off his master's right ear.

#

If you remember, I told you back along that in a weak moment I sort of volunteered to be the Constable, Fence Viewer, Deputy Fire Warden and Animal Control Officer of Skedaddle Gore, which explains how I got involved in this whole mess to begin with. Anyway, little Shorty Devereaux came banging on my door on one of the coldest mornings since "eighteen-hundred-and-froze-to-death." Shorty's job is to plow and sand the twenty-three-and-a-half miles of public roads that make up the Gore. The "good citizens assembled" on the town budget committee have repeatedly declined to put a radio in his truck and he's given up trying to figure out how a cell phone works, so when he noticed that Frenchy hadn't dug out his outhouse for a week, which is lazy, even for Frenchy, he drove over to my place.

"You're the constable," Shorty said. "You should go check on him,"

"Why don't you call the sheriff, or the staties?"

I looked past him at the thermometer on the old maple tree in my yard. It was below zero, but the bottom end of the scale was obscured by an icicle, so I couldn't see it.

"They won't think it's important enough," Shorty said. "Besides, they won't come up here anymore since Frenchie shot at them two years ago. They're all scared of him!" He whined faintly. "I'm not going in there, either. The last time I hit his mailbox with the plow he told me he'd shove a grenade up my ass the next time I came near his property."

"He'll probably do the same to me. Why should I go?"

I was feeling a little sick to my stomach and whiny myself.

"Because that's what we pay you for." Shorty snorted.

Why did I know he was going to say that?

Well, Hell.

#

The deputy sheriff they sent up looked to be about as old as my daughter. Even so she didn't flinch when the wind banged the door shut behind us as we stepped into Frenchy's cabin. I'd held the door and politely let her go in first. She'd been nice enough to me so far, considering I was technically a civilian with no real police standing, despite my glorious title.

Most of Frenchy was still sitting upright on the floor in front of the open wood stove. His head was cranked sharply to the left as if he was looking at the front door. He had a filthy rag wrapped around his left hand and an unlit lucifer match in his right. The stove itself held a full charge of kindling and birch wood blocks, probably from Fletcher's Mill over to New Vineyard. The cold half-light from the two filthy windows did a real poor job of illuminating the powerless cabin, so we both pointed our flashlight beams into all the corners. She was probably looking for clues, I thought. I was watching out for porcupines.

The place was almost empty, just a few open shelves with some canned goods scattered around, a dumped-over tin of loose tobacco and couple of old plastic five-gallon water buckets that were also frozen to the floor in the near corner. A half-full bag of the same birch blocks sat by the door and a few bundles of familiar-looking dried "vegetation" were draped off the rafters. There was also a faintly familiar smell that I imagined would be a lot stronger once the place warmed up.

"Just you been in here?" she asked, all businesslike.

"Think so. The path to the road was just one boot wide, but there was a dusting of snow over it. Didn't see any tracks."

"Snowed last night up here too, right?"

"Enough to justify a couple of hours overtime for Shorty Devereaux," I said.

"Did you touch or move anything?" she asked, pulling a pen out of the breast pocket of her tan parka and a thin spiral notebook out of her hip pocket.

Her name tag read "Wilma Brackett" and she was a "slick arm," having no service hash marks sewed to her left sleeve.

"No, I didn't have to," I told her. "It was pretty obvious after a second or two that there wasn't anything I was going to be able to do for him."

She nodded, peering at the body. "So, this is the famous Frenchy Plourde. Did you know him?"

"Frenchy?" I asked. "Everybody knew him. Didn't you?"

"Never had the pleasure," she said with the hint of a smile. "I was at the police academy when he took a shot at my boss. They probably should have shot him, but my dad tackled him instead."

It suddenly struck me that she was kinda pretty, in an official, professional sort of way, of course.

"He got out of the Correctional Center down in Windham six months ago," she went on as I slapped myself mentally. "Did a year for Reckless Conduct for shooting at the sheriff and he is . . . or *was* on probation. I called his probation officer on the way up. Sounds like he didn't have many friends."

"I'd say his only real friend went with him," I said, nodding at Sumbitch's body.

"Poor thing." She sighed. Looking back up at me she shook her head and asked, "OK, what's the first thing you saw when you walked in?"

"Just his face at first," I said. "He looked like he was mad enough to spit at me until I realized he was dead."

"What else?"

"Saw the dog, obviously. And that."

I pointed at a pile of stuff by the back wall that was probably the bed.

"Could've done with a housekeeper," she said. "He's got something of a reputation as a poacher. Do you know what else he does, uh, *did*?" She blushed and grinned.

Mister man, I thought to myself, a boy could get used to that fairly quick. Then I remembered just how old I was getting to be, regretfully.

"Drink and fight, mostly. Probably some junking, too," I said. "I think he gets SSDI for drugs, but that's just a rumor."

"From Marti Wallace, I expect." She smiled again. Our rural mail carrier, you see, is well known as a wicked gossip.

The door banged back against the wall, I jumped, and what looked like a grizzly bear carrying a briefcase stumbled sideways into the cabin.

"I do wish you people would take the time to shovel out instead of just stomping down a path," it said, grumbling. "Hey, Willie." Its tone brightened. "What we got *this* time?"

"Pretty much what you see, Doc. Meet the late, unlamented Frenchy Plourde."

A fur-lined parka hood flipped back from the bear's head and revealed longish white hair and a corresponding beard crowning a body that was easily a head taller and fifty pounds heavier than me. He reached over Frenchy and shook my hand. He had some grip!

"Eimon Jeffries, boy medical examiner." He looked down at Frenchy. "Legally dead, I'd say from my extensive and exhaustive preliminary examination. At least he still looks relatively fresh. Got pictures yet?"

"I'll go get the camera out of the cruiser," Willie said. "Looks straightforward though. I don't think we'll have to call in the troops."

"Probably not." The doctor wheezed and coughed into his elbow. "But I'll have a look anyway. Need to do something to earn that massive fee the state grudgingly pays to get an aging country G. P. out of bed in a snowstorm, usually in the middle of the night."

He smiled and bent down over the body as Willie went out the door.

"Whoa! *This* is something you don't see a lot in Franklin County.'

"What's that?"

"It looks to me like *Rictus Sardonicus*." The doctor said, scratching his chin through his beard. "I think maybe old Frenchy here finally pissed off the wrong person,"

"Huh?"

"That look on his face is called a poison grin. Usually strychnine if I remember right." He shook his very large head. "I'm beginning to think that maybe we *should* call the troops after all."

Well, Hell.

#

"They had to light the fire and warm the place up enough to scrape him and the dog off the floor," I told Nadine, the half owner of Sally's Motel and Bar and Live Bait and Convenience Store, two hours later over my first Shipyard Export. "They took them both down to Augusta for autopsies."

"So, they think somebody did him in?" Nadine looked mildly grossed out but interested, as did the two guys in nice, clean, brand-new snowmobile suits sitting at a table by the front window. Together they rose and slid in on either side of me at the bar.

"Maybe," I said, warming up—I do like an audience. "The state police detective team came in behind us after a bit. They kicked me and the deputy out as soon as they got there. She looked a little pissed to be put on traffic detail."

"That'd be Willie Brackett, Big Jim Brackett's daughter from down in Phillips," Nadine said, shaking her head. "She's a little corker, that one. A month ago she cleaned this place out single handed when the Martinos got into it with the Regan brothers. Handcuffed Dutch Regan so fast he didn't realize it until he was out the door. Then she came back and used a judo wrist lock on Finn Martino that had him crying like a baby."

The snowmobilers edged closer and the older one who smelled like a cigar offered to buy me another beer, which I happily accepted.

\#

I guess I was walking a little close to the middle of the road on my way home sometime later, because Marti Wallace had to pull into the left lane and blow her horn to get my attention when she found me. Luckily there was no oncoming traffic. There seldom is that early.

"Ya got yourself hammered again, din't ya?" she said, shaking her head as she climbed out what should rightly be the passenger side front door. She shoved me into the back seat of her canary yellow Jeep amongst all the mail and her turnout gear and drove me the last hundred yards or so home.

Did I mention she's a "BMW," a "Big Maine Woman?" She had no trouble at all extracting me from her back seat and walking me into my kitchen. Of course, I had to tell her the whole story all over again, which pleased her no end but made her late finishing her mail route because she had so much fresh news to distribute along the way.

#

I swear it happens every damn time. Just when Helen Hunt is about to finally slip out of that tiny little tank top, something wakes me up. My late wife Pam's probably laughing her ass off somewhere, wherever she is.

"Sorry, Hon," I said to her picture on my nightstand.

My fire department pager was screaming like a banshee in heat. Lummox, my cat, headed for the hills. From the length of the sequence of different tones I could tell that this wasn't going to be just a little chimney fire. I started pulling on my long woolies.

I can't remember if I told you but Skedaddle Gore doesn't really have its own *official* fire department. About ten years or so ago, just after I moved here, the insurance company that covers the Skedaddle Ridge Ski Resort up on Skedaddle Mountain, realized that the nearest fire truck was ten miles away in Rangeley and that "The Mountain," which is what the locals call it, was accumulating a lot of expensive and flammable equipment, not to mention all those combustible customers who were paying to sleep—or party hearty—in their fancy trailside condos, each of which has its own rustic, fully stocked fireplace—for the atmosphere, of course. The Mountain sent their professionally attired and outfitted legal representatives to one of our Board of Assessors' monthly meetings. They stood out like a sore thumb and looked a dite nervous. They quite reasonably proposed that we needed a fire truck in town in the worst way. As the assessors were themselves all taxpayers and consequently tight with a buck, they balked up tighter'n a tick until the team of suits said that The Mountain would pick up most of the tab. As a result, after a bit more Yankee negotiating, the Gore had the permanent loan of old Engine Five from Rangeley, along with enough money each year to insure her, keep her in diesel and oil, and heat the town garage enough to keep her water tank from freezing up. Fifteen or twenty good citizens who always wanted to be firemen as kids usually show up for monthly meetings at Sally's and about half of them actually show up for the infrequent fire or traffic accident. All us taxpayers have to do is pay the insurance premiums and minimum wage to the ones who *do* report for duty.

Anyway, the screaming subsided finally and all over Franklin County men and women first responders lifted their pagers to their ears to see which of them could go back to bed.

"Attention, Skedaddle fire. Attention, Rangeley fire. Attention, Phillips fire. Attention Northstar Ambulance Rangeley base. Report of a structure fire, fully involved, at 3700 Skunk Hollow Road in Skedaddle Gore. Skedaddle One is on the scene requesting mutual aid. Rangeley respond to assist for attack. Phillips, respond one mutual aid tanker and stand by at your station. Time out—zero four forty-five."

Since I live across the street from the town garage, I usually drive the truck and run the pump. I had more than enough firefighting experience and training in the Coast Guard to know that I'm no longer interested in climbing ladders or charging into burning buildings. There are enough young kids who get a charge out of that, so I'm content to pass on the actual grunt firefighter stuff. Besides, I like running the old American LaFrance; she's a real gamer for her age.

"Frenchy Plourde's place," Snort Benson shouted, piling into the shotgun seat as I hit the starter. "Weren't you just over there, Bobby?"

"Yeah, Snot. I was." I said as I hit the lights and siren as the old girl warmed up. I pushed the shifter toward first gear. "Sounds like Marti called it in on her paper route. The woman never sleeps!"

Snot's had his nickname since grammar school. He pronounces it "Snort" but says he's used to hearing it the other way by now. Marti Wallace is our fire chief. She's good at it. I did tell you about her, didn't I?

"Skedaddle Five to Franklin. Enroute with two, uh, make that three," Snort spoke into the radio mike as Bear MacGillicuddy landed next to him and slammed the door shut.

"Ten-four, Skedaddle Five." Franklin County Dispatch replied.

Snort grunted as the right turn out of the garage pushed Bear over onto him. Bear's big. Snort's not.

We made it to the late Frenchy's ex-cabin without further incident and set up to pump three main lines at Marti's direction. After checking that nobody and nothing of consequence was in imminent danger, we adopted the ancient, accepted and safe fire-fighting strategy of "surround and drown." With help from Rangeley's attack pumper and the tankers from Rangeley and Phillips we efficiently reduced the cabin to a few standing charred timbers in half an hour. With precise hose handling from the nozzle men, we managed to stop the flames from reaching the outhouse, a feat which, everyone knew, would later be loudly and proudly celebrated at the incident debriefing at Sally's. Curiously, the cabin's stove pipe remained standing when the cabin finally collapsed. Backed by the rising sun it was twisted into the shape of a question mark, as if the place's last comment was, "WTF?"

"Might's well wrap it up," Marti shouted to me as I throttled down the engine to disconnect the power takeoff from the pump. "The fire marshal will be up later to look for a cause and the sheriff's sending a deputy to stand by until they get here."

"Hope they find something to go on," I said as the old engine settled back to a gently purring idle. *God, I love that machine!*

"I think they will. I met a big, black, one-ton pickup with two snow machines on a tilt body trailer booking it out of here just before I came on the fire. No front plate I could see but I think they were massholes 'cause one of them gave me the finger on the way by."

"Gotta be massholes," I agreed, grinning. "Nobody from around here would dare!"

About then I stepped down wrong and slipped on the ice that had accumulated under the pump's output connector. Gracefully I landed on the left side of my face, splitting my lip. My first thought was that the OSHA and Workman's Comp paperwork was going to be a bitch. My second thought was "What the hell is that?"

Lodged in the ice under the truck was what looked very much like a cigar butt.

#

A couple of days later I was sitting in front of the picture window I installed in my front room of my cabin the first summer I was here so I could keep an eye on the spectacular view of Rangeley Lake down in the valley below me. I was working on my flies when a sheriff's cruiser pulled into my dooryard. Buck Champagne, an old Penobscot shaman who was one of the first people in town to come over and say hello after I moved in, taught me how to tie fishing flies my first winter in the Gore. It's a real good way to stay sane and at least semi-sober from November through April up here on the mountainside. Sadly, Buck's no longer with us. Cancer got him during my third year here, but he managed to teach me a lot more than just fly tying while he was still alive. Later on, I took an adult ed course about the internet at Rangeley High School and the kids there taught me how to set up and run a simple website. Believe it or not, I now sell my Wytopitlock Wooley Booger flies all over the US and Canada.

I watched as Willie Brackett got out of the car and walked up to my front door. I rapped on the window between us and waved her on in.

"Mister Wing," she said with a nice smile. "How've you been? How's your lip?"

My day was improving by the minute.

"Healing. I've had worse. And it's Bobby. Mister Wing was my dad."

She grinned at me as she hung her parka on the hook by the door. I waved her into a chair in what passes for my kitchen and poured her a cup of coffee. No rings, I noted.

"I wanted to thank you for preserving that cigar butt and remembering those two snowmobilers at Sally's," she said. "I managed to get a tentative ID on one of them from Nadine's room registration records and the parking lot's surveillance camera. They gave her false names and a bogus plate number when they registered, but the camera gave us a good one. The truck was a rental from Worcester, Massachusetts. It's still missing, and the Mass State Police have just listed it as stolen in NCIC. Luckily, the guy who rented the trailer had to show ID. They told the rental agent they were going to Maine to pick up a couple of snow machines for a guy in Vermont. We think they actually stole the machines from a dealership down near Portland and were headed back home to sell them. If they are who we think they are they're players on the Boston docks involved in all kinds of stuff like fencing stolen property, smuggling, dope—you name it. Our DA says thanks to you we've got a good chain of custody on the cigar butt and the crime lab's doing DNA analysis as we speak. With luck we'll be able to place the cigar guy at the scene in a week or two."

"I'm sure Frenchy would have been pleased," I said, sarcastically.

"That's another thing," Willie took a sip of coffee. "Doc Jeffries called me this morning to tell me that he and the state police have closed his death as a natural causes case."

"Natural causes? It sure as hell didn't look natural."

"Agreed," she said. "But it turns out that one of the other causes of that facial expression is tetanus—lockjaw. He probably caught it off the ax he was using to split kindling. Doc says it's a really painful way to die, with violent muscle spasms and seizures. Frenchy'd probably been alone in that cabin, sick, for a week or more before he worked up enough strength to fill the stove and light it. Doc thinks he had a seizure just before he lit the match and suffocated. He was probably conscious and at least vaguely aware of what was happening until he passed out from lack of oxygen and eventually died."

"I'll be damned," I said, beginning to feel a dite sorry for Frenchy. "And the fire?"

"Was definitely set, probably by our Massachusetts friends. We don't know exactly why yet, but there may be a connection between Frenchy and one of them through Frenchy's prison time. Again, if he is who we *think* he is, the older guy was locked up in Windham at the same time Frenchy was. I think they were looking for something in the cabin and couldn't find it. They burned the place to cover their tracks. Alcohol, Tobacco and Firearms agents have also gotten involved because of the arson and the interstate connection."

"I'll be damned, again," I said softly. "Who would have thought . . . way up here in Skedaddle Gore, Maine . . . of all places."

I shook my head, feeling suddenly anxious. The PTSD demon can be a real bitch sometimes, let me tell you.

Willie laughed. "Come on, now, Mr. W . . . sorry." She paused. "Bobby. I get the feeling there's more to your act than you let on. I heard you were in the service for almost as long as I've been alive. I bet you've seen some things . . ."

I'm not sure what I looked like just then, but whatever it was she picked up on it, along with my admittedly uncharacteristic moment of silence.

"I better get going," she finally said, with a little frown. "I've got a meeting this afternoon on this case with the DA and all the agencies involved. Maybe there'll be new developments. I'll let you know." She stood up and grabbed her jacket off the hook.

"You don't have to. I'm just the local yokel."

"Who's been a big help to us all. Besides . . . I like you. See you later."

She looked at me a bit sadly, I thought, and left.

You know, I thought to myself as I watched her walk down the hill to her cruiser, *she looks just a little like Helen Hunt.*

Well, Hell.

#

Turns out Willie was right. The cigar guy was positively ID'd through the DNA on his butt, putting him at the scene of the fire. Franklin County Consolidated Court issued a warrant for Arson (of a Residence), Class A, for the two of them and the younger one caved as soon as the ATF agents walked into the Boston PD interview room and showed him their badges. Along with a lot of other stuff, they'd been in the business of procuring dried bear gall bladders for Chinese men who think they're an aphrodisiac. They were shipping them off the Boston docks in a clandestine scheme. You can apparently make a mint doing that but it's illegal under federal law. Who knew?

The cigar guy *was* in prison with Frenchy and had offered to buy any bladders he could get when they got out. Frenchy had called him a couple of weeks before and said he had some ready, but they'd found him dead when they got there. They tossed the cabin looking for the bladders and left before the snow started. After they heard my story at Sally's they went back for a second look but still couldn't find anything. They dowsed the place with gasoline and tossed the cigar into the fumes to set it off and cover their tracks.

Willie got a commendation from ATF and Federal Fish and Wildlife. She got her picture in the paper at a county commissioners' meeting shaking hands with the high sheriff himself. She looked pretty good but embarrassed as hell.

#

That March the Board of Assessors got tired of fielding complaints from The Mountain about how bad the fire scene looked to their customers headed up through town to spend money lavishly on all those clean, healthy Maine rustic recreational opportunities, so they voted to take the property for taxes—Frenchy had never paid any—and gave me another of their "commissions" to "eliminate the eyesore," as they told me.

When things had melted off that May I rented an excavator off M & H Logging in Rangeley and went over to Skunk Hollow Road to "reestablish the harmonious beauty of nature." I was almost done when I tipped over the outhouse and a canvas bag that had apparently been hanging under the seat fell onto the now-uncovered pile of now-stinking crap.

Well, Hell...

I shut the machine off and sat with the warm spring sun on my back and stared at that bag for a long while. I thought about money, and happiness, and Frenchy, and fear, and Chinese men, and dead bears and dogs, and Willie, and Helen Hunt, and Pam. Then I covered the hole all up, graded it off and planted some grass seed.

Three: Deadly Discoveries

It was obvious to anyone who cared to look—and there were definitely folks doing just that on a crispy Maine afternoon in mid-September—that Mrs. Grania "Granny" Liberty was a very fine-looking woman indeed for her age. That she was a natural redhead was also evident, as she was standing bollocky bare-ass naked in the middle of Jack Frost Hill Road holding a rope attached to a sad-eyed Brown Swiss milk cow. Apparently completely unfazed by the state of her increasingly public appearance, she was, also obviously, mighty pissed off.

"Noah," she shouted at the top of her rather prodigious lungs as I pulled up next to her. "Noaaah, you lazy bahstid! I've told you and *told* you to check Molly's tether before you come inside. Noah? Get your sorry ass out here and help me!"

Ten minutes earlier Snort Benson had come running into Sally's Motel and Bar and Live Bait and Convenience Store all aflutter, interrupting the consumption of my second Shipyard Pumpkinhead Ale. Breathless as usual, he announced to all three people present that the Skedaddle Gore animal control officer—that would be me—was needed at once for an all-fired big cow-related emergency up on Jack Frost Hill.

Some people think that Skedaddle Gore is a funny name for a town and they're right. The way I heard it is that back in the 1860's, during the Civil War, not everybody who was eligible to join in the military on the Union side was enthusiastic about doing so—sort of like during the 1960's a hundred years later. There were even draft riots in New York City that got pretty brutal. It seems that a bunch of folks who weren't keen on getting blown to bits on some cow pasture in Pennsylvania or Georgia decided to head for the hills—or "skedaddle," as they called it then. Also sounds sort of like the 1960's, doesn't it. What goes around, comes around, as they say.

Anyway, those "skedaddlers" wound up in the northwestern Maine mountains, of all places, where they hid out in a big cave on the side of a mountain and almost froze to death that first winter. If it hadn't been for the local Indians and a few sympathetic Quaker farmers in the area, they would have. Somewhere along the line later on a surveyor came through and mapped out the whole area. He laid out one patch that was roughly triangular in shape, something those surveyors apparently call a "gore"—I don't know why. Since that was the area where the "skedaddlers" hid out in their cave, it came to be named Skedaddle Gore. Oddly, nobody has ever found that big cave on what came to be called Skedaddle Mountain, despite years of trying. It's probably just a myth.

Being the Constable, Fence Viewer, Deputy Fire Warden and Animal Control Officer of Skedaddle Gore isn't all that big a deal. Basically, I get paid minimum wage and mileage to spend a couple of hours a week taking care of the odd "stuff" that needs doing in town. "Stuff" like Granny Liberty's cow standing in the middle of a public thoroughfare, where she, and now Granny, could easily be hit by traffic, if there had been any traffic, which, to be truthful, there seldom is.

Actually, traffic did look like it was beginning to pick up as word got around about all the goings on. As I pulled up I counted three old beater pickup trucks, a shiny new green Subaru with New Hampshire plates and a pulp truck with half a hastily tied-down load—all of them lined up in the road next to the driveway into the Libertys' landscaped and well-tended gentleman's farm.

Bailing out of The Beast, my new pickup—I'll tell you that story later—I grabbed my old wool army blanket from the space behind the front seat and tried to drape it over Granny's shoulders as she shouted louder and increasingly profanely after this Noah fellow. Since I know her husband's name is Wilbur and that he was most probably at his office on Jersey Street in Boston, I began to wonder just who "Noah" might be.

Granny, God love her, suddenly looked at me as if she thought I'd stepped off a flying saucer. Her hair was damp, and I could smell jasmine and bourbon. She looked at the cow, the blanket over her shoulders and the gathering crowd and began to scream. Then she laughed. Then she screamed some more.

"He's dead, the bahstid," she yelled, in between shrieks. "He's finally dead! I finally did it!"

Well, Hell?

Out of the corner of my eye I saw the canary yellow Jeep Wrangler belonging to our rural mail carrier, town gossip and fire chief, Marti Wallace, pull in behind The Beast. "Granny," I said, trying to keep the blanket covering her critical bits. "Grania! It's Bobby. Bobby Wing. Listen to me. We've got to get the cow out of the road before she gets hit."

Surprisingly, that's all it took. Granny looked around again, stopped screeching and let me lead her and the cow toward Marti's Jeep on the shoulder of the road. Marti put her arms around Granny's shoulders, pulled her over to the rear door and sat her inside amidst the mail and turnout gear. I spied Bear McGillicuddy, the owner of the pulp truck I mentioned earlier, in the crowd and handed him the cow's tether. Bear's on our one-truck volunteer fire department with me and Marti and fifteen or so other good citizens. He's also the biggest man in the Gore by six inches and a good fifty pounds. Luckily for all of us his disposition pretty much matches that of the cow I now entrusted him to secure back on Granny's property.

"Off her meds again, I'd say," he said, shaking his head as he walked up the driveway with Molly in tow.

A few in the crowd solemnly nodded in agreement. About then I heard a siren from the direction of Rangeley, the next town over where Northstar Ambulance has its regional base.

"Franklin County Dispatch got a 911 call on her a few minutes ago," Marti said from beside her Jeep where she was holding Granny's hand. "I heard it on the fire channel and came right over. Looks like Bear's right about the meds, though. Too bad."

Granny's usually a very nice, refined lady. She's about my age—"fiftyish"—and most everyone in town likes her and her mister, even though they're from away. Her gardens are famous locally and she's even started giving free horticulture lessons since the state extension named her a Master Gardener.

Her husband's Will Liberty—"Wave'm in Willie"—the third base coach for the Boston Red Sox. They have an apartment in the city where Will usually stays during the season. If the Sox don't make the post-season, which already didn't look real likely that year, he should be arriving in a few weeks to settle into his off-season role of rugged outdoorsman, gentleman farmer and ski instructor. He's a good guy to have a beer or two with—full of baseball stories.

Anyway, somewhere along the line Granny got bit by the "Demon Rum." Shortly after the two of them bought their place here five years ago, we noticed that she started having wicked temper tantrums in public for no particular reason. She'd also do strange stuff and say weird things. I heard that one time, at a board of assessors meeting, she made a proposal to require that all the cats in town had to wear bells to warn away the chickadees. Finally, Will threw out the liquor and took her down to Boston for a while to see a doctor the team uses. He gave her some meds and, after a couple of noisy relapses a while ago, she slowly got better. Now she goes to Alcoholics Anonymous meetings in Rangeley once a week, sees a traveling counselor at the Rural Health Center and generally seems to be pretty normal, at least by Skedaddle Gore standards—or at least she had up until about fifteen minutes ago.

Just as the ambulance pulled up Bear came booking it back down the driveway, his face just feather white.

"Bobby!" he shouted, gasping for air as he skidded to a stop. "You gotta come look. There's a dead guy in the hay barn!"

Well, Hell!

After briefing the paramedics, I walked—kind of reluctantly I'll admit—up the long, curving, flower-lined driveway toward the Libertys' impressive, colonnaded house. Bear didn't come up with me, as he was busy being sick in the ditch behind the ambulance. It didn't take me long to find out why.

After twenty-five years in the Coast Guard as a machinist and Gunner's Mate, I've seen more than my share of death, in more forms than I can count, but, mister man, this turned out to be a new one. The sliding door on the front of the big red hay barn behind the house was part way open and I could hear the deep bellowing roar of a good-sized diesel engine at full throttle. Stepping into the dimly lit space I saw Will's big Kubota tractor nestled up tightly to the front row of a hundred or so round hay bales which filled about three quarters of the place. Stepping over a puddle of Bear vomit, I spied a man's head with a mess of dried blood around his nose and mouth and open goggle eyes staring down at the six-foot-long steel bale spear which had the rest of him skewered between the loader frame on the front of the tractor and the center of the bale behind him.

Well, Hell!

The barn was full of exhaust fumes, and I coughed and retched a bit myself as I reached up into the cab and shut off the engine. Mark Blake, one of the paramedics from the ambulance, appeared with a jump pack of emergency medical equipment in each hand. Seeing what I was looking at, he sighed and set them down as they were obviously going to be useless in this situation.

"Geez, Louise," he said. I shared his opinion.

"How's Granny?" I asked him as we stood there thinking about what to do next.

"She'll be fine. We'll take her to Franklin Memorial Hospital for an evaluation, but I don't think it's anything more than acute ETOH."

"Huh?"

"That means she's blind drunk," he said with a cough.

"Oh. Not off her meds?"

"She says she's not, but the hospital will check. My partner's with her and I called in for a police response. The sheriff's sending a deputy. Do you know this guy?"

Mark pulled on a pair of blue rubber gloves from a pouch on his belt and carefully climbed up onto the loader mechanism of the tractor.

"I'm guessing he's the Libertys' hired hand, but I've never met him, so I'm not sure," I said, watching in case he slipped.

Mark reached over and felt for the guy's jugular. "No pulse, cool to the touch, stake through his heart." He shook his head. "I don't think this boy's riding with us today." Hopping to the ground he coughed again and said, "This place is probably full of carbon monoxide. Come on. We'd better go outside and let it air out."

"Sounds good to me."

The two of us shoved the door all the way open and headed back down the driveway to wait for the sheriff.

"I almost forgot," Mark said. "Granny wants you to call her husband. She says her cell phone is on the kitchen counter and he's number one on her speed dial."

Mark trotted off and I detoured into the kitchen, where I could hear what sounded like a washing machine running in the back room. The phone was right where Granny said it would be, sitting on the counter—right next to an empty pint of Jim Beam's best and a baseball bat covered with blood and hair.

Well, Hell.

Will answered on the third ring. "Hi, Hon. Bad timing. I'm in the pregame staff meeting. Can I call you back?" He sounded stressed. The season was petering out and, sadly, so were the Sox.

"Will, it's Bobby Wing from up in Skedaddle Gore. It's important."

"Bobby? How'd you get Granny's phone? Is she OK? Give me a minute." I could hear him making his excuses to the manager and then heard a door close. "Hello?" he said as he came on the line.

"She's OK, Will. Physically anyway."

"The middle of the road?" "Naked?" "Drunk?" The pitch of his voice rose a little with each question as I told the sad tale. Finally, he sighed. "I guess I don't know what to say, Bobby. Thank you. I'll be up there as soon as I can. Tell Noah to make sure everything is locked up and the animals are tended to before he goes home tonight."

"That's another thing, Will . . ."

#

"OK, you people," Deputy Douglas Elvin Berry—as proclaimed by the extra-large shiny brass name tag pinned to his rather tight uniform shirt—hoisted himself out of his cruiser. "I'm taking charge here now. What's going on?"

Pulling up on his gun belt and down on his campaign hat he peered at the bunch of us with something, I thought, bordering on contempt.

"Oh, God!" I heard Mark say softly to the other paramedic, who looked like she might still be in high school. "Deputy Dog. How'd we get so lucky?"

Thankfully, Marti took the lead. I stayed busy trying to keep a straight face.

"Hi, Dog," she said. "It sounds like we've got an unattended death in Mrs. Liberty's barn. It's full of diesel fumes right now and we're letting it air out so it's safe to enter. The medical examiner's been called, too."

"Who's the stiff?" Dog asked, chomping down on a wad of gum, which popped loudly.

At that point I lost it.

He rounded in my direction and gave me a look that would have made a lumberjack cringe. Unfortunately his campaign hat kept turning, stopping sideways on his head, which didn't help me regain my composure.

"Who the hell are you and what the hell are you laughing at?"

He grabbed his hat again with one hand and his holster, which had slid around until it was covering his prominent butt, with the other. I wondered if they were somehow connected.

"Sorry, deputy," I choked out. "I'm Bobby Wing, the Gore's constable. I got the original call and sort of helped to find the body. It's been a tough hour or so." I shrugged, swallowed a chuckle and tried to look contrite.

"Constable, huh?" he glared at me with a pretty good *Heat of the Night* Rod Steiger impersonation. "I heard about you. You've never been to the training academy, have you? I'd be really careful what I called myself if I was you. Impersonating a Law Enforcement Officer is a serious offense!"

"I'll be careful, deputy," I said.

Somebody behind him snickered and Dog jerked his head around again, actually sneering at the crowd. This time his hat stayed in place, thankfully.

"We're not sure yet *who* it is," Marti said, pointedly interrupting. "Bobby, Bear McGillicuddy and the paramedic here are the only ones who've seen the deceased and they don't recognize him. He might be a guy named Noah. We don't know his last name. He's Mrs. Liberty's hired hand."

"Noah? Noah's deceased? Noah's dead?" Granny started shrieking again from the ambulance where Mark and his partner had, thankfully, just gotten her strapped in for transport.

"Oh, crap!" Marti said. "That's Mrs. Liberty. Let me go talk to her."

"You do that," Dog said, raising his voice as she walked away. "And tell her if she doesn't quiet down, I'll take her to jail for Disorderly Conduct!"

"Jail!" Granny screamed.

Marti hurried to the back of the ambulance.

"His last name is Stevens," I said. "Noah Stevens. I talked to Granny's husband on the phone. He's driving up from Boston and should be here later tonight."

Dog extracted a notebook from his back pocket and pulled a stubby pencil out of the wire spiral that held it together. Squinting a bit, he checked his watch.

"Right. 14:33 on scene. Deceased ID'd as a Noah Stevens." He scribbled in the notebook. "Got a date of birth, *constable*?" he said, drawing out the last word a bit longer than I thought necessary.

"No, and I'm not sure that's who it is, either." I managed to register only a slight, hopefully innocuous, smile. "Will says he lives up at the Chicken House."

"Oh, for the love of Pete!" Dog threw up his hands, dropped his pencil and then had to grab for his hat again, which was threatening to tumble off the back of his head. "Not another one of them friggin' hippie commie friggin' cult chicken freaks. Great! I can't ever get a straight answer out of any of them crazy canucks."

I held my tongue as he squared away his hat again and retrieved his pencil. The Community of Satin on the Skedaddle Lake Road has always struck me as a nice, steady bunch of Newfoundland chicken farmers with a funny name and a good collective ability to judge character.

"Carbon monoxide poisoning, you said. Farming accident, right?" Dog sounded eager but the light in his eye was fading a little. It also started to sound like he was looking for an easy out. I guessed that his forte was writing traffic tickets—nothing too complex.

"Sorry, I don't think so," I said. "The place was full of exhaust smoke from the tractor, but I'm betting the M.E.'s going to say that the cause of death was a two-inch diameter steel stake rammed through his heart."

His face fell. "The hell you say. Oh, this is just friggin' great! I'll never get home for supper at this rate!"

A handsome old white Mercedes sedan pulled into the line on the shoulder behind the New Hampshire Subaru. I watched with a twinge of envy as the single occupant slowly unfolded himself from this very fine Teutonic masterpiece of diesel-powered engineering.

"M.E.'s here," shouted Mark from the back of the ambulance.

Eimon Jeffries, MD, stepped up onto the ambulance's high tailgate. He had to duck his large, rather shaggy white head to look inside.

"Hey, guys," he said to the paramedics. "Hey, Grania. How you feeling, my girl?"

Granny, strapped to the gurney and basically immobile, raised her head and gazed at the doctor with unabashed affection, and attraction—as did the young female paramedic. Back in the day, you see, Doc Jeffries worked his way through med school as a male stripper.

"I'm much better, Doc, but they're taking me to jail!" A touch of panic crept back into her voice. The doctor glanced at Mark, who shook his head.

"ETOH, Doc. Her vitals are stable but we're running her to FMH for an eval."

"It's OK, Grania." Doc's voice rumbled from deep in his barrel chest. "You're not going to jail. I'll come down to the hospital in the morning and check on you, OK? You'll be fine. You'll be safe. Don't worry."

"Good," Granny finally broke a smile. "That's good. I'd like that."

Even I felt better. Doc has a way of doing that to you.

"Hey, Dog," Doc said as he walked over to us. "What you guys got *this* time?"

"I don't know—yet." Dog sounded nervous as we watched the ambulance roll away. "I thought we had a farming accident. Maybe carbon monoxide. But the constable here just told me different."

"Hey, Bobby," Doc turned to me and grinned. "How's The Beast running?"

Doc and I both like big diesel engines and the solid steel that tends to surround them. I filled him in on my new hitch-mounted winch and the events of my afternoon so far as the three of us walked up the driveway.

We all stopped at the barn threshold and looked around. The door was now fully open in the afternoon sun and most of the diesel smoke was gone, so the visibility was a lot better. I pointed at the drying puke pool on the pole barn's hard packed clay floor.

"I stepped over that and walked straight to the tractor and shut it off. Mark came in the same way and we both left as straight as we could after he checked the body."

"Well, this is a new one for me," Doc said, raising his bushy eyebrows. "From here he looks pretty dead to me." He gazed around the barn. "Does it look like anything has changed since you left?"

Without moving my feet, I looked carefully. The field treads of the tractor had dug themselves six inches into the surface of the floor and sprayed loose dirt all over the wall behind it, which I hadn't been able to see through the diesel smoke earlier.

"Looks to me like the guy jumped off the tractor while it was still in gear and it shishkabobed him," Dog said before I could answer Doc's question. His eyes were wide and his face was going pale.

"No, I don't think so," I said. "I tinkered this tractor for Will last spring. Thanks to the feds' safety regs it has an electric interlock that kills the engine if the driver gets out of the seat with the transmission in gear. Since it was running full blast when I shut it off, it had to have been in neutral."

"Which means," Doc said slowly, "that our friend here did not meet his demise as the result of a terrible, tragic farming-related accident."

"Nope," I agreed. "Somebody had to have been sitting in the driver's seat."

"Well, la-dee-frickin'-da!" Dog had a happy grin on his face. "That makes it a *suspicious death* and *that's* a case for the staties! I won't have to go talk to them commie frickin' chicken farmers after all!" He looked like he was about to dance a jig—something I did not want to see, frankly.

Doc called the Chief Medical Examiner's Office in Augusta from his Mercedes while Dog happily wrapped everything he could see in yellow "Sheriff's Line—Do Not Cross" tape and then parked his cruiser directly in front of the driveway with all the emergency lights going. It was all a little unnecessary, I thought, given the lack of traffic—but he *was* the professional.

Marti left to finish her mail route, the rest of the rubber-neckers got bored and drifted away and Bear drove his pulp truck back to his woodlot.

Strangely the New Hampshire Subaru didn't move. I brought this to Dog's attention. He was sitting in his cruiser reading an old Spiderman comic book.

"Probably nothing at all. Don't worry. Somebody will be back for it."

I shrugged and walked to The Beast, where I sat and waited for the cavalry.

#

It was well after dark by the time I got to the Chicken House, more formally known as the Mother House of the Community of Satin. I'll tell you all about the "Community," as everybody calls them, another time. They're an interesting bunch.

I'd been interviewed twice by two different state police detectives, fingerprinted and had my shoe treads photographed. I'd also submitted a handwritten statement describing my afternoon. The detective sergeant in charge glanced at it, warned me to be quiet about what I'd seen and told me to go home. I didn't do either.

Happily, the first person I ran into was Tangerine Gilchrist. Angie runs the home school for the Community kids and is the single mom of two, a boy and a girl. She graduated from McGill University up in Canada with a master's degree in Education and she likes beer and baseball—except she's a Blue Jays fan. I still like her anyway. And she's a wicked looker.

"You're here about Noah Stevens? Why?"

I told her. She laughed.

"That's impossible. Your victim can't be Noah Stevens. I just had supper with him in the dining hall."

I asked her if she was sure. Oddly, she paused, peered at me closely and quietly said, "Things are seldom what they seem."

"Yeah, and skim milk masquerades as cream."

My mom was a Gilbert and Sullivan fan, and *H.M.S. Pinafore* was always one of her favorites. The classic 1950's D'oyly Carte Opera LP album played a lot in the house when I was a kid. I always liked that particular song.

Her eyes widened and she smiled. Somehow, I felt a warming in the air.

Well, Hell.

#

My phone started ringing pretty much as soon as I got to sleep. First the state police detective sergeant in charge of the case wanted to know why I'd gone up to the Chicken House without his permission. I told him that it was wicked dark out, I was half asleep and I wasn't aware he was my boss. He seemed to take offense at that for some reason. Then he wanted to know why I hadn't called him about Noah Stevens being alive. I reminded him that it was late, I was tired, and I *still* wasn't aware he was my boss. He told me about Maine's Obstructing Government Administration law. I don't think he likes me much.

Next Will Liberty woke me up to tell me that the hospital had put a deputy sheriff on guard outside Granny's room who wouldn't let him in to see her or tell him why. I told him to call Woody Bernstein, a lawyer friend of mine down in Farmington.

Finally, Doc called to tell me, in confidence of course, that he was watching when they rolled the tractor away from the barn wall before de-spearing the guy by now known to *not* be Noah Stevens. Under the left front wheel they found a loaded and cocked Colt M1911 .45 caliber semi-automatic pistol, which turned out to be stolen. Oh, and that New Hampshire Subaru out front was also stolen.

#

I knew they were feds as soon as they pulled into my dooryard. I was sitting on my screen porch in the morning sun with my old Maine Coon cat, Lummox, enjoying the view of the early fall foliage in the valley toward Rangeley Lake, drinking my second cup of coffee and reading the *Daily Bulldog* on my iPad. Our local on-line newspaper had a picture of the Liberty house surrounded by "State Police Line—Do Not Cross" tape, which had apparently replaced Dog's at some point, and a four-line non-story which declared that state police detectives were investigating an "incident" at the home of Red Sox coach Will Liberty and the story would be updated as more information became available.

Two guys in gray windbreakers got out of their gray sedan and walked up to the porch screen door. Lummox raised his head, peered stonily at them from his perch on the porch railing and yawned.

"Bobby Wing?" asked the older looking one.

"Yup."

"Can we come in?"

"Do I need a lawyer?" I asked, mindful of the numerous legal warnings I had received in the past few hours.

"Do you think you do?" the younger guy asked.

"I sure as hell hope not," I said. Lummox sighed and rolled his eyes—I swear to God.

I realized that they looked beat. I offered coffee and Country Kitchen donuts from the Rangeley IGA.

They glanced at each other and the older one shrugged, "Yeah. That would be good. We've been up all night."

Lummox, two deputy U.S. marshals and I sat on my porch for the next hour drinking coffee and discussing the situation. They told me a bunch of stuff which is wicked confidential, so forget this next bit.

It turns out that "Noah Stevens" was living at the Community of Satin as his cover identity with the Witness Protection Program. It seems that the Community, since they moved to the U.S. from Newfoundland six years ago, has provided the most secure and problem-free placement of its type in the whole, entire country. The marshals wouldn't say so, but I got the distinct impression that they had other "clients" in residence besides "Noah." I was amazed that this was possible given the extensive Skedaddle Telegraph and its primary driver, Marti, and I told them so.

Without missing a beat, the older marshal said, "Martha Wallace has been a great asset to us over the years. We hope you will be, too."

Well, Hell!

It turns out that Noah had called in to them as soon as he got back to the Chicken House yesterday afternoon. The dead guy was a known professional shooter who had somehow tracked Noah down and tried to collect on the substantial contract bounty out on him. Having developed a few professional survival skills of his own over the years Noah successfully used the only weapon available to defend himself, the bale spear on his tractor. I was impressed by his guts, and his ingenuity.

Finally, the marshals told me the challenge and countersign to use if I ever needed to talk to a Community member about their little "sideline" in future. Whoever thought that one up must have been a Gilbert & Sullivan fan, too—and the information went a long way toward explaining Angie's sudden, and welcome, change in attitude.

Despite her self-incriminating public rant, Granny was cleared as a suspect when Will told the detectives that she's afraid of his tractor and won't go near it. Also, there were no prints on it except Noah's—and mine.

The state police detectives at the scene had all been briefed on a "need to know" basis and agreed to close the case as self-defense. Dog Berry, who didn't pass muster, I guess—I'm not super surprised somehow—was told to forget everything he'd seen or heard that day because if he ever talked about it to anyone, he'd wind up just another piece of fat virgin ass sitting in a federal super-max cell somewhere in Colorado for the next twenty years. Later the sheriff gave him a week off without pay for missing the stolen car, especially after it had been pointed out to him. I admit I chuckled a bit when I heard that. We haven't seen him much since.

#

A new recruit was introduced at the October firemen's meeting at Sally's—one Noah Stevens from the Community of Satin. He told us that, although he was born and raised a city boy, he'd really become very fond of life in Skedaddle Gore and everybody he'd met there so far. Seems like a real nice guy.

After CPR and First Responder re-qualifications were finished and the bar was reopened, Marti asked to talk to me outside.

It seems Granny told her weekly AA meeting that, after sixteen months of sobriety, she had a slip. She'd been trying all summer to fend off a groundhog that was chowing down on her beloved gardens, even trying one of those humane cage traps to no avail. She finally resorted to an old-fashioned leg hold trap, which had worked on the day in question. When she saw that the poor thing was rolling in pain and trying to gnaw off its paw to escape, she panicked, grabbed one of Will's souvenir baseball bats and beat it out of its misery. Turns out that's what she'd been screaming about. Covered with blood and gore, she ran to her laundry room and threw all her clothes in the washing machine. She also dug out her security stash, a pint of Jim Beam she had hidden inside the motor compartment of the drier and jumped into the shower with it. After sixteen months her tolerance for alcohol was non-existent and she quickly blacked out, coming to in the back of Marti's Jeep. She exchanged her sobriety chip for a beginner's model and started all over. The group gave her a standing ovation.

#

A month later the Board of Assessors paid me thirty-four dollars and fifty cents, less withholding, for my time on this case. They cut my mileage request in half, though, reasoning that my initial response to the loose cow report was indeed something they should pay for but getting home after everything was over with was my own responsibility.

Well, Hell!

Four: Wicked Lust and Dismay

It's not as if I'd never seen a severed head before. The first time was the result of a boat explosion on the west coast when I was still in the Coast Guard. We had our forty-seven-foot-long MLB fast patrol boat temporarily moored a few slips over when a local marina's fuel pump jockey forgot to switch on the bilge exhaust fans on the charter fishing boat he was filling up. The resulting blast blew him and the boat to smithereens. His head—which had a look of surprised annoyance I'm never going to forget—landed at my feet on our fantail. Luckily, I'd thoroughly emptied my stomach a few minutes earlier as a result of my bar crawl liberty the night before, so I didn't puke. That fact alone made me a grizzled tough guy to the kids in the mess for the rest of that posting, which, at the time, pumped up my middle-aged ego no end.

I'm afraid that I wasn't quite that lucky this time around.

#

As I think you know, Marti Wallace is our rural mail carrier, fire chief and town gossip up here in Skedaddle Gore, which is normally a pretty peaceful and thoroughly respectable little piece of the woods of western Maine. I thought her voice had a curious lilt to it, considering it was 4 A.M. and sounded like it was pouring rain out as I picked up the phone.

"Want some moose meat?"

Now, I have *got* to tell *you* that I consider Maine moose meat to be right up there with that hand massaged, hot-tubbed super beef the Japanese put out, so my initial grumpiness at being woke up early evaporated some quick.

"What happened?" I asked as I reached for my pants.

"I'm up here on the Skunk Hollow Road delivering papers and this big honkin' bull pops out in front of me with no never-you-mind, just past Frenchy Plourde's old place. I took out his legs and broke his neck, but he sure mangled up my front end. Luckily, I wasn't going too fast, and his head was down, so he didn't wind up in my lap." She stopped to catch her breath.

"The carcass is in the ditch and Pug Eugley is on the way up to pick up my wreck. I called Franklin County Dispatch on the fire channel, and they've sent over Mike Hawkins. He ought to be here in a few minutes but I'm sort of up against it without my ride. I've only got about ten more papers to deliver. Can I borrow you and The Beast?"

"Be there in ten minutes, Marti. You OK?" Visions of pan seared moose steaks already had me salivating.

"Yeah, just a couple of bruises and ticked off as hell. I'll probably friggin' need a whole friggin' new friggin' front end."

"The Beast" that Marti asked me for is actually the second by that name. I came out of the Coast Guard with a three-quarter ton Chevy pickup truck of ancient, uncertain and slightly twisted lineage. She had a wooden stake body behind the cab and an interesting, kind of random paint job. Despite her looks and lack of pedigree, she was a piece of work underneath. She'd pretty much go anywhere I wanted and her winches, fore and aft, could always get me home from the hills. Since I was a kid I've always loved machinery and I spent hundreds of happy hours lying under her frame tinkering and tweaking until old age and last winter finally did her in.

I was down at Sally's Motel and Bar and Live Bait and Convenience Store about the end of February plowing out my now-traditional personal parking space—along with the rest of the place—when a loud bang and a thick puff of black smoke accompanied by a mechanical death scream gave me to suspect the worst. Sadly, I was soon proven right.

Pug Eugley, with a catch in his voice, told me the old girl would never again make it up Moxie Hill, which is our main drag, much less pass state inspection. I considered throwing a proper wake at Sally's, as most of the Gore's population had made fun of, ridden in or been hauled out of a snowbank by The Beast over the past several years, but I decided it would be more humane to just trade her in, although it *would* be like shooting a good old horse.

I got hold of Wally Backus down in Farmington, a nice fellow who owned the county Dodge dealership at the time. He did pretty well by me, even giving me a trade in allowance for the junk value. I only had to go a short way into debt for The Beast II—a brand new bright red Dodge Ram one-ton, four-wheel drive pickup with a big, bad, blown hemi diesel engine, a modern every-which-way plow, dual winches, snatch hooks out the wazoo and even a small crane in the bed that I bought off Fly Fleance. She's some nice, let me tell you.

Now bear with me here but I really should back up and tell you a little about Pug Eugley before I go much further. He runs a garage and towing service the next town over in Rangeley. Pug is a true gentleman who understands fine machinery and a man's love for it. Unfortunately, how he got his nickname is obvious if you just look at him. His family is an old and respected one in this area, right up there with the Hinkleys and the Hoars, but he is, without a doubt, the ugliest man I've ever seen, which is saying something, given all the places I've been in this world. Buck Champagne, my late Passamaquoddy shaman friend, used to say that when Pug was born the doctor took a look at his face coming out and thought he had a breech birth. His looks haven't stopped him, though, because, mister man, he is married to one of the finest looking women in three counties and he's got three girls coming up who can knock your socks off with just a smile. He's also a man who can hold a prodigious amount of Gritty McDuff's finest IPA and still change a drive shaft on the side of a hill in a snowstorm.

Well, anyway, Pug had Marti's Jeep on the hook and out of the way by the time I arrived. Mike Hawkins, our local game warden, had already done the accident report, given her the roadkill permit and beat feet. Marti said he was in a hurry because he had a meeting in Augusta with some Hollywood types who want to do a TV show all about him and his Maine warden buddies. I'll believe *that* when I see it.

You see, you need to get a permit tag in Maine if you want to legally keep the remains of a game animal which unfortunately meets its end on a public way. Most locals do if they find themselves in that situation—it softens the blow of having to get your frame straightened—but Mike can usually find someone who can use the meat if the occasional Mister Fussy Pants from away doesn't want to get a little blood in his trunk. Mike's a nice guy in or out of uniform. Nobody but a poacher would ever have a problem with him.

Our late friend Mr. Moose had been quite obliging in his last moments, as he had managed to land belly up and spread eagled just off in the ditch. He was good sized and pretty much in a perfect position to gut and roll out the paunch, which is what we decided to do before finishing up Marti's route. I hooked The Beast's crane to the old boy's offside hooves while Marti—who'd been honing her skinning knife ever since Pug arrived—climbed over the guardrail and opened that puppy up like he'd come factory equipped with a zipper. She cut away the innards and gave me the high sign to hoist away. The plan was to dump out and bury the guts, pack up the tasty organs like the heart and liver in some Ziploc bags Marti always carries "for emergencies," and then let the carcass bleed out and cool while I drove her around the rest of her route.

I'd just swung the crane boom out enough to roll the carcass over when I heard Pug swear.

"Jesus, Mary and Joseph!"

Since that was the foulest language I'd ever heard out of him, even when he was hammered—him being the head Congo church deacon and all—I stopped to look. I wished right off that I hadn't. Remember what I said a while ago about severed heads? Well, this one was staring back at me from the bottom of the hole in the soft ground that the moose had just vacated. Flies were crawling from its lidless eye sockets and the gaping, slack jaw still had junk which I supposed used to be skin hanging off it.

Well, Hell . . .

This time I puked for fair.

#

Marti's newspaper customers didn't get their papers until late that afternoon because we all had to do up statements for the state police crime scene folks while they photographed and combed through the area for a quarter mile in every direction. They even brought in a dog to look for the rest of the body, but they didn't find squat. The moose was nice and cool by the time we got back to my place, where we hoisted him up into the rafters in my garage to cure. I locked the place up tight afterwards because I'd seen the Regan brothers eyeing the carcass from behind the crime scene tape. I don't trust those boys.

The next morning, I called Lucille Castonguay, the butcher at the Rangeley IGA and she gave me an appointment in a couple of weeks to bring the carcass in after it had seasoned up properly. I knew she'd make nice, neat paper-wrapped and labeled packages out of him that'd fit just perfect in half a dozen freezers around town.

#

When Tangerine Gilchrist and her son Jack walked up to my front porch one sunny morning a week later, the latent seventeen-year-old boy who still lives inside my aging skull perked right up. Angie is the Community of Satin's school teacher and counselor. She's got a master's degree from McGill University up in Canada, two kids and fine-looking legs under those long, flowing rainbow-colored skirts those Community women tend to favor in the summertime.

I put down my iPad, waved them on in and offered coffee from that K-Cup thingy my daughter sent me Christmas before last. It makes pretty good Joe, but the useless little left-over plastic cups sure fill up my trash can fast. I hoisted Lummox, my Maine Coon cat, out of his porch chair and offered it to Jack. Lummox gave me one of his looks, but he must have liked Jack because he hopped up into his lap after giving his shoes a thorough sniffing. Angie smiled at them as she sat, which curled my toes. Did I mention she's a fine-looking woman?

We chatted while the coffee machine flashed its lights, groaned like a foghorn and dispensed two Carrabassett Valley Sunrise Blends. Jack asked for sugar and put enough half and half in his cup to qualify the thing as a milkshake, which interested Lummox no end. I judged him to be about sixteen, just shooting up into his adult body—which promised to be tall. Angie gave him the look Pam used to use on our daughter, shook her head and took hers black, like I do. Lummox sighed, hopped up onto the porch railing and settled down to nap in the sun, his best trick.

We chatted for a while, exchanging daughter data. Mine was living in Oregon with her soon-to-be-second ex-husband. Hers was staying for the summer with her father in Victoria, British Columbia. After graduating as salutatorian from Rangeley High School a few years ago, she's in veterinary school out in Calgary. Angie schools some of the Community kids through high school if their parents request it, but she'd wanted her own children to have a wider social experience, which seems to have worked out pretty well so far. All in all, this was turning out to be a pleasant, neighborly visit.

I'd been thinking for a while about asking her out. *Maybe now would be a good time? Carpe Deum, as they say.*

"I'm afraid we've got a problem up at the Mother House, Bobby," Angie said, her voice turning serious.

Damn, I thought. *I knew it!*

"One of our people is missing and I heard about what you and Marti found out on the road last week. I'm worried it might be him, eh?"

"One of the Community members?" I asked.

"Not yet." She paused, then sighed. "We actually kind of think he might be a spy."

Well, Hell...

Now, I think I need to give you some background on the Community of Satin before I say much more. Some say they're little weird. OK, they actually *are* pretty weird—about some things—when you come to think of it. Six or seven years ago a couple of moving vans and a bunch of Saabs and Volvos with Canadian license plates showed up in town. Turns out they had bought up old Beanie Butz's chicken farm about halfway up the Skedaddle Lake Road from where it meets the Ridge Road. They are communal organic chicken farmers and I mean to tell you they are *some* serious about it. Sometimes I think it's almost like they worship the jeezley things.

Now don't go jumping to conclusions. They aren't a cult. They don't even have a church, mind you, but they do have a humongous barbeque pit in front of their main house, where in summer there is almost always some chicken cooking, which they are quite free with—and it's quite tasty.

When they first got here there was a bit of a to-do. They put up a sign on Moxie Hill Road, which is the main drag up into the Gore from State Route Four, that said: WELCOME TO THE HOME OF SATIN. They stuck it next to the WELCOME TO SKEDADDLE

GORE sign the Board of Assessors put up. Well, mister, I want to tell you that *that* got a whole mess of people *some* wound up. Suddenly everybody in town was talking about cults and midnight rituals and human child blood sacrifice and all that. There was even a petition set up in Sally's to have them thrown right out of town, although nobody could agree on just *how* that could be done.

I wasn't constable yet then, but I decided to go over and say hi. Among other things I was somewhat curious. I mean—"Home of Satin?" Really? Don't Canadians have to pass fifth grade spelling like American kids do? Well, it turns out they're actually a group of fifty or so very nice, friendly folks—including several pretty well-behaved kids—who are followers of a pacifist fellow named—honestly, I am *not* making this up—Satin Phavogue. He lives in St. John's, Newfoundland, not to be confused, which they tell me it usually is, with St. John, New Brunswick, which is also in Canada.

This guy is the "Satin" the sign talks about, not "Satan"—who's something else entirely. Nobody local has ever actually met him because apparently he still lives in an apartment over a bodega he owns in St. John's. The U.S. Customs and Immigration Service won't let him into the country because he's a convicted felon in Canada. Some tax thing apparently. They did let most of his followers in, though, so the sign should probably read: WELCOME TO THE HOME OF EVERYBODY *BUT* SATIN. I pointed this out to them and told them about the big hooraw in town. They had a meeting and voted that very evening. The sign came down the next day and they invited the whole town to a big barbeque with a couple of kegs the next weekend. That went over like gangbusters and these days the Community is pretty well thought of, considering they're *actually* from away.

"A spy?" I said, putting down my coffee cup.

"We don't really know. There are some well-meaning animal rights groups *and* a few outright whackos who sometimes send undercover agents into operations like ours to see if they can claim we mistreat our flocks." She shifted in her chair and leaned toward me. I reciprocated. It felt comfortable and friendly. Jack was looking over my iPad and didn't seem to notice.

"I know it sounds odd to some—Lord knows we've heard about it enough—but we in the Community really *respect* the chicken. All over the world this one humble species has done more to enable and enhance the process of life on Earth than any other, including the human species, eh?" She leaned in closer. "It feeds us with its eggs and body, even leaving us its droppings and remains, which can be composted to grow even more food to nurture us and countless other beings on our planet."

Jack yawned. Angie's face colored a bit and she sat back. "Sorry. I don't usually get this wound up, but the reverence for life we have, especially for the life of what many consider to be an insignificant, ubiquitous food species, is at the very core of my personal values. It boils my *knickers* that anyone would want to destroy that."

Her forehead wrinkled, her jaw clenched, and she was so cute at that point that I lost my train of thought for a second.

"Boils my knickers," I thought. *That's a new one on me. Wonder if it's a Canadian saying, eh?*

"It's OK." I chuckled. "I tend to respect folks with strong beliefs, even if I don't share them." I grinned at her. "But in this case I agree with you. I love chicken, too. But mostly with barbeque sauce."

She laughed and sat back. Her shoulders relaxed against her chair. She was silent for a moment as she looked at me. I met her gaze. She had these big hazel eyes, with gold flecks . . .

"So, who's this guy who's missing?" I finally asked.

She shook her head. "His name is Frank Lopez. He walked in last spring and asked us about joining the Community. We took him in because he said he was homeless and hungry. He looked it. We do that sometimes—take people in—I know you know that." She glanced down at her cup and set it on the porch rail.

Now if you've known me for a while I may have told you about the Community's little sideline, but if you're new in town or just up for the fishing over the holiday weekend, forget everything I'm about to tell you because it's wicked confidential. It seems that the Community of Satin, since it moved here, has operated a secret safe house for the U. S. Marshal's Witness Protection Program. The two deputy marshals who run it out of Portland say that the Community has provided the most secure and problem free placements of this type in the whole, entire country. How about that?

I had a sudden vision of the marshals sitting in these very chairs last fall, drinking coffee and discussing the New England mob.

"I do."

"Frank is not in that program. We don't get a lot of applicants at the Community and we don't recruit. Most of us came down from Newfoundland and Labrador with the migration and we're very much a big family now."

"Did you hire him?" I asked.

"No. Sometimes we hire contractors for things we aren't able to do ourselves, but we don't hire people to work in our business day to day. We share everything in the Community, including the labor." She gazed out over the Rangeley Lakes in the valley below. "Most of us do own small items, usually things that mean something to us personally. Family photos, wedding rings, underwear. Things like that, eh?" She shrugged.

Underwear? Uh huh. I shook my head as I absorbed the thought. She didn't seem to notice.

"Other than that, everything we need is provided by the Community—held in common by a written Compact all the members have signed."

"Has Frank signed it?" I asked.

"Not yet, but he said at a meeting last month that he would when the time came. We have sort of a probationary period that takes about a year. We get to know new people gradually. We answer their questions. We help them with personal issues if they want. We're not a church and we don't preach or proselytize. We just live and let live—and glory in it. We gather at meals, especially supper, where we discuss anything we want to. We talk a lot." She smiled. "We do yell sometimes, but we work out disputes in peace. We help each other. We sing."

I nodded. I've heard them sing many times. They do a bang up four-part *a capella* job on "The Star-Spangled Banner" and "Oh, Canada" before each Little League game.

"And Frank?"

"I thought he was serious," she said. "He seemed happy whenever I talked to him, just a bit odd. Sort of detached. He's been a hard worker in the field and the barn. Never complains. Asks good questions. Doesn't talk much about his past, but many don't. Understandable, really."

"When did he go missing?"

"Two weeks ago. He just stopped coming to supper. He was on our utility crew, and he used to drive the reefer truck around for deliveries, sometimes as far as Boston. It's not unusual for those who are off working to miss meals for a day or two, but the truck is here, and he never signed out any other transport."

"Did he leave anything behind?"

"We haven't been through his things." Her face colored. "You see, we're in a quandary." She looked into my eyes. "Satin teaches strict respect for the private things and thoughts that everyone holds dear. That's why I stopped in. We'd like you to go through his room for us. Maybe you could even see if what you and Marti found is him, eh? You're a constable, aren't you?"

"In name only, actually," I said. She frowned. Then I remembered what a constable is in Canada.

"It's a long story but . . . sure. I'd be happy to help." She smiled.

#

We took The Beast up to the Chicken House, which is what most locals call the Mother House of the Community of Satin. Jack called shotgun and sat tall, looking around as we pulled in to ensure that the other kids could see him. Some things never change. Angie sat in the middle, next to me. It was a little tight, but we managed. She smelled nice.

The main house has been expanded since Beanie's kids sold it. The Community has also built a big modern barn and processing facility and several smaller cottages, where families like Angie and Jack live. Most of the few unattached residents like Frank, Angie explained, stay in private rooms in the old farmhouse.

The second story room assigned to Frank Lopez was larger than I'd expected, but sparsely furnished. Unlocked, as Angie told me all internal rooms are, it held a comfortable looking bed which was neatly made. By the single window sat an old-style upholstered chair with a floor lamp and side table. A good-sized dresser and a tall wardrobe cabinet rounded out the furnishings. There was a utilitarian, almost institutional-looking rug on the floor which didn't look as if it would do much to protect your feet from the cold hard pine floors on Maine winter mornings. No curtains in the windows and nothing hung on the walls. No radio or TV. No feeling at all about its occupant. A plain, clean room. Like a monk's cell. Odd, indeed.

From the doorway I peered at the ceiling, into all the corners and around the light fixture in the center of the room. Then I looked at the walls, then the floor. Nothing jumped out at me, no loose wallpaper or lifted floorboards.

"Looks to be a good housekeeper," I remarked.

"He has a good one," Angie answered from the hall behind me. "'Elizabeth the Third' we call her. She's for hire, you know."

"Really?" I actually was a bit interested. I can be a little lazy about housework and my place could use an occasional dusting—or hosing out.

"Yup, but your sex could be a problem, eh?" Jack said.

"My sex?"

Angie laughed. "She won't work in a man's space if he's there. You have to be elsewhere when she shows up."

I glanced over my shoulder. Jack was hiding his mouth behind his hand.

"I'll bite. Why?"

"She works in the nude," Angie said.

I shrugged. "That's not necessarily bad."

"She's sixty-five and has a mustache," Jack said with a giggle. Angie made a face at him.

I laughed. "OK," I said. "You two kids stay here in the hallway while I look around." Angie nodded and grinned. My toes curled up—again.

I figured that if I could find something with Frank's DNA on it, I could get the sheriff's office to have it tested against the head. I reasoned the dresser would be my best bet and I hit paydirt on the first try. Right in the top drawer, where everyone having a Y chromosome who shares a common bathroom puts it, was Frank's toilet kit.

"I'll need a plastic bag," I said.

"Jack," Angie said. "Go down to the kitchen and get one from Deuteronomy."

"Right," he said.

"Make that a half dozen or so," I said.

"OK." He ran toward the stairway.

"Deuteronomy?" I asked.

"We don't get to choose our names in Canada." She stuck out her chin. "And he's a very good cook."

Hmm.

I pulled out the other four drawers in the dresser but found only clean underwear and work shirts in the top two. The others were empty. I moved over to the wardrobe and pulled open the door. Hanging on a hook was a plain, non-descript baseball cap that looked like it had been used to wipe out a chicken coop. I grabbed it and flipped it over just as Jack came bailing back down the hall. The hat was heavier than it should have been.

Well, Hell . . .

"Looks like you were right, Angie."

"About what?"

"About there being something odd about Frank."

I turned back the cloth flap inside the brim of the cap and showed her the video camera hidden underneath.

#

After that, things got a little hectic in the Gore for a while. I called up Willie Brackett, the local deputy sheriff. It turned out that she was next door in the town of Madrid, and she skipped right up. She asked a few questions, listened, and took some notes. I noticed that she wrinkles her nose when she's thinking, like Helen Hunt did in *Twister*. She told us that the John Doe head I'd found was still unidentified and the state police were waiting for a report from the medical examiner's office. She took the plastic bags with the toilet kit and the ball cap and gave me a receipt. Angie told Jack to go get a padlock and a hasp from Elizabeth the housekeeper and I screwed it to the door. Willie pasted some evidence tape over the padlock and kept the keys.

The next day she and a state police forensic team showed up with a couple of detectives and gave the room a thorough shakedown. Angie says Elizabeth is still steaming. They didn't find anything more than what I found, but they were a whole lot messier about it.

Frank Lopez, whose real name turned out to be Scott E. Smith, had a criminal history in Jackson Hole, Wyoming and was in CODIS, the FBI's national criminal DNA database. Turns out he was indeed an undercover agent for an animal rights group. He'd been recording his experiences with the video camera in his hat. Ironically his final recording turned out to include a statement telling them that he had really found no fault with the way the Community of Satin treated their chickens, even calling them a model operation.

He was also a bit of a rounder. His camera's memory card held a few rather revealing photos of Lucille Castonguay, our butcher. Remember I mentioned her a while back? Anyway, when Willie and the state police detectives went over and showed her the pictures, she broke down and admitted that she'd fallen for Frank. He'd dropped dead "in the saddle"—as they say—at her husband's fishing camp up on the Dead River, where they'd gone to consummate whatever it was that she thought their relationship was. Since she was also the daughter of the minister of that strange Love of God Church up in Hogan's Goat Township, she panicked. As Willie joked with typical black cop humor, she "filleted" him, scattering choice bits all over two counties. Eventually they did get most of poor Frank/Scott back. He'd died of a massive brain hemorrhage, as it turns out. Lucille paid a fine for Abuse of a Corpse, a Class D misdemeanor, and moved to Vermont after she was excommunicated and her divorce was finalized.

Marti got a new front end on her Jeep from her insurance company, but we had to find another butcher for the moose.

\#

The next month the Board of Assessors paid me seventeen dollars and eighty-five cents for my time and mileage on this case, less withholding. I thought that was fair, all things considered.

Five: Tower Thirteen and the Skedaddle Triangle

She was tall, and brunette, and blessed with the clean, open look I've always called "interesting." Not overtly pretty, she was nevertheless just the sort to catch the eye of the grizzled widower sitting at the next picnic table over in the great room of the main lodge at the Skedaddle Ridge Ski Resort. I was nursing a coffee and the last remnants of a breakfast sandwich in the last few minutes before my shift was due to start. The fact that she'd stripped off the jeans she was wearing, revealing a pair of skin-colored tights, just might have contributed to the fact that I noticed her. Facing away from me she slowly propped one long, well-muscled leg up on the picnic table across from me and leaned over toward the kid with her. Her hair was done up in a long, tightly-woven braid and she wore a fine chain with a tiny cross that looked to be gold around her neck. Artfully worked, the braid fell fetchingly over her shoulder as she cocked her head and smiled at him, lifting an eyebrow. He grinned and, reaching for his wallet, walked away toward the snack bar. No rings that I could see on either of them, but they were obviously acquainted. As I watched her foot drop back to the floor, it struck me that she was a fair bit older than him, late twenties I'd guess. She replaced it with the other and continued her warmup stretches as a bunch of school kids from the middle school in Rangeley came busting through the side door, throwing their gear bags every which way as they shrieked at each other in the excitement of being out of the classroom.

Well, Hell . . .

I recognized the harried form of their teacher, Harriett Tupperman, who followed them through the door, her arms full of notebooks and file folders. I've heard that the braver kids call her "Old Tupperware." Gym class, I thought, has changed little over the years, but at least the kids these days get to have more fun than I used to. Harriett dropped her stuff on the nearest table, nodded at me and blew a blast on the whistle hanging around her neck that would have blown old Max Benno, one of my best Coast Guard gunners—who used to brag that he could sleep through a hurricane—right out of bed. Silence dropped like a soggy blanket over the room as she gave the hoard five minutes to get their gear on and assemble outside at the morning ski school. I admired her technique. She'd have made a good drill sergeant.

The brunette was a little startled at first but then shook her head, yawned and grinned as she bent down to dig her ski boots out of her bag. Mentally slapping myself I briefly admired the view as she pulled a set of quilted ski pants over her tights. A grey sweatshirt with ST. JOSEPH'S COLLEGE printed over her quite adequate but not spectacular chest completed the ensemble. "Catholic girls start much too late," popped into my head. I must have snorted at the Billy Joel lyrics because she glanced at me and frowned for a moment. I smiled my most reassuring smile and nodded, raising my coffee cup. She relaxed and smiled back. Second date for these two maybe, I speculated.

She certainly didn't seem particularly shy around the kid, who'd returned carrying two cups of what smelled like Carrabassett Valley Coffee's Longfellow Dark. He looked over, nodded and dismissed me in a second for what I was—no threat whatsoever to his plan of the day, whatever that was. For an instant I envied him, but that passed. None of my business really. I glanced at the clock on the wall and stood up. Grabbing my backpack with my lunch and fly-tying gear I zipped up my forest-green company parka with the Skedaddle Ridge logo on the back. I tossed my used wrapper in the trash as I clumped toward the door in my old second-hand Tyrolia ski boots. It was starting out looking like a nice day, sunny but colder than hell;

but after a couple years working on the ski lift crew—a "liftey"—I was pretty used to that.

I originally took the job a few years ago as a part-time gig after Will Liberty, a neighbor of mine who's a ski instructor during the winter up at "The Mountain," as the natives call it, told me that I could get a free ticket and lessons if I worked there. I found out later that you can also get a bonus for recruiting new employees, so I'm guessing Will had ulterior motives. Whatever. Good for him.

I'm not necessarily the best skier in the world, but I'm getting there. Not too bad considering I grew up down on Maine's coast and my view of skiing as a kid was that it was some stupid, expensive exercise that rich tourists from away practiced far up in the mountains in the snowy part of Maine. I'm having a lot more fun lately than I originally thought I would and it's good exercise on my off days. Will says I'm already up to the intermediate level and working my way toward advanced. Last week in Sally's he told me I'm doing pretty well, for an arthritic old codger. I threw my beer coaster at him. I've been watching the Ski Patrol, though, and I'm thinking about applying for the training next summer. Their parkas are really cool looking. We'll see.

These days I usually work in the top shack on the old "Buster" triple chairlift that runs up to the summit from the mid-mountain lift junction. Buster got her name because most people called the old T-bar that used to run up that line the "Ball Buster" and the owners decided to leave the name on her when they moved her in five years ago. They finally blasted away the jeezley cliff at the top of the old T-bar line that used to have folks hanging on for dear life as it lifted them almost straight up for the last fifty feet. Then it would dump them off, sometimes in a heap of tangled equipment and bodies. We skiers call that a "yard sale" because there's stuff scattered all over the landscape. I heard that the explosion that day rattled windows as far away as Berlin, New Hampshire and the Community of Satin's chickens stopped laying eggs for a week.

Anyway, Buster's machinery and towers actually used to be the old main lift. They recycled her when they put up the new, fancy detachable quad on the line up from the base lodge, so my girl's already got plenty of time in grade on her. She's slow but still runs slick and she's never failed her state inspection in all her twenty-five years.

By the way, funny story. They named the new lift "Big Poppy" after that famous Red Sox baseball player. I kind of doubt he was actually a skier because he was originally from the Dominican Republic, but you never know. And he *did* spell his nickname a little bit differently. The story goes that the company that built the lift out in Utah called up to find out what name the owners group wanted them to paint on the side of the brand-new base station. They had a meeting and decided it would be fun to name the lift after the Hall of Fame ball player. They did the whole naming deal over the phone, and nobody here saw anything in writing. When the lift arrived, everybody saw that the big guy's name was misspelled. When the owners heard how much it would cost to get the name redone, they decided to leave it as it was. Personally, I think it's turned out to be some clever marketing. Our big boss is one smart cookie, let me tell you. Everybody who lives anywhere north of New Yawk City gets a chuckle out of it the first time they see it.

Originally I didn't think I'd like the assignment way up at the top but being up there above the tree line turns out to be a hoot. The view is amazing if the weather is clear. I can see *Canada* from my shack! But some days the wind can be brutal. I've got a readout thing on the wall that tells me what the wind speed is on the tower just below me. If it hits forty-one miles per hour, which happens once or twice a week on average, we have to stop loading and shut down the lift. The wind resistance of a bunch of people sitting on the dangling chairs could derail the "rope," which is the technical name for the steel cable that carries the chairs up and down. Let me tell you, I wouldn't want to be on a chair that happened to, mister. I hate heights to begin with and a couple of Buster's towers are better than thirty-five feet off the ground. I have to hire Nicki Carson from the stove shop down in Rangeley to sweep my chimney flue every year because I get wobbly just climbing ladders, much less walking on my cabin roof top, and *it's* only fifteen feet off the ground. I don't even like standing on a stool to get something out of a kitchen cabinet. I don't go up top at Fire Department calls, either. Like I said back along, I just keep the pumps on old Engine Five running and let the young kids do the other stuff. When I ride Buster up to my shack in the morning I stare straight ahead when my chair gets to those towers and pretend I'm not about to die.

Most days on the Ridge I sit there next to my "little buddy," the shack's electric heater, tying my trout flies and watching the paying customers slide off the chairs just before the rope takes them around the big revolving bull wheel that sends the empties back down the hill. Sometimes a skier happens to fall or get snagged on something getting off, but that's rare because it's an expert area of the mountain and most of the sports who come up here know what they're doing. If something *does* happen, I hit the big red button right next to my chair and go out and make sure that they're OK. Usually they are, we share a laugh and off they go. Other than that, all I really have to do is wave occasionally, look friendly and rake off the top landing once in a while so that it's nice and easy for the paying customers to be on their way. On the day I'm talking about here, though, all that changed—just like that.

We'd had a weather front move in about mid-morning and the wind had died down, which caused a fog bank to form all the way from Skedaddle Lake at the base of the mountain almost up to where I was sitting. There wasn't much of a crowd on the lifts that day because of the reduced visibility and I was seeing a whole lot of empty chairs coming by. If it hadn't been for the sunshine and fairly mild temps above the clouds, I'd've been bored stiff. I was daydreaming a little about the new barbecue sauce that the Chicken House had just started using when this one chair, the first occupied one in a while, came up out of the clouds. I could see that there were two people on it, one on each end, with a vacant space in the middle. The safety bar was up but nobody was paying any attention. I didn't see either of them move at all as Buster began to swing them around the bull wheel. There's a safety gate there that you can kick to stop the lift if you get into trouble. The gate caught one of their drooping ski tips, and Buster dutifully spun down just before the chair cleared the landing on the downhill side. I set my fly-tying vice aside and went to check. I remember thinking there was something really odd going on. Usually, folks this happens to are embarrassed and laughing. Not this pair.

They were leaning away from one another as the chair stopped swinging. It was suddenly completely silent without the normal background rattle of the machinery. I started to get worried when they didn't respond to my cheery hello as I came up behind them. The person on the outside seat was slumped over and the other one, on the inside, was covered with blood which was starting to drip onto the landing deck.

Well, Hell . . .

I hustled back to my shack and grabbed the phone down to the base station. I started pushing the call button for all I was worth.

Charlie Winchenbach, the crew boss, answered after what felt like an hour. "Judas Priest, Bobby, what's the matter?"

"Charlie, stop loading the lift!" I shouted. "There's people on a chair hurt up here. Call the Ski Patrol and send me some help."

"OoooKay, Bobby," Charlie said. "There's only been one chair loaded in the past fifteen minutes, so there's just them three on the rope. We're damn lucky we won't have to evacuate anybody. I'll get everybody moving. You get those people over to the warming hut if you can. Patrol shouldn't be long."

I ran back to the chair and felt for a pulse on the guy who was slumped over. The other one—the one covered in blood—started to mumble something over and over that I couldn't understand. I couldn't get a pulse on the first guy. His skin was pale and cold, and he really didn't look good. I realized then that he was probably gone. Since the other one was at least breathing I figured that was the priority. I circled around to the front of the chair and grabbed him round the waist, flipped him over my shoulder and pulled him off the chair, skis and all. I was expecting more weight. Maybe it's a kid, I thought. I hoped not. With the body over my shoulder, I stumbled the ten yards or so to the warming hut beside the landing, pushed open the door and laid my load down next to the heater.

I finally got a good look. The first thing I saw was a tiny gold cross and chain. You could have knocked me over with a feather, let me tell you. It was that woman from the base lodge who'd caught my eye that morning. She was breathing slowly but steadily, and her eyes were open, but I could tell that she was actually somewhere else. She had the vacant, glazed-over look in her eyes that I've unfortunately seen all too often in the past. They call it the "thousand-yard stare." Going to be some wicked PTSD for this one if she lives, I told myself as I looked for the source of the blood. As I worked, I saw her eyes focus on me for an instant and she started to mumble again. This time I thought I caught a name, "Peter Foster." She repeated it three times before her voice trailed off and her eyes went blank again.

"Is that your boyfriend?" I asked her. "Peter? Peter Foster?"

I could see it was no use, she'd lapsed back into oblivion. Strangely, I wasn't able to find the source of the blood. I couldn't find any wounds on her anywhere. It looked like somebody had dumped a whole bucket of red paint all over her, except I could tell from the smell that it wasn't paint. I pulled one of those emergency tinfoil space blanket things off the shelf next to the hut's door, laid it over her and headed out to the lift to check again on the first one. I remember thinking that he must be the kid I saw her with that morning. Was that all *his* blood, I wondered? Maybe a lover's quarrel? If that's what it was, it must have been a doozy.

I heard a roar behind me as I ran and turned to see Peggy Gordon and Pete Durrell riding double on a two-up snowmachine. Peggy, who's seventy-five years old if she's a day, was driving like a maniac, which didn't surprise me in the least. She crested the last hump about four feet off the ground and skidded to a stop in front of me. Old Pete was hanging on for dear life. Peggy's the big boss lady at The Mountain. Her dad was the skipper of a combat ski troop company in the 10th Mountain Division of the U.S. Army during World War II. He and six of his buddies who didn't know what else to do with themselves after the war moved up to Rangeley, pooled their money and bought all the land around Skedaddle Mountain from the Great Northern Paper Company. People in town thought they were nuts, but they cut one trail by hand that first summer and set up a rope tow with an old Model T Ford drive train to power it. They still call that trail, which is now the beginner's slope, "Model T." Peggy's the principal partner in the owners group that evolved from that first bunch. And she's got a mouth on her that any old sailor like me can't help but admire.

Pete Durrell is the head of the Ski Patrol and once Peggy cut the engine, I yelled at him that there was somebody hurt inside the warming hut, and I thought the one who was still on the lift was dead. He grabbed his medical kit and headed for the hut while Peggy ran with me to the lift. I knew she'd trained as a nurse as a girl and used to work summers at the Health Center in Rangeley. She checked the guy's eyes and leaned in to pull back his jacket collar to check for a pulse. He was white as a sheet and cold as a dead mackerel—and he wasn't the kid from the lodge I was thinking he'd be.

Peggy glanced down at his legs. "Damn! You're right, Bobby, he's dead," she said with a groan. "He's been stabbed in the nuts."

Well, Hell!

#

The rest of the day was pretty much a blur. The woman was evacuated by the Ski Patrol to the base lodge on a snow groomer, which is a humongous machine that looks like a space alien version of a caterpillar-tracked battle tank with a big snowplow on the front and a giant rototiller behind. Willie Daggett, the local deputy sheriff, who arrived on another snowmachine, shooed everybody away from the lift and fended off the gawkers until Doc Jeffries, the Medical Examiner, could get there to officially declare the man dead. Eventually she got detailed by her sergeant to stay with the woman on the ambulance trip to the Farmington hospital in case she suddenly became lucent, which didn't look at all promising. Then it started to snow blue blazes, of course.

Because there was a suspicious death involved, the state police finally arrived and took charge. I remember giving a written statement to a detective who said his name was Dalrymple. He skimmed over it in the corner of the warming hut where he and his helpers had set up their "command post." Then he said he wanted to talk to me in private.

As soon as they'd shooed everybody out into the cold and we were alone, that numbskull asked me flat out if I'd stabbed the dude myself. I was astonished. I tried to answer all his questions, but I don't think he believed anything I told him. He told me in no uncertain terms that it didn't make sense to him that I didn't do it because, to his way of thinking, I was the only person who *could* have. Finally, he told me not to leave town. Honestly, just like in the movies. I laughed at that point, which I immediately realized was a wicked stupid mistake.

Then and there he had me searched for weapons—stripped right down to my wooly drawers out in the falling snow in front of God and everybody—by a couple of his goons, who weren't too gentle about it, either. Then he had them take my fingerprints and scrape a DNA swab off the inside of my mouth. He kept everybody penned up inside the warming hut for hours after that and wouldn't let anybody leave until the "crime scene" could be "processed." He even ordered Peggy Gordon to shut down operations on the whole mountain for the rest of the day, which earned him a dressing down that would have made a Marine Corps Master Gunnery Sergeant blush. Gotta love that old girl!

I finally got home after midnight. My old Maine Coon cat, Lummox, was almost as pissed about missing his dinner as Peggy had been at Dalrymple. I fed him a whole big can of the extra stinky stuff he loves and cracked a Shipyard for myself. Then I fried myself a bacon cheeseburger, drank two more beers and fell asleep on the couch in front of the TV with the dishes in the sink and the cat curled up on my chest.

It was already daylight when I woke up. I was afraid I'd be late for work, and I didn't have time to fix myself anything for lunch, so I dug out my biggest thermos and filled it with a whole pot of the strongest coffee blend that I had in the cupboard. The first place I went when I hit the base lodge was the kitchen, where I was just in time for the first daily shouting match between Peachy Keene and Snort Benson. Snort's the head cook—the "Chef de Cuisine," he calls himself. Peachy is his baker and his gigantic chocolate donuts are legendary in Franklin County. Snort thinks Peachy is a fat glutton and Peachy thinks Snort is a dink. To some extent they're each right, but all I had time to do that morning was step between them, grab a sixpack of Peachy's Moose Turds, and run for my life.

I had my arms full, and my backpack slung over one shoulder when I climbed onto Buster's first chair a few minutes later for my ride to work. On my way up in the morning it's part of my job to check each tower visually to make sure that nothing looks out of place or needs attention from "Frick and Frack," the two-man lift maintenance crew. Everybody calls them that because they're always together. I'll tell you a funny story about them sometime.

Anyway, looking up while doing the visual inspection also helps me over that height thing I was telling you about. Everything was fine until I got up close to tower thirteen, which is halfway up and is the shortest tower on the lift. I heard a sharp noise below me. It sounded like a single dog bark, but I'd never heard of a dog this high up, almost 4,000 feet. I've seen squirrels, rabbits, chipmunks and once even a bobcat up there, but no dogs. Startled, I looked down. Then I shook my head and gulped back a quick bout of nausea, even though I knew I was only ten feet off the ground.

Right under me I saw a jumble of about half a dozen ski poles, some stuck upright and some lying halfway deep in the fresh powder. They looked like they'd fallen from the lift. That happens a fair amount when skiers shift in the chair, but I couldn't remember seeing that particular bunch the day before. We call that spot the "Skedaddle Triangle." It's the point where the rope runs up over a hump on the hill. Riders tend to feel stiff and "antsy" at that point and start squirming around trying to get comfortable. Often, they drop stuff when they do that. Every summer the maintenance crew takes an ATV with a dump body up to tower thirteen to pick up all the accumulated trash. They've found water bottles, ski poles, hats, hypodermic needles, gloves, used condoms (think about *that* for a minute), mittens, books, beer cans, underwear (both sexes) and even a few cell phones.

I called Pete Durrell when I got to the summit.

"Hi, Pete, I wonder if you or your patrol crew can go check something for me?"

Pete has a *real* slow way of talking that can make you want to shake him by the shoulders sometimes.

"I don't know, Bobby," he drawled. "Seems like you've got the whammy on you these days, don't it? Wouldn't want one of my guys to catch it." I hoped he was joking.

"It's no big deal," I said. "I just noticed coming up this morning that there's a bunch of ski poles sticking out of the snow at the base of tower thirteen. I remembered that that chair load yesterday with the dead man on board didn't have any poles with them. If it turns out to be nothing they can go to the lost and found, but I'm curious."

"OK." Pete chuckled. "You been watching that CSI show on the TV, aincha? Ya think maybe I can find the murder weapon and solve the whole case, once and for all?"

"Yeah, Pete," I said. "Then maybe we could get rid of that dumbass Dalrymple character. He gets on my nerves."

"You're not alone there, Bobby Boy. You should've heard what Peggy had to say about him when she called up his headquarters in Augusta last night. Mister man, I'll bet his ears are some burned up this morning."

"I hope so. Couldn't happen to a nicer guy."

"Got that right," he said. "I'll swing over that way on my first sweep this morning. Any of them Moose Turds left?"

"I'll save you one."

"If you can eat that whole friggin' sack full I saw you with this mornin', you're a better man than I am. I'll let ya know what I find," Pete said and hung up.

Peachy's Moose Turds are basically a chocolate raised donut filled with chocolate pastry cream and covered with a chocolate frosting, with chocolate sprinkles. Gotta be a thousand calories each. I'd eaten two already that morning and was starting on my third. I could already feel the sugar rush pushing away my drowsiness. I'd pay for it later, I knew, but at least I wouldn't need to eat again until supper.

After about fifteen minutes my cell phone rang. Pete found something alright. He told me that next to one of those poles, half buried in the snow, was an open switchblade stiletto knife with blood all over it. He said he didn't touch it, thinking back to what *he* learned watching CSI.

Well, Hell.

I called Willie Brackett on her cell phone and told her about the knife. She sounded groggy but she said she had Dalrymple's number and she'd pass on the information. She told me to have Pete stay put and keep anybody away who might be curious. I told her I would.

When I asked her if she was OK she told me that she'd just spent the night sitting with the woman from the lift in her room at Franklin Memorial Hospital, waiting to see if she'd wake up. She'd been relieved that morning by a brand-new young state trooper named Chad Fairchild who's just been assigned to Franklin County. She told me she thought he was "dreamy." I joked that she'd better watch out, he'd only break her heart.

"I wish," she said, with a yawn.

Oooh, boy.

#

About two that afternoon, Detective Dalrymple showed up at the top of Buster on a groomer with Charlie, my crew boss, and Mike Hawkins, our local game warden, in tow. Charlie said he'd been told to take over my job while I "discussed a few things" with the detective.

Well, sir, that friggin' jackass started in on me *again*. Right then and there, in the middle of the landing—with people getting off the lift all around us, mind you—he laid into me for "telling" Pete to

go to tower thirteen and "corrupt" the scene. Then he accused me
of "compromising" his investigation. Then he wanted to know how
I'd known the knife was at the foot of tower thirteen anyway and
implied that maybe, just maybe, I'd thrown it there myself. A crowd
of skiers gathered around us to listen.

Between my lack of sleep and the amount of caffeine and sugar
I'd consumed that morning, I began to get just a little huffy at that
point. I told him—I thought in a perfectly civil tone—just what
I'd seen and what I'd done about it. Then, mister manny, he told
me—right there in front of all those people, mind you—that I was
the one who discovered the body and "statistics" say that the person
who finds the body like I had is usually the "perp."

"In my view, *you*, Mr. Wing," Dalrymple shouted at me, "are the
only other person besides that woman he was with who *could* have
killed that man, and she's too traumatized by what she saw to say
anything about it."

The crowd started to murmur at that and I gotta tell you *that* did
it, mister man! He'd got my full Irish up and my "civility" went right
out the window.

Before I could stop myself I spit out, "You damned, friggin'
stupid idiot! Why would I friggin' tell anybody where the friggin'
knife was if I friggin' did it? There was friggin' witnesses right there
to see me all the time after I found the guy."

I could see Dalrymple's face getting redder and redder. I should
have known enough to stop there, but . . .

"Your friggin' buddies all but friggin' strip searched me yesterday
and I didn't have anything on me," I shouted, throwing my hands in
the air. "When the frig did I have time to get down there, drop the
friggin' knife and get back to the friggin' top? That doesn't friggin'
make any friggin' *sense!*

(I may actually have used stronger words then "friggin'" and
"frig.")

Mike Hawkins put his hand on my arm at that point. "Easy, Bobby. He's just doing his job."

Dalrymple ignored Mike, grabbed my other arm and bellowed, "Frig it. You're friggin' coming with us."

(Yes, he used those stronger words, too.)

Well, Hell!

\#

I don't think I've told you, but I was arrested once before when I was still in the Coast Guard. I was on a training detachment on a Marine base in Yuma, Arizona when a bunch of us wandered out of the NCO club and headed back to the barracks after an evening of socializing and indulging in a few "adult beverages." That was where I was introduced to tequila, which is nothing but a Mexican headache in a bottle, let me tell you. On the way we came across this beautifully maintained lawn next to the roadway that seemed to go on for miles. We could see that the barracks we were assigned to was just the other side of it, so, being sailors, we took a bearing and set a course. By the time we staggered to the other side you'd have thought World War III had broken out. There were four Jeeps sitting there bearing a total of eight very large, very pissed-off Marine MP's who were in no mood to party. We were "politely" escorted to the base administration building where the duty Master Gunnery Sergeant "instructed" us in Marine Corps customs and traditions. It seems that *NO ONE* walks across the parade ground on a Marine base unless he or she is on parade or mowing the grass. I took a quick informal poll and determined that none of my Coast Guard colleagues present were aware of this. We were then treated to a classic Marine dressing down, fined twenty-five dollars each and turned over to our duty officer, a young ensign who laughed so hard he pissed himself.

This was a little different.

Mike Hawkins loaded me into the passenger seat of the groomer next to Cruiser Muldoon, the head groomer driver, who's the size of two full-grown Saint Bernard dogs sitting side by side. Smells like one, too. Mike squeezed in beside me but there was no room left for Dalrymple, so he stayed where he was, which was fine with me. I was starting to cool off and reflect on my situation. When last seen Dalrymple was talking on his cell phone and gesturing toward the warming hut. He looked chilled, which I found somehow comforting.

Cruiser delivered us to the VIP parking lot next to the lodge, where Mike's warden service pickup truck was parked. Mike didn't say a word on the ride down to the jail and neither did I. I spent the time going over what I knew about the rights of someone who's been arrested, which they'd touched on at the Citizen's Police Academy course that Farmington PD had put on a couple of years before. I remembered that I had the right to remain silent in a situation like this and that seemed the best course of action for me just then.

Mike turned on the radio in his truck when he got down to Phillips and we listened to Golden Oldies on WKTJ FM and the cop chatter on the two-way the rest of the way to Farmington. He picked up the radio mike and announced to Franklin County Dispatch that he was on "final approach" as he turned onto the access road to the jail. The oversized overhead door on the side of the jail, which looks like an unadorned, rectangular two-story brick shoebox, was already open when we got to it. Mike pulled in, shut off the truck and waited until the door closed behind him. I heard him take a deep breath.

"Bobby," he said softly, "I don't agree with Dalrymple. I think I've come to know you pretty well since you've been up here, and I seriously doubt that you've done anything wrong." He shifted around in his seat to face me. "Dalrymple called the Augusta dispatch center and asked for backup up at The Mountain. I was in the area, and

I took the call. It's what we do for each other." He sighed. "I don't know Dalrymple except by reputation, which, I'll tell you in confidence, isn't very good. Just go with the flow for the next few hours and we'll see what happens. OK?"

I nodded.

He handed me a pair of handcuffs and said, "Put these on. It's jail policy. Not too tight or they're hard to remove."

"Don't worry," I said, breaking my vow of silence.

Mike climbed out of the truck and walked over to a row of small lockers bolted to the wall as I fitted the cuffs around my wrists. He pulled one open and placed his service weapon and the pepper spray canister from his duty belt inside. Then he put the locker key in his pocket and walked back to my side of the truck. He pulled the door open, took a look at me and sighed.

"You put the handcuffs on with the seat belt latched, didn't you?"

I looked down. "That's what you told me to do."

He reached over me and unlocked one handcuff with a little key on his key chain. Then he unlatched the seat belt and let it retract.

"For future reference, Bobby, if you do that you can't get out of the truck; you're caught in the seat belt." I shrugged. He shook his head. "Come on."

Somebody must have been watching us from somewhere because I heard a clang and one of the doors on the wall opposite the overhead door popped open. Mike steered me through it and as soon as it closed behind us another one opened in front of us, like an airlock.

"Beam me up, Scotty."

"And a good day to you, Mr. Wing," said the fresh-faced young fellow standing next to an ancient grey government issue metal desk in the middle of the room we'd stepped into. "We've been expecting you. Do you have any weapons or drugs on you? It would much better if you give them to me now because, if I find any . . ."

"I know. Sorry, nothing." I'm afraid I was staring up at him with my mouth hanging open.

The embroidered name over his right breast pocket read "Rivers." Over the other pocket was an embroidered badge that read "Correctional Officer." He was huge, as big as Bear McGillicuddy from town. He seemed friendly, though, and I was thankful for that. He swiftly collected everything I took out of my pockets and put it into a plastic container on the desk. Then he patted me down and confiscated my boots.

"Long laces, Mr. Wing. We don't want any accidents now, do we?"

A line from Arlo Guthrie's classic sixties folk song "Alice's Restaurant" popped into my head unbidden. *"Obie, did you think I was going to hang myself for Littering?"* I kept it to myself, but I must have chuckled a bit, because he gave me a curious glance.

He kept up an almost constant chatter of questions, explanations and warnings for about twenty minutes as he took my picture and fingerprints as well as my medical and employment history. By then I'd learned that, within reason, I had a right to call as many people as I wanted—provided they'd take the call, of course. I'd also learned that he had just graduated with a degree in Sociology from the University of Maine at Farmington, just down the road. He cordially confided in me, a total stranger, that he had high hopes of becoming a patrol deputy soon as he had great plans for quick advancement in his law enforcement career so that he could help "improve the human condition." He was also proud of the fact that he had been the captain of the University rugby team, who had won the New England championship his senior year. All I know about rugby is that it's sort of like football, except without pads, helmets or common sense. I looked up at his smiling, almost cherubic face and mentally shook my head. I'd promised myself I wouldn't say or do anything to get myself in more trouble, so I didn't.

All this time Mike Hawkins had been standing at a shelf bolted to the back wall filling out forms and talking on the phone to someone, but I couldn't catch what he was saying because of the unceasing monologue. He disconnected, put down his phone and said, "You can call the bail commissioner, Clyde. He's got somebody coming."

"Excellent!" Clyde said with a big rosy-cheeked grin.

Clyde? I thought. I hadn't expected that. He didn't look like a "Clyde" to me.

Mike paused at the airlock door and turned to me. "You'll be OK, Bobby, you're in good hands. See you later."

"Thanks," I said as he cycled through the air lock.

"I'm going to have to ask you to step in here, Mr. Wing." Clyde easily pulled a cell door open that looked like it weighed half a ton. It had inch-thick plexiglass windows top to bottom, which looked bulletproof. "This is called our drunk tank. Sorry about the name," He shrugged and grinned. "Our regular holding cell isn't available because we currently have a young lady in residence, and I'm not allowed to let the two of you meet. I doubt you'll be with us much longer, though." He shrugged, still grinning.

I glanced at the matching cell door on the opposite wall, where there were a set of eyes peeking out under the venetian blind that had been drawn—for privacy, I assumed. The eyes were bloodshot and watery.

"No problem," I said. The door clanged shut behind me.

The "drunk tank" actually wasn't all that bad. It was clean and well lit. The walls *were* painted a god-awful shade of pink and there *was* a drain in the center of the concrete floor, but I've certainly been in worse places. I didn't want to even think about what that drain was for. Over in the corner there was what I can only describe as a piece of modern art metal sculpture crossed with a plumber's nightmare. It appeared to be a stainless-steel cross between a toilet, a sink, and a drinking fountain. Next to it was a speaker grill with a tiny black pushbutton. A sign next to the grill read, ASK FOR FLUSH. Thankfully I didn't feel the need at that moment.

I sat on a wide wooden bench bolted to the wall for what felt like an hour until Clyde pulled the door open again and cheerfully announced that my "friends" were here to bail me out. He didn't say who they were, but at that point I didn't care. He gave me my boots and my wallet back and had me sign a form titled, "Personal Property Inventory." Then he pulled open another door in the fourth wall and said, "Have a wonderful day, Mr. Wing. I hope we don't meet again. No offense?" He smiled again.

"None taken," I said.

Behind the door was a tiny room with two chairs and another of those grey government desks at which sat a small, fidgety man in a black and red checkered wool hunting jacket and L.L. Bean Hunting Shoes. I have a pair just like them. They're useless on ice. Behind him stood Woody Bernstein, my sometime lawyer, and Peggy Gordon.

"Are you OK, Bobby?" she asked.

"At the moment," I replied.

The man in the Bean boots introduced himself as a bail commissioner and proceeded to go through a well-practiced speech detailing what I had been charged with (Disorderly Conduct, a Class E misdemeanor), the amount of the bail ($100 cash), and his fee ($50.) "Set by law, not me," he assured me.

"Oh, shut up, Myron," Peggy said. "My car's running in the parking lot and I've got a friggin' business to run."

Myron looked back over his shoulder at her at her and hurriedly said, "I'm-required-to-advise-you-that-if-you-don't-show-up-in-court-a-warrant-will-be-issued-for-your-arrest-and-your-bail-will-be-forfeited."

"Are you *done* yet?" Peggy bellowed. Behind her Woody turned his head and put his hand over his mouth.

"Sign here and give me the money," Myron said, looking startled.

Peggy reached into her purse and peeled a hundred and a fifty off a roll of bills.

"This is my happy hour money, Bobby. I'll be after you if you don't show up."

I shivered as I signed the form in front of me.

Myron picked up the phone on the desk, punched a number and said, in a grateful tone, I thought, "We're done." The door behind Woody popped open and Peggy sprinted for the lobby door, followed by Woody and me.

"Don't make any statements to the police without talking to me first from now on, OK?" Woody said as we walked into the freedom of the parking lot.

"Don't worry."

Peggy ran the window down on her blaze orange Range Rover and hollered, "Get in here, dammit. I'm taking you home."

Woody shook my hand, wished me luck and told me to stay in touch as I climbed in.

Neither of us said a word on the trip north, which is unusual for both of us. We pulled into my dooryard, and I opened the passenger door.

"See you at work tomorrow, Bobby?" Peggy asked.

"You mean I'm not fired?"

"Of course not, you blockhead. I should give you a damn medal for telling off that pompous little dink. Get some sleep."

She spun all four tires on the Rover as she backed out. Gotta love her!

There was a note pinned to my front door. "I fed your cat. I think he likes me. He's nuzzling my feet as I write this."

You old pervert, I thought.

A while ago I showed Willie where I hide my emergency key. In case I die of a heart attack, and somebody needed to get in, I told her. Yeah, right! Hey, I can dream.

"I've got news," the note went on, "Call me. Willie. PS: but not tonight, I have a date. Woo-hoo!" There was a little heart doodle at the end.

Oh, well, I told myself. *There goes one more old man's fantasy shot to hell.*

Then from out of nowhere came a memory of my Grampy Mac singing an old Scots ballad, *"Oh, bonnie Bessie Logan. She's ower young for me."*

I winced, locked the door behind me, took a shower and went to bed. I slept pretty well, considering.

#

The next day passed quickly and quietly. Everybody I met asked how I was doing. News travels fast in the Gore. I told them all that I was fine, which was mostly true. Then they drifted away to their own jobs and lives.

It was what they call a "bluebird" day—sunny and in the low thirties. Business was brisk "On Top of Ol' Buster" and the lift was pretty full most of the day. I finished up filling an internet order for my Wytopitlock Wooly Booger fishing flies and only had to hit the kill switch once all day, for a drunk who fell asleep and hit the safety gate. I shook off my sense of déjà vu, dusted him off and asked him if he was alright.

"Right as rain, Boy-o. My ex-wife finally kicked the bucket and I'm celebrating my freedom. No more alimony!"

Then he pulled out a flask and offered me a snort. I politely declined. He took one for the road, sang two choruses of "Ding, dong, the bitch is dead," and skied off unsteadily. I called his description in to the Ski Patrol, just in case.

Halfway through the morning I figured that however Willie's date had gone the night before, she'd be recovered by now, so I called her. When she answered I swear she was purring louder than Lummox lying in a sunbeam.

"Oh, Bobby, Chad is *soo* nice. And a perfect gentleman, too."

"Perfect?"

"Yes, he took me bowling at Moose Alley in Rangeley. I let him think that he let me beat him three games to one. He's so funny. He told me a joke about a Frenchman and a bear and I was rolling on the floor."

"I'll bet that looked some cute," I said, feeling a little jealous.

"Oh, *you*. Then he took me to the Gingerbread House up in Oquossoc for dinner. There was a band and we danced. He's really graceful, and very athletic. Did you know he played basketball in college?"

"No. I haven't even met him yet. Remember?"

"I'll introduce you. I think you two will be the best of friends. He's *soo* nice."

She sounded like one of those California "valley girls" in heat. My daughter gets a little like that on the phone sometimes too, when she's spotted a new target. I sighed. This was getting ridiculous.

"Yes, you just said that. You have some news?" I asked, hoping to get her off the subject of Chad.

"What? Oh yeah. Sorry. But Chad was so—"

"Willie," I said. "If you don't come back down to earth, I'm going to call your father on you."

I didn't know if that would work but it was all I had.

She laughed. "Actually, Chad and my dad already know each other. Chad was back-up for him and Dog Berry at a domestic last month and Dad was impressed with how he talked to the female. He told me Chad calmed her right down even though she'd thrown her boyfriend's clothes, stereo and TV out the front window and threatened to castrate him in the street. Had her eating right out of his hand, Dad said."

"Charming."

"Yes, he is." She sighed again.

"The news . . . ?" I repeated.

"Right. Sorry," Willie said. "I really should tell you in person. Are you home tonight?"

"Sure." My mood instantly improved.

"I'm off at four. Can I tell you about it at your place? I'd love to see Lummie again."

Lummie?

I improvised. "OK, I'm having spaghetti tonight. Why don't you come over and I'll make some extra?"

"Sounds delish. I'll be there around five," she said and hung up.

Delish?

Suddenly I realized I needed to go shopping after work.

Well, Hell.

#

Willie was a little late for supper but that was OK because I got home only about fifteen minutes before she pulled in with her twelve-year-old Subaru beater. Pete Durrell was a man short that day, so I was recruited to help with the final trail sweep for stragglers before the snowmaking crew and groomers were cut loose on the mountainside to work their wonders unimpaired. Once I finally got to the employee locker room, I realized that it was going to be an iffy proposition that I would be able to get to the Rangeley IGA in time to buy spaghetti, a bottle of sauce and meatballs from the deli and then get home before Willie showed up. I wasn't about to just crack open that can of Chef Boy-R-Dee's best that I'd had in the cupboard for two years.

I changed to my civvies as fast as I could and was headed for the employee parking lot when I had a thought. I made a quick pivot past the loading dock through the back door to the kitchen, where Snort Benson was sweating over a hot griddle and swearing a blue streak at his prep cook. When he stopped for breath, I asked him if he had any spaghetti sauce I could "borrow." He cocked an eyebrow and wanted to know why. I said I was having somebody over for supper, which drew guffaws from all over the kitchen.

"It's not what you think," I yelled over the noise of the dishwasher in the corner. "It's business, you bunch of horny jackasses."

"Aren't you a little old for that kind of business?" asked Peachy Keene with a big grin. "Who is she, you old whoredog?"

I stuck out my chin, looked down my nose at him and said, "A gentleman does not discuss such things."

Snort laughed so hard at that that he had to grab hold of the table he was working at to keep standing. When he'd calmed down after a minute or two of hysterics, he looked at me, grinned like a knowing old dog himself and started barking orders. Five minutes later I had five pounds of dry spaghetti imported all the way from Italy, a two-quart container of Snort's special handmade sauce and two dozen monster handmade meatballs, along with cooking instructions and several suggestions about what—or who—to have for dessert. I grabbed the stuff and ran—with what little dignity I had left.

#

"Hi, Lummie," Willie said to Lummox as she came through the door carrying a loaf of bread in a paper sack. "Would you like some num-nums?" she asked in that baby talk voice that women get sometimes when they spot something that jogs their motherly instinct. She pulled a packet of kitty crack out of her jacket and shook it. I'm damned if Lummox didn't start acting like a jeezley kitten, rolling over and over and nuzzling her ankles as she hung her coat up on the peg next to the door. It was disgusting. She put the sack with the bread on my kitchen counter, bent over and put a handful of evil on my kitchen floor. From Lummox's reaction you would have thought that I never fed the fat old lying fleabag.

"Oh, you're such a love," she cooed, petting him as he gobbled. She hadn't even looked at me yet.

"Hello?"

"Oh. Hi, Bobby. I brought a loaf of my mom's Italian bread. She just made it today and it might even still be warm. What a coincidence, right? I was going to pick up a bottle of Chianti, too but it was already too late to get to the IGA. Sorry." She pouted. I melted, of course.

As per Snort's instructions I had already filled my biggest kitchen pot—which I inherited along with the cabin from old Filthy Phillips—with water and put it on the stove. Snort had suggested that I wait until my "guest" arrived and then turn the heat on under it and add a handful of salt as soon as it hit a boil. Then I dumped in all the spaghetti he gave me. I already had the meatballs and sauce in a saucepan, bubbling away at what I hoped was a simmer.

"It smells wonderful," Willie gushed. "I had no idea you could cook."

"Well," I said, looking over my shoulder at her from the stove. "When you live alone you learn to cope."

Her face fell. "Oh, Bobby, I'm so sorry." She walked over to me and touched my elbow. "You must miss your wife so much. I didn't mean to . . ."

"No problem. It's been a long time."

OK. I know I was milking it at that point, but I just couldn't help it.

She sat down at the table and "Lummie" jumped into her lap and started to purr like a diesel locomotive. She scratched him behind the ears and you would have thought he was in heaven. He's always been an idiot around females, and I've often wondered how many kittens he fathered before he left his balls in a cup at the Franklin County Animal Shelter.

I'd decided, after that first lonely winter alone in my cabin, that I needed some kind of companionship and, since there weren't a lot of human females in the area who appeared to be available or willing, I decided to follow Harry Truman's advice: "*If you want a friend in Washington, get a dog.*" So, I drove down to Farmington to see if the shelter had one I could adopt. I did look at a beagle and an old basset hound before I made the mistake of walking through the cat room. In the back corner I saw this big ball of black and white fur in a cage that was way too small for him. He was glaring at me. He grabbed my hand through the bars as I walked up to him and it felt like he was sending out brain waves screaming, *"Get me the hell out of here, NOW!"*

Willie and I chatted during the meal about this and that. She told me about her parents, and I told her the history of The Beast. The meatballs and the sauce were delicious, and it got me to thinking that maybe I should do more of my own cooking. Then I remembered that I'd just accidently boiled up enough spaghetti to feed Cuba for a week. *Nah.*

"You had something to tell me?" I said as I ran my third slice of her mother's crusty Italian bread around my bowl, sopping up the last of my "old family recipe" sauce.

"Yes, I do. Just a second."

She walked over to the door and took a notebook out of the pocket of her jacket. She sat back down at the table, and I watched as she became a cop again.

"You know that I was assigned to sit with that woman you found with the dead man on the lift?"

I nodded.

"Well, she was quiet the first night. She slept until Chad relieved me at 0700. He brought me breakfast. He's so considerate . . ."

Her voice trailed off. After a few seconds I cleared my throat and her eyes focused again.

"The second night she was quiet until zero two hundred. I was brim full of coffee by then and I'd just got up to go to the bathroom when she started mumbling again. This time I was able to figure something out." She flipped a page in her notebook and her voice became totally professional. "You had advised that you heard her say a name, remember?"

I nodded. "Peter Foster."

"She was actually saying, 'Pater Noster,' which is Latin for 'our father.' It's the first two words of the Lord's Prayer in Latin."

"How'd you know that?"

"We learned the Pater Noster in catechism class when I was in sixth grade. They used to let us Catholic kids out of school one day a month to go down to Saint Joe's in Farmington where Father Paul taught us about our faith. He was an older man and very traditional, so he taught it to us in both Latin *and* English."

"I didn't realize you were Catholic. Sorry. I guess I just assumed . . ."

I realized how stupid that sounded. I hadn't been inside a church since I married Pam.

She grinned. "Yeah. I come from a long line of good Irish Catholics. I was born with knee pads, as they say. No bother."

The professional voice returned. "I thought that she was trying to pray, so I took out my rosary beads—"

"You carry them around with you?" I asked.

"Yeah. They can be a comfort, sometimes . . . when I get lonely. . . or scared."

She paused and looked at me. For once I had the sense to shut up.

"I started up the Pater Noster and after the first line she joined in, very faintly at first, but she got stronger as we went along. When we finished, she started the Hail Mary and I recited it with her. We did five of them and she stopped. Then her eyes focused on me, and she said, 'Thank you.'"

"She did seem somewhat aware at that point," Willie continued. "So I decided to ask her some basic questions. She told me that her name is Angeline St. John. Then I asked her, 'Angeline, what happened on the chairlift?' She said, 'Our father' again and I thought she was trying to say the Lord's Prayer in English, so I said, ". . . who art in Heaven?" and she said . . ."

Willie looked at her notes.

"No. No. He was *our* father. Paul's and mine. He killed my mother."

"Wow"

"You can say that again," Willie said. "I started writing down everything verbatim. She didn't stay with me long, maybe five minutes all together, but I found out that the man you saw with her is her brother, Paul, and she's a nun."

"A nun!"

Oh, great, I thought. *Now I'm going to hell for admiring a nun's legs! Sheesh!*

"Yes," Willie glanced back at her notebook. "Then she said, 'Paul killed our father. He fell. There was so much blood!' Then she went quiet," Willie said, flipping her notebook closed. "She didn't say anything else all night."

"My God!"

"Indeed!" Willie said. "After Chad relieved me that morning, I took a chance and called St. Joseph's College in Standish from the office. The sweatshirt she was wearing. Remember?"

I nodded.

"I talked to Father Morton, her spiritual advisor. He sounds very nice," Willie continued. "He was concerned when I told him she was in the hospital, but I could tell that he was skeptical of me at first. He said he wanted to check something before giving me any information."

"He called the S.O.'s routine line a few minutes later and asked the secretary if they had a Wilma Brackett working there. They confirmed my ID and put him through to me."

Smart priest, I thought.

"He told me that Sister Angeline always wears a small gold cross on a chain that her mother gave her when she was a little girl. I told him that matched. He asked how she was and sounded very relieved when I told her she was OK physically, but her mind seemed in and out. He told me that she and her brother, Paul Freeman—actually he's her half-brother—decided to take a week off and go skiing to relax after a rough patch for both of them. Sister Angeline's a graduate nursing student enrolled in Saint Joe's. She was working as an RN at Mercy Hospital in Portland when she decided to go back to school and become a family nurse practitioner. She wants to work with traumatized and grieving children."

Great, I thought. *She's studying to be a saint to boot.* "Beelzebub has a devil set aside for meeee."

"Then Father Morton told me that Sister Angeline grew up in an extremely abusive home." Willie was reading directly from her notes. "She was sexually abused by her father, Matthew St. John, from the age of six until she hit puberty. Her father beat her mother to death one night when she was ten and buried the body under a concrete floor that he poured in the basement of their house. He told people that she had run off with another man and at the time there was not enough evidence for the local police to investigate any further."

"My God," I mumbled.

"After a year or so Matthew took up with another woman and eventually fathered Paul. He physically and psychologically abused Paul's mother so badly that she drowned herself when he was four. But again there was no real evidence for police to investigate."

"Wow," I said. "This is starting to sound like a Stephen King novel."

"No kidding," Willie shook her head and read on. "When she was fourteen, Angeline realized that she and her brother couldn't go on living with Matthew. She was sure that he'd eventually kill them, too. She went to her parish priest and told him the whole story. The priest went to Human Services, and they got Matthew to agree to give up custody. The church's social service department then got them placed in a foster home out of state."

"Can a priest do that? I mean, isn't that confidential? Sanctity of the confessional, or something like that?"

Willie looked up from her notes. "She didn't actually confess the information to him, so it wasn't privileged, and, even if she had, the church makes exceptions. Danger of death to a child is certainly one. Plus, Maine law makes the clergy mandatory reporters. If they learn of or suspect child abuse they have to call Human Services."

"Right," I said.

I felt a shiver run down my spine. I gotta tell you, I was getting more and more horrified the more I thought about it.

"These days," Willie said. "Sister Angeline and her brother live together in an apartment in Gorham while she's in school and he works for Whole Foods in Portland. For years they've been telling anyone who would listen that her mother was buried in the basement of that house, but there was never enough basis for a search warrant. Only the long-repressed memories of a traumatized little girl.

"Then, four years ago, Matthew was convicted of a bank robbery in Massachusetts and spent four years in prison. During that time, the town took his house for unpaid taxes and sold it at auction. Father Morton told me that Angeline talked the new owner, who'd wanted to renovate anyway, into giving permission for the police to finally dig up the cellar and they found her mother's remains. Last week Matthew was indicted for Murder and Gross Sexual Assault, for his years of abuse of Angeline. She and her brother were celebrating the warrant's issue."

"I was pretty sure by then that Matthew was the dead man on the chairlift," Willie said. "I passed the info on to Doc Jeffries, the Medical Examiner, after I got off the line with Father Morton. He'll try to confirm his identity. Meanwhile we've put out a statewide BOLO on Paul."

"BOLO?"

"A Be On the Look Out notice. We've got a description of the car registered to him and the Gorham Police are going to check their apartment. Hopefully we'll find him and get his side. I expect that Detective Dalrymple will request a warrant for him through the DA's office tomorrow."

She looked down at Lummox snoozing on her lap like he didn't have a care in the world and smiled.

"I hear Dalrymple thinks I'm trying to horn in on his case. He's not too pleased with me right now."

"Welcome to the club."

We shared a cup of dessert coffee and she complimented me again on my culinary skills. Since I *had* actually boiled the water and heated up the sauce and meatballs on the stove, I did my best "Aw, shucks" act without feeling the least bit of guilt. Well—maybe a little. I offered her some leftovers "for the road" but she declined, having seen the remains in the colander in my sink. After an extended "coochy-coo" chin scratch for Lummox, which produced a reflexive hind leg kick in him and a slight pang of jealousy in me, she retrieved her coat, shook my hand and left.

Well, Hell.

#

I've gotten used to the phone ringing in the middle of the night but that didn't make me any happier two hours later.

"What is it *now*?" I barked into the receiver.

"Bobby? Bobby, is that you? This is Angie, Angie Gilchrist. Are you OK?"

Of all people to yell at.

"Sorry, Angie. I was asleep and . . ." I tried to sound contrite.

"Bobby, can you come over right away? We've got a situation at the Mother House, and we need help."

I didn't even think to ask what it was.

"On my way," I said as I grabbed my pants off the floor.

The Mother House of the Community of Satin is a big rambling old three-story farmhouse where the Butz family raised generations of kids, cows, chickens and pigs for years before old Beanie died. His kids, who weren't into the concept of farming for the rest of their lives, sold the farm to the Community. All the lights in the building were on and most of the members were standing in the front yard as I pulled in. Curly Phavogue, the son of the founder and its current leader, met me as I climbed out of The Beast.

"Bobby, thank goodness you're here." He sounded wicked anxious and out of breath.

"No problem, Curly," I said, a bit surprised. Curley is normally a pretty steady fellow and not prone to getting worked up. "What's going on? Angie said there was a problem."

"Angie's inside, up in the attic, talking to a fellow we took in a day or so ago. His name is Paul. He comes here off and on because he's a buyer for a grocery store in Portland that buys our chickens."

Oh, no, I thought.

"He showed up here dressed in bloody ski clothes and slurring his speech," Curly went on. "Nothing he said made much sense, eh? We asked him if he wanted us to call an ambulance, but he refused. He didn't seem to be hurt. At first, I thought he was drunk, but there was no smell of alcohol on him. Angie checked him over too but couldn't find anything obviously wrong with him, either. We do have a couple of rooms available for people who come to us to explore joining our community—or need a respite. You know about that, eh?" He raised his eyebrows.

I nodded.

"We offered him a bed for the night, and he accepted. We checked on him several times and he looked like he was asleep. He hadn't eaten anything, either. I'd decided to call the sheriff in the morning if he hasn't come to."

"So, what's he done?" I asked.

"I'm not sure," Curly said. "Angie has the fire watch in the Mother House tonight and when she peeked in about half an hour ago, he woke up and went berserk. He said, 'I deserve to die. I need to die.' Angie said he pushed her aside and ran up the stairs into the attic. He keeps saying he wants to kill himself. She's up there trying to calm him down. She said it'd be quicker to call you then wait for the sheriff, eh?"

"OK," I said. "First thing to do is call 911 right now. Tell them we need a deputy and an ambulance. I think I know who this guy is. Show me how to get there."

#

When Curly and I got up to the attic we both had to pause a moment to catch our breath. We were three sets of stairs above ground and neither of us are spring chickens. The only light was a single bulb at the top of the stairs. Angie was kneeling with a flashlight under an open trap door in the roof at the other end of the attic.

"Thank God you're here," she said in a whisper as we walked toward her. "He's getting more and more anxious by the minute and some idiot on the lawn keeps shining some sort of jack light thing at him. That's not helping. Curly, can you go down and get whoever it is to stop doing that? It's just winding him up."

"OK," Curly said, still panting. "I'll do what I can." He took a deep breath and turned toward the attic stairs.

"And see if someone can turn off the extra lights in the house that we don't need to move around, eh? It might help calm things a bit," Angie added.

"Right." Curly disappeared down the stairs.

She turned to me. "Bobby," she whispered. "Did Curly tell you what happened?"

"Yes," I whispered back. "I think I know who he is. He's involved in that death on The Mountain the other day. I think he's the son of the man who was killed. The police are looking for him."

"That explains a lot," she said, shivering. She was wearing only a light bathrobe and slippers.

She gestured up at the open trap door. "Do you think you could try to talk to him? He only gets more and more upset when I try. I told him my name and he called me a liar." She grabbed my hand. "He stared right at me and said, 'No. I killed you!'"

"His sister's name is Angeline. She's in the hospital. He may have hurt her. He probably calls her Angie."

"Oh, my God," she whispered.

"OK," I said. "I'll try to talk to him. The ambulance and sheriff should be here soon. Maybe I can stall long enough."

"Good. Be careful. It's slippery out on the roof."

Out on the roof?

My stomach did a flip flop. I took a deep breath and stood up.

Don't look down! Look straight ahead. Maybe you won't have to actually go . . . out there.

The trap door was next to a massive old brick chimney. It had probably allowed the Butz family to clean out the creosote buildup from wood fires in the kitchen stove and the fireplaces in almost every room before the advent of central heating. I grabbed onto the frame of the door to steady myself and looked around. I could see a figure about ten or twelve feet away sitting with his back leaning on the chimney and his feet pointing toward the edge of the roof. It was eerily quiet. Curly must have been successful because I couldn't hear any more talking from the ground. The sky was just beginning to lighten as the sun prepared to make its appearance. I fought down a sense of panic as I saw the treetops of the old maple trees that stood in the yard.

Straight ahead. I reminded myself. *Don't look down. Stay calm. Breathe.*

"Paul? Paul Freeman?" I said softly. "Can you hear me?"

"I hear you."

His voice was surprisingly calm, considering. "That girl. She claims to be Angie. She can't be."

"Why not, Paul?"

"Poor Angie. Poor sweet Angie. She's dead, man," he said, standing up.

An edge of panic crept into his voice. "I killed her." His voice rose half an octave. "I killed her; do you hear?" Now a full octave. "Don't you see? I have to die. It's time!"

This was not good.

"It's OK, Paul," I said, trying to sound calm and reassuring. "Angie's alive, Paul. I've seen her. She's in the hospital. You didn't kill her."

"You're lying, you bastard. I heard her scream. I saw the blood. Then I fell." His voice rose to a shriek. "I have to die." He turned toward the edge.

"Paul," I said, trying to keep my own growing panic out of my voice. "My name is Bobby. I saw the two of you together in the lodge that day. The day you fell. Before it happened. Remember?"

He turned toward me, away from the edge. I could just see his face. His eyes were squinting at me.

"Yeaahh," he said, drawing out the word. His voice was dropping back to a conversational volume.

He smiled weakly. "You're the old man Angie said was looking at her butt. The 'lecher,' she called you. We laughed about that. 'If he only knew,' she said."

Well, she certainly had me pegged. "Old man?"

"Paul, Angeline is alive. I can prove it," I said.

He peered at me in the gathering light.

"Prove it? No, that's impossible. I heard her scream . . ."

"I'll take you to her."

"No, that's imposs . . ." He turned away.

"Paul," I said. "Look at me."

"No . . . You're trying to trick me." His voice rose again, and he took a half step toward the edge. My heart sank.

"Paul." I heard my voice rising involuntarily. I took a deep breath and stepped onto the roof. "Would Angie want you to do this?"

His shoulders sagged and he turned slowly back toward me. I held my breath. "No. No, she wouldn't." His voice fell to a whisper. "Sweet Angie. She loved life. In spite of that bastard and all he did to us . . . she loved life." He started to cry.

I felt a moment of hope. "I'll take you to her, Paul. You can see her for yourself." I held out my hand.

God, I thought. *I hope he takes it!*

He shook himself, squared his shoulders and walked up the roof to me, grabbing my hand. "Please." He looked into my eyes. "I want to see her. Please, Bobby."

Well, Hell!

#

The long and the short of it was that I finally got to meet Willie's young trooper, Chad Fairchild, when he arrived with the ambulance ten minutes later. He was tall, athletic and looked to me to be about nineteen years old. While the paramedics checked Paul, Chad listened to everybody's stories and took notes. After a few minutes on the phone with his headquarters, he walked over to where I was standing on the porch with Angie, who had put on a long coat and a pair of boots.

"Mr. Wing. I've got to hand it to you. I haven't been doing this job all that long, but I don't think one of our own trained negotiators could have done that any better."

"Thank you," I said. I think my face was red with embarrassment at that. Or maybe it was the big bear hug Angie gave me in front of the Community and the rest of the rubberneckers from the Gore. "What happens now?"

"Well, there *is* an active warrant for Mr. Freeman's arrest, so I'm going to have to take him into custody. Given the shape he looks to be in, I'm guessing the ambulance will probably transport him down to Franklin Memorial, where he'll be checked out, mentally and physically. Once he's medically cleared I'll take him to the jail. It looks like he'll need a shower and a hot meal, and the jail can provide those. After that it's up to the lawyers and the courts. Do you know if he has a lawyer?"

"No," I said, "but I'm going to call Woody Bernstein. I promised Paul I'd take him to see his sister. Hopefully she's still in Farmington."

"Nope, sorry. Willie Brackett and I sat with her in opposite shifts at the hospital for three nights running but now she's been transferred to the psychiatric unit at St. Mary's in Lewiston. I've heard they're good at their job and they'll probably take especially good care of one of their own."

"When do you think I can take him down there to see her?"

He sighed. "You still have pending charges, Bobby. The jail won't let you in to visit him and I'm guessing he won't get bail for a while, if ever. He *is* facing a murder charge." He shrugged.

"But we can prove it wasn't murder."

"The decision about that is way above my pay grade," Chad said. "The lawyers will have to straighten it all out. And it *is* still Detective Dalrymple's case. I've heard he doesn't like people stepping on his toes. I wouldn't take that chance if I were you."

"Thanks," I said. "But I promised Paul, and I have to back that up."

"I think that's admirable, Bobby." He patted me on the shoulder as we walked together to his cruiser. "Willie told me you're a good guy and that's enough for me." He paused. "Everybody is safe and more or less healthy right now. If I were you, I'd just let the powers that be do their thing. I think it will work out." He climbed into the driver's seat.

"OK," I said with my fingers crossed. "I will."

"Good."

He pulled his cruiser in behind the ambulance and they both headed south.

#

"Well," Woody Bernstein said, looking over the top of his glasses at me. "That's quite a story."

He'd given me an appointment that same afternoon. He had his Naval Reserve officer's commission in the Judge Advocate General corps on the wall of his office. It gave me a good feeling.

"I'll need to talk to the Attorney General's office. They handle all murder cases in Maine. I'll try to get an order attached to Paul's bail conditions allowing him to be transported to St. Mary's for a visit with his sister. He'll have to be transported by a sheriff's deputy—or probably two because it's a murder case. That's the best I can do for now."

"Could I go, too?" I asked.

"Probably not. Trooper Fairchild was right to tell you that your pending charge would prevent that. I'm working on that, too. I have a meeting with our local Assistant DA this afternoon to review your case. I've read Dalrymple's report and, frankly, I don't think he's got a case. We'll see on that. In the meantime, sit tight and get on with your life. The jail will take care of Paul just fine. Young Clyde Rivers up there was on the rugby squad that I coached last year. He's a good kid, if a little naive still."

I left his office feeling cautiously optimistic.

Woody *was* able to arrange an escorted visit for Paul with his sister in the hospital on humanitarian grounds a week later. Willie's father, the chief deputy, assigned her and himself to the transport and escort duty. The next day she saw The Beast parked in front of Sally's and came inside looking for me. We sat by ourselves in Nadine's private function room, which doubles as her dojo three afternoons a week when she teaches karate to little kids. There was a shelf of trophies on the back wall that seemed to grow every time I saw it. Willie had a coffee and I was nursing a Molson.

"I was surprised at how nice the psychiatric unit at St. Mary's is." Willie said. "It was the first time I've been there. One of the sisters there was one of Sister Angeline's instructors in nursing school."

"How is she?"

"Before we went in, her ward nurse told us that she's still in and out sometimes, but she's been a lot better now that they have her in treatment. She's been diagnosed with severe PTSD, depression and generalized anxiety disorder. My dad sat with Paul in the waiting room while I went in to tell her he was there. She actually remembered me. She brightened up and wanted to see him right away. I told her what his legal situation was, and she agreed that I could record the conversation on my cell phone.

"They had a great visit. There was a lot of crying on all sides, including me, I have to admit. They were able to confirm each other's story and Paul's remembered a lot more, too."

"So, what did they say actually happened?" I asked.

She flipped open her notebook.

"Matthew St. John *was* the dead man in the chair. Doc Jeffries has positively ID'd him. Paul and Angeline essentially repeated Father Morton's statement to me about the deaths of both of their mothers and how they tried for years to get someone to believe them. Then Sister Angeline confirmed the statement that Paul gave to Detective Dalrymple last week at the jail with Woody present."

"Which I heard that Dalrymple doesn't believe."

"Right, I heard that too," Willie said. "It appears that Matthew tracked his children to their present apartment in Gorham after his release from prison and had been stalking them for some time. Sister Angeline thinks that he followed them to The Mountain and waited until he could slip onto the chairlift with them. Halfway up he took off his goggles and they recognized him. 'What were we going to do?' Angeline said. 'We were trapped on the chair with him.'

"She said that she made the mistake of telling her father that there was a warrant out for him. He flew into a rage and pulled a knife. Paul said that he remembers grabbing for the knife as Matthew swung it at his sister, who was sitting on the other side of him in the chair. He deflected the knife enough that it missed Angeline but swung down and around, lodging in Matthew's groin."

"So, he cut his own femoral artery," I said, mentally wincing.

"Right," Willie went on. "Paul remembered that Matthew started to bleed 'Like a fire hose,' he said. Paul lost his grip in all the blood, slid out of the chair and landed in the snow under tower thirteen."

"Then," I said, "he must have skied down to the parking lot, probably with a concussion, got into his car and drove to the Chicken House, which was the only place he knew where he could count on finding some help and someone he knew.

"Exactly," Willie said.

"Meanwhile Matthew must have bled out all over Angeline."

Willie nodded. "Doc says that he would have lost consciousness almost immediately and it would only have taken ten minutes for all the blood in his body to flow out."

"About the time the chair would need to get to the top," I said.

"Angeline said that she remembers screaming when Paul fell but doesn't remember anything after that until she saw me in her room at Franklin Memorial. Then she blacked out again until she got to St. Mary's."

"Wow. So, what happens now?"

"I gave a copy of my report and the recording to the Attorney General's Office. They reviewed it this morning and decided to dismiss the charges against Paul. He was released from the jail an hour ago and is on his way home. Sister Angeline will be going to a nursing care facility until she's able to go back to school." Willie paused. "Happy ending!"

She looked up at me and flipped her notebook closed with a snap. She grinned, like the proverbial cat that ate the canary.

"But wait. There's more!"

"And?" I prompted.

"I found out through the grapevine this afternoon that Mike Hawkins was so upset at how Detective Dalrymple handled his interview with you at the top of the mountain that he dropped a dime. He called his boss, who then called Dalrymple's boss. It turns out that our favorite gumshoe was already on *very* thin ice for his temper. I've heard, unofficially of course, that he's been "counseled" about it at least twice before.

"This morning, before his lieutenant could reach him, Dalrymple confronted the Assistant DA in Farmington in the courthouse parking lot when she arrived at work. He'd found out that she'd dismissed all the charges against you for lack of credible evidence. He flew off the handle and took a swing at her. Chad happened to be in the parking lot at the time and had to restrain him. Dalrymple's been relieved of duty pending an internal investigation.

Well! Hell!

Six: Twinkle, Twinkle Little Star. How I Wonder . . .

With my fists clenched I watched as the best hitter the Red Sox had moved farther back in the box and dug in with grim determination. It'd been a wicked poor season so far and wins were a bitch to come by. Down a run and it was three and two with two outs in the last inning with runners on second and third. The tension was as thick as the air on that sultry July afternoon. The Orioles pitcher looked in, wound up and delivered.

"Yeeer out!" bellowed the umpire.

The batter's helmet slammed to the turf with a high-pitched scream as Morningstarr Phavogue, our star catcher, spun in protest, her ten-year-old blonde curls flying.

"He's not s'posed to throw curve balls!" she shouted to the overflow crowd of maybe fifty friends, family members and fans of the Skedaddle Gore Red Sox. "It's against the law!" She stamped her feet and started to cry. "Daddyyy!"

Her father, Curly Phavogue, our head coach, stood along the third base line with his head down and his shoulders slumped. I shrugged at him in sympathy from my spot across the diamond in the first base coach's box. Secretly I thanked my lucky stars that my own daughter hadn't showed the slightest interest in sports growing up. A pure "girly girl," her only sweaty interest had briefly been golf when her now first ex-husband was hired as the pro at the local muni course in Florida where I was stationed with the Coast Guard at the time. Her second husband's status was still pending an Oregon judge's decision.

Curly straightened his shoulders and clapped his hands. "Huddle up, you guys! Let's go." He trotted toward the home dugout, shaking his head.

While he went through the post-game drill of lining up the team and running the gauntlet of sulky high fives with the winners, I gathered the equipment. Pulling up the second base bag I noticed a movement in the woods beyond the left field fence. It was just enough to catch a glimpse of someone I don't ever see unless he wants me to.

I like baseball well enough, but I never played it after the seventh grade when Stinky Burlingame broke my front tooth with a line drive to the face. After that I tended to shy away from anything hit or thrown my way, which pretty much ruled out any contact or flying missile sports. It also helped me to develop what to this day I consider to be a very helpful attitude toward dentistry. After sitting through three root canals and reconstructive dental surgery after a newly minted U.S. Navy Dental Corps ensign split what remained of that tooth clean in two during what must have been his first attempt at unsupervised drilling, I still break out in a cold sweat when I see a surgical mask and hear that sucking sound. I also brush and floss—a lot.

Anyway, despite my lack of baseball skill and knowledge I let Curly talk me into helping out when the Community of Satin decided to sponsor the Skedaddle Gore Little League team. Admittedly we did have a few beers during the conversation.

Curly and the Orioles coach finished up the post-game ceremonies and we sent most of our kids off home or into the arms of their parents, who were by now pretty much resigned to another loss. It helps with that, you see, to live in "Red Sox Nation."

"Thanks, Bobby," he said, shaking my hand. "I really thought we had a chance there for a while. Until . . ." He shrugged and looked embarrassed.

"Yeah, I know." I patted his shoulder. "Starr did a good job, Curly. She's quick, smart, has a good arm and she really gets into baseball."

We walked to the parking lot and stowed the equipment in the back of The Beast, my nearly new, shiny red Dodge one-ton four-by-four.

"Yup, I know. We just have to work on that temper of hers a bit more, eh?" He closed the tailgate and sighed. "She worries me at times. She's been getting these . . . spells, eh? She's started defying her mother and lately she's making up a bunch of weird stories and such."

"Ah, Curly, she's still just a kid." I smiled, remembering the rows my daughter and Pam got into around that age. "Believe me. She'll grow out of it."

"Even Angie has remarked on it," he said with a frown. Angie, actually Tangerine Gilchrist, is the Community's school teacher. She's got a master's degree from McGill, two kids of her own and wicked fine-looking legs.

"That reminds me." Curly brightened a bit. "This morning Angie asked if I saw you to tell you she wants to talk to you, eh? Said you should come up to the schoolroom when you get a chance."

After a couple of very nice rejections a while back I'd finally talked Angie, who's currently unattached, into dinner last month at the Gingerbread House in Oquossoc followed by a movie over at the Lakeside Theatre in Rangeley. It went well. We shook hands and she hugged me when I dropped her off. She said she'd had fun. I got the feeling she'd like me to come around again but I hadn't gotten to it yet.

"Thanks, Curley. I will." I hoped I wasn't grinning too much like a teenager in heat.

#

The next day was the hottest day of the summer so far, which it always is when you're working up firewood. I somehow felt him come up behind me. Normally I've got just enough PTSD to hate it when that happens without warning. On more than one occasion

I've been known to jump and hit my head on that jeezley low-slung ceiling beam over my favorite booth at Sally's Motel and Bar and Live Bait and Convenience Store.

Anyway, the few people in town that our resident hermit's comfortable enough to interact with have gotten used to most of his quirks. Most of us call him Squatch, because he's never told anyone his name, or much of anything else for that matter. Despite his nickname he's not a particularly hairy fellow and he apparently bathes fairly regularly as he usually smells pretty decent, sort of like balsam fir trees in the winter and wild raspberries in the summer. Nobody knows where exactly he lives, or how, but Nadine, the co-owner of Sally's, has sold a pile of his bird carvings to the tourists and online. Marti Wallace, our RFD carrier, holds his mail for him until he flags her down for it every now and then. It's usually addressed to "Eiam Noone" in care of Sally's. Marti thinks it's pronounced "I am no one" but nobody is sure. Looking to be in his thirties, he's pretty good sized. I'd say he's about six foot two, with a sturdy, well-muscled build.

I hadn't heard him, of course, because you never do and I was running the wood splitter, which makes a wicked racket anyway. He usually just sort of appears and disappears unexpectedly. If I was the poetic sort, which I'm not, I'd say he was a lot like the morning mist over a still valley on a quiet spring morning. I'd been expecting him since the ballgame.

I didn't turn around, just kept feeding the splitter and tossing the offload onto the rising pile to be stacked near the back door later. Wood warms you three times, the old saying goes—when you cut it, when you split it and when you burn it. I'd personally add when you stack it, but some lazy folks just let it rest after the splitting and then have to beat apart the frozen junks in mid-January, something I have no taste for. Eventually I got to a good place to pause and stood up, stretching my back and shutting off the splitter.

"Water?" I asked as I turned slowly to see him, as expected, standing next to The Beast. As usual he was holding his hands crossed in front of him and staring at the ground at his feet. He doesn't make eye contact and has never, in anyone's experience who knows him, said more than two words in a row.

"Yup."

I tossed him my Poland Spring squeeze bottle and headed in the back door of the house to get myself a Shipyard Monkey Fist from the fridge. I'd been anticipating the IPA's hoppy bite for the last ten minutes anyway. Grabbing a towel out from under Lummox, I wiped the sweat off my face. My old Maine Coon cat never shifted, just raised his head and glared at me, as usual.

When I went back outside I found Squatch stacking wood in just the right place and in just the way I like it done. He'll do stuff like that for folks out of the blue sometimes and it's uncanny how he can anticipate the way people want things to be. I set my beer down on the open tailgate of The Beast and we worked companionably for the next ten minutes or so until the day's jumbled pile became an orderly stack.

"Hose?" he said as we finished up.

"Help yourself. You know where it is." I replied.

"Yup."

Like me he'd stripped off his shirt while working. Walking over to the hose reel on the wall he grabbed the nozzle and cranked the sill cock open. Throwing his head back, he gave himself a pretty fine all over shower of my nice, cool well water. I think he almost smiled, but I'm not sure. Since he usually has the same flat expression on his face, I expect I was wrong. I know him well enough by now to let him take things at his own speed.

"Batter . . . cried," he said slowly, turning toward me and running his fingers through his hair. It took me a minute to realize he was talking about Starr's meltdown the previous day.

"Yes, she did," I said. "But she's OK. She's a good kid, just a little full of herself."

"Trouble," he replied, without looking up.

"Starr?" I said, surprised. "She's no trouble. Usually she's pretty cool, actually, for a ten-year-old."

"In . . . trouble."

He looked up at me then and his eyes glistened.

"What do you mean?" I asked.

"You'll . . . see."

Just then I heard my fire department pager start squalling from where I'd left it on the kitchen table. I turned toward the door. When I glanced back he was gone.

Well, Hell . . .

#

Several hours later, I think, I came to with a miserable headache. On a normal day I'd have written it off as another hangover, but then I realized that I had a bandage wrapped around my head that was holding an ice pack. On top of that I was some startled to find that I was being stared at, from about two feet away, by a wolf. You know, as in a tear-out-your-throat-and-eat-your-liver type wolf. Not a dog, mister man. I saw a pack of wolves in the wild tear up a caribou carcass once when I was stationed in Kodiak, Alaska. I know the difference.

Well, Hell!

"No worries, Bobby," a soft gravelly voice said. "He likes you."

"I should for damn sure hope so!" I sputtered.

"Sit, George," the voice continued.

Amazingly the wolf complied, opening his mouth and letting his tongue loll out. If I didn't know better, I'd think he smiled at me. At least he looked well fed.

"Go on, George," the voice continued. It seemed to come from overhead, but my brain was still a little foggy and my attention was still focused on that set of big, white, sharp-looking teeth.

"I think you've spooked him. Let me talk to him alone. Go and check on the cabin. OK?"

The wolf cocked his head, pulled in his tongue, seemed to nod and disappeared. I could breathe again.

I was lying on what felt like a soft leather sofa in what looked to be some kind of fancy wood-paneled room. It was fitted out like a rich English lord's library, the kind that you might see in one of those classy historical dramas on PBS. Bookcases full of what looked like real books lined the walls, floor to ceiling. There was a nice, expensive looking woven rug on the hardwood floor, a couple of comfortable looking chairs in the center of the room and an old-fashioned roll-top desk in the corner. The lighting was subdued, and I couldn't tell where it was coming from. It was comfortably cool. There were no windows.

I was still foggy but the last thing that I could recall doing was walking slowly through the woods poking through the pine forest duff on the north side of the Gore near the access road to the Navy base. A bunch of other volunteers and I had been set out on a search line looking for little Starr.

Squatch had been right. She *was* in trouble. Her mother had reported her missing along with her school backpack and a bunch of her clothes. She'd left a note saying she was going to walk home to see her Grampy in Canada. She's Satin's granddaughter, you see. The surrounding fire departments had been toned out for manpower and Mike Hawkins, our district game warden, had organized a grid search through the woods along a line north of the Community's Mother House. It's the most direct line toward Newfoundland and would put us, hopefully, in her tracks.

Since before World War II there's been a U. S. Navy training base taking up nearly all of Redington Township, which shares a town border with Skedaddle Gore on the north side. It's a small, secure facility in the middle of thousands of acres of wicked mountainous timberland. As far inland as we are it seems weird that the Navy owns it, but they need to train their fly boys and "others"—international spies is the local legend—who might need to know how to survive intensive "interrogation" if captured by an enemy. I myself doubt that spy rumor, but these days you never know—there could be some truth in it.

The place is mostly staffed by Navy personnel who wear civvies, along with a few outside contractors who can keep quiet, although it's no big secret. We see their plain dull grey trucks and minibuses all the time. I've heard that the C.O. is a bigshot clinical psychologist. I've been in there once for a fire department orientation. They've got their own truck, but they wanted us to be familiar with the layout of the place in case they needed help. I was stationed in some backwater places in the Coast Guard, but I can tell you that I would not have been happy to do a tour of duty at that place.

Every now and then they get a student who actually manages to escape from their "simulated" prison camp. They usually come stumbling out of the woods near Sally's. Nadine calls a number she's been given and feeds them a cheeseburger and a few beers while they wait for a couple of big ugly types who show up to take the "escapee" back into the loving arms of Uncle Sam's Yacht Club. Not a bit like *Hogan's Heroes*, she says. Sucks to be them, I'd say.

"How's your head, Bobby?"

That voice finally manifested in the form of, of all people, Squatch. He walked out from behind me over to the roll top desk with a coffee mug in his hand and sat down. I realized there was another mug on the coffee table in front of me. I sat up, winced, and took a swallow. It was perfect, fixed just the way I like it.

Well, Hell . . .

"You can talk?"

He chuckled. "Yes. I can talk. But I *am* a little out of practice, so I hope you'll excuse me. George is a good friend, but he's not much for prolonged conversation."

"George? The—?"

"Wolf? Yeah. Actually, I think he's a wolf/dog hybrid. There was a woman over in Stratton a few years ago who was breeding them, but the State shut her down. I think one of her pack jumped the fence and George is the result."

"But you can actually talk." I sputtered. "We didn't think. . ."

He frowned and held up his hand. "We're a little pressed for time, Bobby, so I'll give you the short version." His voice was low pitched and a bit raspy. "When I was a kid I was very shy and quiet by nature. I hated being in school. I got teased and picked on every day because I was different. Eventually I stopped talking at all except at home. My folks took me to get evaluated and they diagnosed me with something called "selective mutism." It's part of the human heritage. Hard wired into our DNA, apparently." He smiled, another first. "When you think about it, early humans would have had precious few natural assets in the wild. We weren't the fastest or the strongest species, so we developed a fight or flight response to survive."

I nodded. The coffee was clearing my head quickly. I pulled off the ice pack. I didn't see any blood on it, which was a good sign.

"I've heard of that," I said. "When you're in danger the natural reaction is to run from it, unless you can't for some reason and—"

"You have to fight," Squatch finished. "Yeah. Back then that usually meant that something hidden in the dark was going to make a meal of you—which could cause some serious anxiety. You know what I mean?"

I nodded. I was familiar with the feeling, though it was fading with George out of the room.

"Unluckily for me, my normal anxiety level is so high that it results in the inability to speak outside of a place where I feel safe." He held up his hands and looked around the room. "Here."

"Where are we?"

He sighed and looked at me sadly. "Bobby, I've always liked you. You are one of only a handful of people I feel comfortable enough with to approach, much less speak to. I can only do that after years of therapy that I'd just as soon not get into right now." He leaned forward, cradling his cup in both hands. "Let's just say that this is my home. My sanctuary. It's the only place on Earth where I feel completely safe. I can't tell anyone where it is. I'll have to ask you to trust me.

"I was shadowing you. I saw you fall into that hole and I pulled you out. The rest of them didn't see. They just kept going. Nobody would ever have found you and you might have died right there. I couldn't let that happen. I took a chance bringing you here. I hope that won't cost me my home." His eyes were glistening again.

I thought on that for a minute, shrugged and set down my mug. "OK, sort of like Superman's Fortress of Solitude. I think I get it. I guess I don't need to know where it is anyway. It doesn't really matter to anyone but you, does it?"

He shook his head and smiled again. "No, not really."

"Can I go home now?"

He laughed. "Sure. But first we need to help that little girl. From the ball game?"

"Starr? Do you know where she is?"

He sat back in his chair.

"That I do. George found her yesterday wandering through the woods. He came and got me. Unfortunately, before we could get back to take her home she walked up onto a shack that those two brothers who cause all the problems around here use as a poaching blind."

"You mean the Regan brothers?"

"Yup. They're the ones. They're holding her. She's OK for now, but I heard them talking." He paused. "They're not too bright."

"Don't I know it," I said.

Dutch and Damien Regan are the local dinks who are the cause of most of what little crime there is in Skedaddle Gore ever since Frenchy Plourde died. They are collectively dumber than dirt, but they like to drink and pick fights and probably wouldn't hesitate to steal an elderly childless widow's last nickel.

"They plan to send the Community a ransom letter."

"We need to call the sheriff," I said, standing up just a little too fast. The room spun.

Squatch stood and grabbed my shoulders. "Easy, Bobby."

The dizziness passed.

"No. I'm sorry but I can't risk that. They'll find out about me and George and our lives won't be worth living anymore. We can do this ourselves, I think, if you're willing. Then George and I will disappear again and we'll all get on with our lives. Please?"

He looked at me again with those glistening eyes. So, sue me, I agreed.

Squatch went over his plan quickly and it made sense, *if* we could catch the Regans by surprise. Given what I knew of their intellectual capacity, I thought that probably wouldn't be too difficult. By the time he finished, I had the rest of my balance back, which was good because he asked if I'd mind being blindfolded until we got a piece away from wherever it was that we were.

He led me by the hand, and I could tell that I was climbing some stairs with metal railings and treads. Somehow it all felt strangely familiar. Deprived of my vision I realized that it was the metallic, slightly oily smell in the air and the faint hum that I'd gone deaf to from years of living with it in the Coast Guard. Nonsense, I thought. We're at least a hundred miles from a body of water big enough to float something that big.

"The Navy and the Coast Guard are friendly rivals," I said, half joking. "I won't tell them you stole their ship!"

I heard a soft laugh. "It's hardly a ship."

Then I heard what sounded like a watertight hatch close behind me.

Well, Hell . . .

#

We walked for a bit before Squatch silently removed my blindfold and led me what must have been a couple of miles in the dark through pretty dense woods to the edge of a tiny clearing with a ratty old tar paper shack in the middle of it. I judged that it was well after midnight but there was some moonlight that night, for which I was grateful. Two beat-up four-wheel ATV's sat in front of the shack, but I saw no other signs of life. George met us at the edge of the clearing and he and Squatch looked at each other for a minute before they both nodded. Squatch pointed to the front door and headed around the back with George. Being as quiet as I could, I crept up to the door and counted silently to ten, as per the plan.

"Police," I shouted at the top of my lungs, pounding my fists on the door as hard as I could. "You are surrounded. We have a warrant. Open the door!"

At that point I heard George begin to howl from out behind the cabin. I knew it was all an act but still the hair on my neck stood up! Squatch reared, let out a blat and chucked a junk of Maine granite the size of a basketball through the window. George jumped in through the hole and undertook what sounded like a very effective display of lupine ferocity. Luckily, I'd had the presence of mind to step back from the door because the next thing I knew the Regans came barrel-assing through it with their faces just feather white and their eyes as big as saucers. Screaming at the top of their lungs they hopped on those ATVs and booked it out of there like a thousand pitchfork-toting devils were on their backsides. It was just George. I swear to God he was grinning when he went by me.

#

Starr was a little scratched up but otherwise fine once she recognized me and figured out that she'd actually been rescued. She started talking a mile a minute at that point and never even stopped when the two of us finally walked up to the front gate on the access road to the Navy base just at dawn. The sentry there called his boss, shared a thermos of coffee with me and listened with wonder and no little amusement to Starr's story of the evil woodsmen, the friendly giant and his magic wolf that had saved her from being cooked in an oven and eaten by the wicked witch that lives by Skedaddle Lake. I think he was happy to get off the hook when Mike Hawkins showed up with Curly, Starr's mom and most of the Community of Satin in tow.

#

The Regan brothers stole Jeep Niemi's rusty old Pontiac station wagon over in Oquossoc and lit out in the general direction of British Columbia. The first night they stopped at a motel in Colebrook, New Hampshire where Dutch decided they should disguise themselves by dying their hair. Not having any prior cosmetology experience their efforts produced the prettiest bright orange hue you're ever likely to see, which caught the attention of an alert New Hampshire state trooper. Those boys'll be at the Maine Correctional Center in Windham for the next several years.

#

The following weekend Angie and I went to a honky tonk dance at Poacher's Paradise, a dance hall in Madrid, a town a little south of us. *She* asked *me*! She's got some surprising moves after a few beers, that woman. Between dances she told me that Starr's not homesick anymore, but she keeps telling wild fairy stories about a magic talking wolf named George. Imaginary playmates aren't unusual, Angie says, and they're working through that together. I discreetly kept quiet, but I *did* feel a little guilty.

By the way, Angie's teenage son Jack, who's quite the budding artist, designed a new graphic for Engine Five as a thank you to the town from the Community. It's a polar bear hugging a moose. The moose looks just a dite startled.

Seven: A Butcher, a Baker . . .

Agnes Heikkinen's voice always gives me the willies. I mean, talking to her is like eating a pizza with a spoon. It's exhausting work and most of the time you don't get much out of it in the end. For some reason I've never really understood, Agnes is our town clerk in Skedaddle Gore, Maine. Almost everyone in town is afraid of her, which is understandable when you consider that she used to be the commandant of a Nazi prisoner of war camp. (No, not really, but she *could* have been.) Everything about dealing with her is difficult and time consuming, so when I realized it was her on the phone that July morning, I groaned silently to myself.

"Robert Wing . . . is that you?" she barked. I had to pull the phone away from my ear. "Where have you been? I have tried to reach you forever."

Since my mom died Agnes is the only person in the world who still calls me "Robert."

"And a bright shiny good morning to you, too, Aggie," I said, with more than a little sarcasm, I'll admit. "I've been right here, just south of heaven."

And how was your commute up from Hell this morning? is what I didn't say, aloud.

"Very funny, Robert," she said, without the slightest trace of humor in her voice. "You are such a hoot. And *don't* call me Aggie. Your presence is required at the Town Office immediately. We have a situation."

"What kind of a situation?" I asked reasonably, I thought.

"I cannot discuss it over the phone, you idiot!" She growled. "Get your buttocks down here *now*!" The line clicked and buzzed. I looked at the receiver in my hand, then I looked out the window at the gorgeous sunlit morning view out over the pristine green valley nestling the azure blue Rangeley Lakes just north of my little cabin halfway up the side of Skedaddle Mountain, where I *had* been lazily enjoying my second cup of Carrabassett Valley Sunrise Blend coffee.

"Do I go?' I asked Lummox, my old Maine Coon cat, who was lounging in his accustomed spot in the sun out on my front porch railing, "or do I just commit ritual suicide?"

He looked at me, shrugged his shoulders and yawned.

#

Our town office used to be a one-room schoolhouse back in the day, where most of the citizens of Skedaddle Gore who have now passed their seventieth birthday spent their primary school days studying penmanship, mathematics and existential philosophy within its storied walls. From the outside it looks much the same as it did then, a small, white, post-and-beam barn-like building lacking only a hay loft. The only real change since those days has been the removal of the student desks and the installation of an indoor restroom and a furnace, both of which are much appreciated by the townsfolk in February during the annual town meeting.

As I pulled in Agnes was standing in the old "boys' side" doorway on the left side of the front wall facing the street. Back then boys and girls used to each have their own door into the schoolhouse because, I'm guessing, using the same entrance would have corrupted their juvenile morals and resulted in precocious premature romance, total moral anarchy and who knows what else. Anyway, these days practically everybody uses the boys' side. For some unknown reason, using the old girls' side on the right is looked down upon locally as politically incorrect. There's even an article being considered on next year's town meeting warrant to board that door up for good. It probably won't pass because Jake Beaverstool, our First Assessor, who runs all the town's daily affairs, thinks the two-hundred-and-fifty dollar estimate that Agnes got from her long-suffering husband

Toby, our local handyman and the building's janitor, is "outrageous" and "violent nepotism run wild."

"Hi, Aggie," I said as I climbed out of The Beast.

"Robert, I *told* you not to call me that," she snapped. "The most egregious blunder that this town has ever undertaken was to appoint you as constable. Tobias could have done the job much more efficaciously than you."

This is pretty much the same thing she says every time she sees me, but "efficaciously," was a new word. I'll have to look it up. By the way, I do happen to know that Toby turned the job down flat years ago.

Speaking of looking things up, when I was just starting high school down in Thomaston on the Maine mid-coast, my parents decided that it would be a good idea to buy a full set of the *Encyclopedia Britannica* from the traveling encyclopedia salesman who used to hit town almost every year in August. He was a very good salesman, and he moved a lot of encyclopedias all along the Maine coast over the years, even though many of them were sold on credit to poor families who really couldn't afford them. Like most parents, my folks reasoned that my high school studies would benefit from having a copy readily available for reference in the "stylish custom-built modern bookcase" (included for a modest additional charge) which was given a place of honor in our living room right next to our brand new Philco television set, also purchased on credit. Sometimes I liked to open it at random and just read for a while. I learned a lot of new words that way.

It turned out that I did indeed benefit greatly in my schoolwork until Mrs. Swanson, my history teacher, noticed that my essays on the American Revolution looked suspiciously well written. She checked one against her own newly purchased copy of the *Britannica* and I learned another new word, "plagiarism." I received a D minus for the course and was grounded for the rest of the school term, which severely crippled my emerging social life. My mother eventually sold our whole set, including the bookcase, to one of our neighbors for half price. But I digress. Don't you just love that word, "di-gress?" Sounds like something a smarty pants college professor would say who's noticed a fine pair of legs in the front row and has to bail for a minute because he's lost his train of thought.

Anyway, there was a black plastic garbage bag lying at Aggie's feet.

"What's in the bag?"

"Garbage, you imbicile," she said.

Silly me, I thought.

"Fly found it in the ditch next to the gate to the new transfer station."

Fly Fleance is our dump guy. I've mentioned him before.

"Isn't that where it goes?" I asked.

"I don't know why I put up with you, Robert," she spit out. "You are such a numbskull. It is highly illegal litterbugging to leave this in the street and we want you to find out the perpetrator."

"We? Who's we?" I thought it was a reasonable question.

"Me . . . *and* the first assessor," she said, looking down her nose imperiously at me.

"Sooo, . . . you . . . and Jake . . . want me to *investigate?*"

"Naturally, that is your function as constable. It is not important enough to involve the sheriff at this juncture. Should you *somehow* be successful it shall be referred to the proper authorities for further action." Agnes sniffed officiously.

That certainly would have blown away my sense of pride in my lofty office, if I'd had any.

"And how should I . . . ?"

"Once again you are wasting my time, Robert. Do your job. Fix it!" She wheeled and stomped back inside.

Well, Hell . . .

#

Back home in my garage that afternoon I put on a pair of rubber gloves and dumped the garbage bag out on my work bench, which I had luckily had the foresight to first cover with one of those blue Marden's tarps that you see all over the place covering wood piles, roofs and old cars. Marden's is a statewide chain of discount department stores that mainly deal in items salvaged from fires, earthquakes and other disasters, natural and manmade, all over the world. Mickey Marden, the late founder, is still famous for once buying a shipload of Ferrari sports cars that were water damaged somewhere down in South America. Sadly, he couldn't ever sell them due to import and environmental laws, so they rusted on a pier until they were finally scrapped. I'm told that Mickey just shrugged and moved on to his next deal.

Anyway, I figured I'd see if whoever had perpetrated this heinous crime against humanity had stupidly left behind a clue, such as an envelope with his or her name and address on it. No such luck. The pile of potential evidence consisted of a half-rotted dead squirrel and a bunch of stinking, fully rotten mashed-up fruit of some kind—apples, I thought, or maybe pears, which were mixed in with about ten pounds of sawdust, floor sweepings, a few scraps of paper, a dozen orange peels and a medium sized rock. There *was* a separate paper shopping bag from the Rangeley IGA in amongst the trash, though. Inside that I found a wadded-up sheet of copy paper. Flattening it out I saw that it was a printed note which read, "I got you now, Benson. You can't stop me. Be warned, you pervert!"

Well, Hell.

The only "Benson" I knew of in Skedaddle Gore was Snort Benson, who, with his wife Mitzi, owns the Skedaddle Lake Lodge on Skedaddle Cove, which is at the end of the Skedaddle Lake Road. Snort and I are on the Volunteer Fire Department together and he's the only other firefighter in town who can drive Engine Five, because she's got a finicky old stick shift and most of the kids in the department who grew up on automatics get anxiety attacks when they see three foot-pedals in any vehicle. In the winter Snort runs the kitchen at the Skedaddle Ridge Ski Resort and Mitzi runs the gift shop which, thanks to the fact that she can charm the birds out of the trees and is one seriously hot-looking blonde, has an amazing sales record. I decided that a visit out to the lake was definitely in order.

During the summer Mitzi oversees the whole Lake Lodge operation, checking guests in and out, running the housekeeping, working the Lodge's computer website, taking online reservations and arranging for local guides who take "sports" from away on trips all over the region, which is famous for being some of the best fishing grounds for trout and land-locked salmon in the State of Maine.

When I pulled up in front of the large log cabin style main lodge, she was sitting in a lounge chair on the wraparound front porch in a pink halter top, a big floppy sun hat, sunglasses and short shorts that looked painted on. She had a drink glass in her hand with a straw and an umbrella sticking out of it. I knew it was probably a ginger ale with ice. Mitzi doesn't drink, ever. She does enjoy a good party, though.

"Bobby Wing, you old sweetheart," she shouted as I climbed out of The Beast. "I wondered when you would be back for more." An older couple on the other end of the porch leaned forward in their own lounge chairs. The lady looked vaguely disapproving but somewhat curious. The guy was grinning like an idiot.

"Mitzi, you little tease," I shouted back. "You wore me out last time. There's nothing left in the tank."

"You flatter me, sir," she giggled and propped up one very shapely leg, showing it off to its best advantage. She lowered her chin and looked at me over the top of her sunglasses. "But then stamina was *never* your strong suit."

I laughed. This is pretty much Mitzi's hello to anything male in her vicinity. It might lead some to wonder, but she's well known as being "totally devoted" to her "little Snotzy."

"Boss around?" I asked.

"You're looking at her, mister man." She leaned forward and her brows knit together in a pretty frown. "But if you're looking for that lazy slug that I had the misfortune to hook up with some twenty years ago, he's in the kitchen poisoning the guests' lunch." The "guests" on the far end of the porch were laughing now. All part of the act.

"When you're done with Old Numbnuts," she cooed. "Come back and see me . . . mister." She did her best Lauren Bacall hair flip.

"Not a chance," I said, laughing. "I value my life too much."

"Chicken! Puck, puck, puck," she shouted as I walked around to the kitchen door at the side of the building.

I was still chuckling to myself when I literally ran into Charlie Winchenbach coming out. He was carrying a good-sized stock pot with a large cardboard box balanced on top.

"Hey, Charlie. What's up?" I said, as he struggled to maneuver his delicately balanced burden through the door. "What you got there?"

"Hey, Bobby," he replied. "Just borrowed this off Peachy for a few days." He set everything in the bed of his old rusty pickup truck and hooked the length of nylon boat rope that passes for a tailgate across the back. "I'm making a special brew this week and I needed an extra pot to boil the wort in. I'm experimenting with using these here blueberries and bananas in this next batch" He nodded at the box. "It should give the stout a wicked extra kick."

Charlie is my crew boss in the winter on the Buster chairlift on The Mountain. He works summers at the Lodge and the Kowabunga Kampground next door doing grounds work and taking care of Mitzi's string of rental fishing boats and canoes. This summer he's caught the home brewing bug. I tried one of his early runs, something he called a "Canadian Crapshoot." He told me that he used maple syrup in the recipe along with another "secret ingredient." I thought it tasted a lot like a sour Orange Nehi soda. Much as I admire Charlie's sense of adventure in life, his brewing experiments so far have been a bit, shall we say, disappointing.

"Sounds good," I lied.

"I'll save you a couple of bottles." He grinned and nodded toward the front porch. "Did you see Mitzi's outfit this morning? Those legs sure go all the way up, don't they?"

"Sure do," I had to agree. "Snort inside?"

"Yup, him and Peachy are inside trading punches as we speak."

"Not for real, I hope."

"Not yet anyway, but you know how those two are. I keep expecting to find one of them face down in the steam kettle. I don't know why they keep working together, being as they hate each other's guts so bad."

Charlie turned and climbed into the cab of his truck. "Gotta make some tracks. Boogie's got me on a short leash. We've been fighting a wicked rodent problem in her attic all this past week. See ya."

"Don't work too hard," I called as he roared off in a cloud of dust and oily exhaust smoke.

Monica "Boogie" Mann is the owner of the Kampground. Charlie lives year-round in one of her little housekeeping cabins. A true child of the sixties, back in the day she was a groupie for one of the second level touring R & B groups. She'll tell you right up front that she got her nickname after a memorable night of "boogie-woogie-oogieing all night long" with the band on a gig in L. A. She's tall and thin and has a face that, these days, would stop an eight-day clock dead in its tracks. You remember the Wicked Witch in the original Wizard of Oz movie? That's what she looks like if you imagine the witch dressed in torn bellbottom jeans, tie died t-shirts and bangle bracelets up and down both arms.

Just about then I heard a loud bang from inside the kitchen and the kid from the college down in Farmington that Mitzi hired as a dishwasher for the summer came bailing out.

"Judas, mister," he gasped. "Don't go in there. Somebody's gonna get killed. I gotta go see Mitzi. This is too much. I'm friggin' quitting. I need the money for school, but I want to live long enough to graduate!"

I looked through the open door to see Snort standing behind his prep table waving a butcher knife at the only other person left in the room. Besides Filthy Phillips, my late Coast Guard buddy, Peachy Keene is one of the best bakers I've ever had the pleasure of knowing. He and Snort have worked together for years but they've never been able to be in the same room for more than ten minutes without arguing, usually loudly, about something.

"You scum sucking S.O.B.," Snort was screaming. "I *told* you not to lend out any more of my gear to that friggin' Winchenbach idiot. It always comes back stained up, dented and smelling like the inside of a latrine. That's expensive professional equipment."

"Well, at least he makes something with it that wouldn't gag a maggot," Peachy screamed back as he waved a three-foot-long tapered French style rolling pin.

"That stuff he makes is the vilest horse piss I've ever tasted," Snort yelled.

"Aha!" Peachy said. "So, you *did* try it. You lied to me. You said you'd rather drown in a septic tank than drink Charlie's beer. I ought to—"

"OK, you two," Mitzi bellowed from the porch. "For the six thousand, two hundred and twenty-fourth time, knock it off. We've got guests out here who can hear you. You sound like two ten-year-olds on a school playground. You've got lunch to make and I'm hungry. Get to it!"

"Yes, Mitzi," they singsong chorused together like two contrite little kids. I chuckled to myself.

Peachy turned back to his granite countertop, where he was rolling out what looked like pie dough. Next to it was a shallow pan with a detached bottom which I recognized from those cooking shows on the satellite TV as a tart shell.

Hey, don't you judge me. They're fun and I've even learned a few things!

"What's on the menu, Peachy?" I asked.

"For some reason that miserable hog sticker over there decided to try to make a Quiche Lorraine for lunch. I'm doing him a favor by making a decent crust for it." He glared across the room at Snort. "Unlike the ones that normally manage to escape from this glorified greasy spoon."

Snort glared right back.

"Smells good," I said as the aroma of crisping bacon wafted from Snort's oven. "Need a taster?"

Snort looked at me with a raised eyebrow. "What do you want, Bobby? Unlike some, I have to work to make a living here."

"Me, too," I said. "I'm here on an investigation."

"*WHAT?*" Snort started laughing and I heard Peachy behind me join in.

"Peachy, old man," Snort said, between guffaws, "We might's well start packing it in. The world's coming to an end."

"No, really, Snort," I said. "Aggie from the town office wants—"

Now Peachy guffawed. "Oh, no. Not 'Agony Agnes?'"

"The same." I admitted. "Fly Fleance found some trash in the ditch in front of the dump gate when it was closed. Aggie wants to know who dumped it. She gave me a commission from the assessors."

"Well," Peachy said, still laughing. "You've certainly come to the right place. Nothing but garbage comes out of here."

Snort looked daggers at him. "Only that side of the room," he growled. "Is that the trash in question?" he said, nodding at the bag in my hand.

"Some of it anyway," I said. I pulled the smoothed-out sheet of copy paper out of the bag and passed it to him. "Is this yours?"

Snort peered at the paper in his hand. "*Pervert?*" Snort said. "Here, Peachy, this must be for you."

Peachy walked over to Snort's station and looked at the paper. He laughed. "Well, Snort, It looks like somebody's finally got your number."

"Sit on it, Peachy." Snort passed the paper back to me. "No, Constable," he said sarcastically, drawing himself up to his full height, which wasn't that far. "I have never seen this missive before in my life. I'd venture to say it's *somebody's* idea of a sick friggin' joke." He looked pointedly at Peachy.

Peachy just grinned and shook his head. "Don't look at me."

"Any other Bensons in the area that you know of?" I asked Snort. "Just Mitzy," he said.

"And who would know better than anyone else about all of your weird habits?" said Peachy.

Snort shook a fist. "Why, you—"

"OK, guys," I said, moving between them. "Let's call it a draw. It's not worth calling in the sheriff, so I'll just file this in case something comes up later. Now . . . about lunch."

#

Two days later a siren going past the house woke me up at 5 A.M. About five minutes later I'd climbed out of bed and was looking out the front window when a sheriff's cruiser went flying by with all guns blazing. I picked up the phone.

"They're at the Lake Lodge," Marti Wallace told me. "I heard on the county channel that somebody found a body in the walk-in cooler."

Well, Hell . . .

#

The fire department got toned out to help direct traffic at the scene, so I parked old Engine Five diagonally across the middle of the Lake Road and spent most of the day turning away rubber-neckers and the occasional camper or lodge guest who wanted to get to their room or campsite. Marti, our fire chief, redirected the grumpier ones to Sally's Motel and Bar and Live Bait and Convenience Store with a note to Nadine, the bartender and Marti's partner, for a complementary cheeseburger and beer. That soothed a lot of ruffled feathers and even made some new summer customers.

Putting together the bits of rumor and speculation I picked up throughout the day I figured out that Mitzi had gone to the Lodge's kitchen very early in the morning when she realized that Peachy hadn't started work yet. She was surprised that no one was there as Peachy usually opens up the kitchen at five when he fires up the oven and starts the bread and pastry planned for the day. Snort comes in about an hour later to prep for breakfast for the guests. That morning the lights were still out, and the ovens and flattop grill were cold. Mitzi had turned on the lights and started looking around when she stepped into the walk-in cooler and found Peachy hanging by the neck from an overhead electrical conduit. She ran upstairs and told Snort, who immediately collapsed in hysterics, leaving Mitzi to call 911.

Well, Hell.

#

"What makes you think it's not a suicide?" Big Jim Brackett said as he sank into my ancient living room couch. It groaned.

I'd met Jim, Franklin County's chief deputy, a few times at accident scenes and fires and the like, but he'd never been to the house before. The couch groaned again as Lummox climbed up onto his lap. Jim set his notebook aside and scratched the perfect spot behind Lummox's ears, which got him a head butt under the chin and a lap full of cat hair as the Thing From Hell that I call my Cat settled down contentedly for his afternoon nap. It *was* his spot, after all.

"It just doesn't fit with what I know of Peachy," I said. "He never struck me at all as the suicidal type. Outside of his constant rows with Snort, I always thought he was a happy, easy-going guy. He must have hung himself up with butcher's twine, right?"

"No," Jim picked up his notebook. Lummox squirmed. "Actually, it was a piece of nylon rope, about five feet long. The Medical Examiner—"

"Doc Jeffries?

"Right. Doc left it on the body. He'll remove it during the autopsy at the hospital in Farmington."

"I would have thought he'd have used the twine. It's handy. I think there's a dispenser for it right in the kitchen by Snort's workstation. It would have made more sense. I wonder where the rope came from."

"Good question," Jim said. "But sometimes suicidal people aren't acting on impulse. Many of them actually plan pretty far in advance."

"Did he leave a note?"

"Yeah. There was a sheet of copy paper pinned to his shirt."

"Copy paper?"

"Yeah," Jim said, "like computer printers and photocopiers use. Eight and a half by eleven inches."

"What did it say?"

Jim looked at his notebook. "I CAN'T WORK LIKE THIS ANYMORE, I QUIT!!!" he read. "All in capital letters."

"That sounds like Peachy."

"What do you mean?"

"Peachy and Snort were always fighting about something in the kitchen. I bet he's quit a thousand times over the years." Something struck me. "You know . . ."

"What?" Jim said.

"I just realized that I've rarely seen Peachy outside of a kitchen. And Snort's almost always been with him. I don't even know where he lives."

"Mitzi told me he lives at the Lodge with them."

"With them? That's a surprise to me."

"Yeah," Jim said, looking at his notebook again. "Mitzi says they've been joined at the hip since they met in the Army. They were both in Desert Storm."

"Really?" I said, startled. "So was I. Neither of them ever mentioned that. Wow."

I didn't know what else to say. I just sat silent for a few minutes.

"Bobby?" Jim finally said. "You OK?"

"Yeah, that's just such a surprise. How's Snort taking it?"

"Not very well at all. Mitzi told me she's never seen him cry before. He won't go near the kitchen. She may have to close the Lodge and give everybody refunds."

We sat quietly for several more minutes. Jim scratched under Lummox's chin and was rewarded with a loud purr. Hearing that made me feel a little better.

"You said the note was printed on copy paper?" I asked.

"Right."

"By a computer?"

"Yeah, I'd say," Jim said.

"And pinned to his chest? That seems an odd thing to do. Why didn't he leave it on the counter?" I had a thought. "Wait here."

I went out to my shed and dug out the note I'd shown Snort and Peachy. I carried it back into the living room.

"Look at this," I said as I handed him the note. "Fly Fleance found it in the ditch outside the gate at the dump."

Jim looked at the note, then at me.

"Maybe you're right, Bobby," he said slowly. "Maybe it's *not* a suicide after all."

Well, Hell . . .

#

Jim called in the state police at that point, because they are the ones who investigate all suspicious deaths in Maine. So far, Jim told me, that's all it was, suspicious, but he agreed with me that there were enough things about the circumstances that didn't quite fit to warrant a closer look. Of course, that meant that the next few days were hectic. The state police mobile crime lab van showed up, followed by the news media trucks that always seem to follow it around. Everyone even remotely involved in Peachy's demise had to be interviewed again by state police detectives in neat suits and ties, which made them wicked conspicuous in the Gore. Heck, I don't even *own* a tie anymore.

The forensic people came to my house dressed in white plastic suits with hairnets and little blue booties over their shoes. They took possession of the note and the rest of the contents of the bag and gave me a receipt for the garbage, of all things. I heard later that they also interviewed Aggie and Jake Beaverstool, who said he really hadn't known anything about the big garbage scandal investigative commission before Aggie gave it to me. It had all been her idea. I expect it was all so she could boss me around. No surprise, actually.

#

A couple of days later I was in the bathroom finishing up business after breakfast when I heard a knock on my front door. Zipping up, I shut off the light, walked through my living room and looked out to see Willie Brackett standing on my porch.

I pulled the door open. "Deputy Brackett," I said with a grin. "What brings you to my humble abode this morning?"

"Hi, Bobby," she said. "Can I come in for a minute? You're not busy, are you?"

"Not too busy for you, my dear," I said as I bowed and waved her inside. "Come on in. Don't mind the mess, my housekeeper is late this morning."

She smiled, a little sadly, I thought, which was unlike her.

"What's wrong, Willie?" I said as she plopped down next to Lummox on the couch. True to form he pawed at her elbow until she made a lap.

"Oh, nothing really," she said. "I'm just tired and a little out of sorts, I guess. I'm coming off a week of nights and I'm sick and tired of chasing 911 butt dials. I must have had over a dozen in the last three days alone. I need a break for a few minutes. Do you mind."

As if I would.

"No. Of course not. Butt dials?"

"Yeah," she said as she stroked Lummox. "The newer cell phones have a feature where they'll dial 911 for you if you press the right series of buttons, or the wrong ones, for that matter. The phone calls in by itself and when the dispatcher answers, nobody's there. The 911 software can usually find an area where the call is coming from and sometimes an address. We're required to try to locate the phone and the caller to see if it really *is* an emergency. Most of the time it's a complete waste of time, but we can't take the chance. Around here it usually happens the most in the winter when skiers up at The

Mountain stick their phones in their pockets and then sit on them, hence the 'butt dial.' I've already chased down two of them this shift at the opposite ends of my patrol area, both false alarms."

"OK," I said. "I'll make us a coffee and you can get all the rest of that 'nothing really' off your chest."

"Thanks," she said. "I appreciate that, but could you make mine tea? I'm so full of coffee I'll probably be up all day."

"Got it. K-cup tea OK? I don't have any bags."

"That's fine," she said. "One sugar, OK?" She reached down to accommodate Lummox, who was settled firmly in her lap and pawing at her arm for more attention. She petted him with a sad, tired smile as I busied myself in the kitchen.

"How's your dad?" I asked. "I haven't seen him since he stopped in day before yesterday."

"He's good," she called from the couch. "He says that state police CID have taken over Peachy Keene's case completely now. The preliminary autopsy results are in." She paused. "Did you know him very well?" she asked as I set her cup down on the end table next to the sofa.

"Not well enough, I guess. I had no idea that he'd been living with Snort and Mitzy for years. I still don't understand it completely, but your dad said they were buddies in the Army. I had one like that in the Coast Guard." I gestured around the room. "He's the guy that left me in all this luxury."

She smiled and sipped at her tea. "Oh . . . hot," she said, startled.

"That's about all you can say for it," I said as I settled into my TV-watching chair across the room.

She set the tea down to cool. "It's bothering me that Peachy's BA—his blood alcohol level—came back at a point two *nine*. That's over three and a half times the legal limit for drunk driving in Maine. Dad says that the worst offender he's ever had in twenty-two years on the road was a point two *six*. Dad found *that* guy upside down on top of a snowbank in a Subaru, swearing that he was in Milwaukee headed for a Bucks game."

I chuckled.

"If that was Peachy's normal, he must have been a super heavy drinker," she said.

"To be honest, I don't think I can ever recall seeing him drunk. Every once in a great while he'd come into Sally's and shoot the breeze with a bunch of us, but I never saw him stumble or slur his words. He'd usually nurse a beer or two for an hour or so and then leave. He was a pretty quiet, friendly guy."

"Except around Snort."

"Yeah." I shook my head. "I never could figure that out." Neither of us said anything for a bit.

"So," I said. "How's Chad doing. Has the romance progressed?" Chad Fairchild, our newest area state trooper, had piqued Willie's interest last winter when he first moved into the area, and they'd had a couple of dates back along.

"No." She sighed. "Oh, Bobby," she said, hanging her head. "I've seen him a few times, but nothing at all lately. He's still friendly and all but he hasn't even called me in going on *three months*. I've pretty much given up. He must have met somebody else."

"Sorry, Willie," I said, hoping I sounded reassuring. "Somebody else will come along for you too."

"Uh, huh. Sure," she said, frowning. "Sometimes I think I'm bound to die an old spinster lady. Who would want me, Bobby?" she said, her voice rising. "Look at me. This uniform and all this duty gear doesn't exactly accentuate any of my 'feminine charms' and I haven't met a guy yet who's bowled over by my firearms qualification scores."

"Don't sell yourself short, kid."

I suddenly remembered having a similar conversation a few years before with my daughter. Considering how *her* love life has turned out, I decided not to dispense any more advice to the lovelorn.

"Why don't you go home and get some sleep?"

"Yeah, thanks," she said. "You're right. I'm just tired. Things will look better tomorrow. Right, Lummie?" She looked down at Lummox, who squirmed around to lie spreadeagled face up in her lap. He batted at the wisps of her hair which had come loose from her bun. We both laughed. He purred louder, the old moocher.

As I watched Willie pull out of my dooryard a few minutes later I remembered what she'd said about Peachy's blood alcohol level. Now, I admit that I have drunk a lot of beer over the course of a lot of years and I think I'd probably qualify by now as an expert on the art. I can tell you that it would take a whole truck load of beer to get that drunk. It was just one more thing that didn't quite add up.

#

"Thank you so much for coming, Bobby," Mitzi said as she opened the door. "I really need your help. I don't know what to do at this point." In all the time I've known her it was the first time I'd ever seen her looking upset. Her eyes were red and puffy, and she looked exhausted.

"How's he doing?"

"I don't know," she said. "He won't talk to me, or anybody else, for that matter. He just sits up in our living room and stares at the wall. He eats a little now and then, but . . ."

"What can I do to help?" I asked as we sat together on the sofa in the lodge reception area. Aside from us it was deserted.

"I just *don't know*," she said again. "I've tried to make him an appointment with the VA in Togus, but they're backed up so much that the soonest I can get him in is three weeks from next Tuesday. I don't know anybody local." Her voice trailed off. "Bobby, I'm afraid for him. This is something I've never seen in him. I'm afraid . . ." She took my hand and started to cry.

"It'll be OK, Mitzi," I said, not at all sure that I was telling her the truth. She smiled wanly. "Where's the coffee pot?"

"I've got a Keurig in the apartment," she said. "I haven't been able to go down to the kitchen since . . ."

I patted her hand and tried to look reassuring, but I was feeling totally out of my league.

"Let's go get a cup."

She nodded and stood up, a little shakily.

I held her elbow. "Are *you* OK?"

She shook her head and looked at the ceiling.

"Yeah, I think so. I haven't had much sleep. Every time I start to drift off I see Peachy's face." She looked at me with tears in her eyes. "Bobby, I woke up screaming this morning. I'm so scared." She moved toward me, and I hugged her.

"Let's go see him," I said. "Maybe a cup of coffee and a familiar face will help."

"OK. Thanks."

Snort was sitting silently in a recliner staring at a blank TV. The living room had a homey, woodsy feel, with landscape paintings on the wall and what looked like family pictures on the mantle over a small fireplace on the outside wall.

Mitzi headed toward the kitchen to get the coffee as I looked around. Between a brace of candles in the middle of the mantlepiece was a framed eight by ten photo of the three of them, Snort, Mitzi and Peachy, on a sand beach about a thousand miles from Skedaddle Gore. Mitzi was striking a showgirl's pose in the middle, looking like a million bucks in a bikini and sandals. Snort and Peachy were standing on either side of her, grinning and holding up Corona beer bottles with lime wedges in the necks as if they were toasting her. They really looked like they were having a good time.

"He liked Cabo," Snort suddenly said behind me. Surprised, I turned toward him.

"Hi, old man," I said. "How's it going?" I took a knee on the floor and put my hand on the arm of his chair.

"That was six, or was it eight years ago," Snort said slowly as he nodded toward the picture. "Peggy Gordon gave us a week off from The Mountain in March for our anniversary—Mitzi's and mine. She even paid for the flight. Peachy didn't want to go at first. Said he'd be in the way. I insisted." He lapsed into silence.

"Mitzi said you guys met in the Army?" I said, trying to keep him talking.

"Yeah." Silence.

"Did you know that I was just offshore in the Gulf during Desert Storm?" I said, trying for an opening. "My cutter was doing anti-aircraft radar picket duty for the fleet."

Snort shifted in his chair and looked into my eyes for the first time.

"No," he said slowly. "I didn't know that."

"Yeah. We were getting buzzed a lot by those Revolutionary Guard suicide boats," I said. "They'd come out and run rings around us, harassing us; just looking for an opening."

"Yeah, I remember hearing that."

I took a deep breath. I don't talk about this much. Hell, I don't even like thinking about it.

"One day I was running a Ma Deuce turret midships at General Quarters when one of them peeled off and headed straight toward us. I guess he got sick of waiting to meet the martyr's promised seventy-three virgins." I let myself down until I was sitting on the floor in front of him with my legs crossed under me in a tailor's seat. "It felt like he was zeroing in on me personally, but I guessed that it was the command bridge behind me that he was focused on."

Snort leaned forward. We held eye contact.

"He started shooting at a thousand yards, small arms. You know, to keep our heads down." I paused, remembering. "My loader was a kid from Nebraska, believe it or not. He'd only been in ship's company for three months. Never even seen salt water before."

"Fresh meat," Snort said, nodding. He was holding onto the arms of his chair now and his eyes were bright.

"Yeah," I said. I felt my own eyes welling. "We opened up on the bastard and I raked his bow with my first burst. Then the Mark 75 Rapid Fire on our foredeck came online and blew him out of the water on the third round. When I looked around for a reload the kid was slumped back against the bulkhead, staring at me. He'd taken one right between the eyes. I still see those eyes sometimes . . . in my sleep . . ."

I heard Mitzi gasp behind me. Snort looked at her, then at me and then down at the floor. He sighed. There was a long pause.

"I was upside down in the back of a burning Humvee, trapped in my seat belt." Snort said softly. "Peachy was my driver. We hit an IED, and he was thrown clear. He was hit in the knee by shrapnel, but he came back and dragged me and the gunner out just before it blew." He shuddered. "I can still smell the smoke. I see the flames." He looked up. "He saved my life."

"Peachy?"

He nodded. "Martin Luther Keene was his full name, believe it or not," Snort said, with a sad smile. "He couldn't cook for beans . . . but what a baker he turned out to be!"

"You were buddies."

"More than that. Brothers. But not at first," Snort said, sitting back and looking at the ceiling. "When he was first assigned to my unit I thought he was a fat, lazy slob." He chuckled ruefully. "After we got out he told me that he thought I was an insufferable dink to him at first. And I was." He looked over at Mitzi. "Still am, I guess, sometimes." He shrugged. "Sorry, honey."

"Oh, Snotzy," she said as she walked in front of me, climbed into his lap and hugged him.

I let myself out.

#

It was a dark, damp morning the next day. I'd lit a small fire in my wood stove to take off the chill when Lummox went on alert and hopped into the front window. I walked over to the window just as a tall, auburn haired woman in dark slacks and a suit jacket climbed out of a plain looking white Ford SUV in my dooryard. She looked around as I watched, then walked up to my front porch door and knocked.

"Can I help you?" I asked.

"Constable Wing?"

I chuckled. "In name only, I'm afraid. Just Bobby most of the time."

She smiled. She looked fit and was nice looking in a sharp-edged, professional sort of way. She reached into the black leather purse hanging over her shoulder and pulled out a badge holder.

"I'm Detective Sergeant Sheila Norton. I'm with the State Police Criminal Investigation Division. Can I talk to you about Martin Keene?"

It took a minute but then I remembered.

"You mean Peachy?" I asked. She nodded.

"Sure. Come on in before the rain starts."

I held the door open. As she moved through it Lummox head butted her in the shin. She stopped, looked down at him and smiled.

"What a beauty," she said. "Maine Coon?"

"Of decidedly mixed lineage." I nodded. "Sorry about that. This is Lummox. He does that sometimes to people he likes."

"I've got a pure white female Coon at home named Snowdrift. He probably smells her on me. I spend half my time brushing her fur off my work clothes."

"I know the feeling," I said. "Coffee?"

"Sure, thanks."

"Welcome to my mountain estate. Come into my formal kitchen," I said, waving at the corner of the room where my stove and refrigerator sit. Lummox was already sitting in one of my kitchen chairs next to the table. He looked up at her expectantly.

"Just push him off. He thinks he owns the place."

"If he's anything like Snowdrift, he does," she said, reaching down to scratch his chin. After a few seconds of that he politely hopped down onto the floor and offered her his seat. She nodded at him with a smile, brushed off the seat with her hand and sat.

"Black, please," she said.

"A woman after my own heart." I slipped the Skedaddle Ridge coffee mug I use when formally entertaining out of the Keurig and put it on the table in front of her.

She inhaled. "Smells good," she said. Her eyebrow lifted as she took a sip. "Married?"

I chuckled. "Look around, Detective. Does it look like I'm married?"

She smiled as she took in my semi-organized chaos.

"Widowed, actually," I said.

"Sorry," she said, setting down her cup.

"No worries," I said. "It was a long time ago now. I have a grown daughter in Oregon."

"Two kids in high school for me," she said, taking another sip of her coffee. "This is good."

"Thanks. So . . . ?"

She became businesslike. "I've been assigned to look into Mr. Keene's death," she said. "Did you know him very well?"

"Pretty well. I've lived in the Gore about ten years since I retired from the Coast Guard, and I used to run into Peachy and Snort quite often. Snort's on the Fire Department with me but Peachy used to say that running *toward* emergencies had no charms for him."

I realized then how ironic that sounded.

"What kind of a guy was he?" she said, pulling out her phone. "Do you mind?"

"Mind what?

"I'd like to record our conversation. I'm not great at taking notes while I'm drinking coffee."

"The phone can do that?"

"Yeah, you just push here," she said, pointing to a little icon on her screen. I had no idea.

"Sure," I said. "I got nuttin' to hide, Officer."

She smiled. "Good. Thanks. So, what kind of a guy *was* he?"

I thought a minute. "Likable. Funny sometimes. Great at his job. I'm really going to miss his Moose Turds."

"Moose Turds?" she asked, smiling quizzically.

"You probably already know that he worked as a baker at the Lodge summers and on The Mountain in the winter," I said. "He made a raised chocolate donut filled with chocolate pastry cream and covered with chocolate ganache and chocolate sprinkles. They're famous around here . . . or were."

"Wow," she said. "Sounds like an instant five pounds applied directly to my hips. Was he moody, or . . . you know, depressed lately?"

"No, not at all. When I saw him last week he seemed his normal self."

I told her about going to the Lodge kitchen to talk to Snort.

"So, Mr. Benson and Mr. Keene were arguing when you got there? Did they do that a lot?"

"They've been arguing since I've known them. They're like kid brothers, or an old married couple," I said. I thought about telling her about my talk with Snort, but I decided I needed to know where she was going with this first.

"So, what are you thinking? Was it suicide?"

"I was going to ask you the same question," she said.

"I have a hard time believing that Peachy would do something like that. It's a shock, frankly. He always seemed pretty steady, but I'm certainly no expert."

"That's not unheard of," she said. "I've done more of these investigations than I care to remember. One of the most common things that friends and family say is just that. 'I would have never believed he would do a thing like that' or 'I didn't see any signs at all.' Was he a heavy drinker?"

"No," I said. "He was in Sally's a couple of weeks ago. That's the last time I can remember seeing him drinking. He did what he normally does. He had two beers, bought a couple more for the people he was sitting with and went home after about an hour. I can't say I've ever seen him drunk."

"That's one of the things that puzzles me. Just about everybody I've talked to so far has said the same thing. The thing is," she paused, "the autopsy report—"

"Said his blood alcohol was a point two nine, I know."

Her eyes opened in surprise. "How did you know that?"

Oops!

I didn't want to get Willie in trouble, so I white lied.

"Skedaddle Telegraph," I said. It was sort of true. "You get used to it in a place like this. That's a pretty high reading, I hear."

She frowned. "Yes, very high." She paused and took a deep breath. "Mr. Wing . . . Bobby, there are a lot of things that trouble me about this case. On its face it looks very much like a suicide, but with that much alcohol in his system it's possible that he could have been unconscious."

"Before...?"

"Yes," she said. "And then there are the notes."

"Notes? Plural?"

"Yes. The one pinned to his chest and the one you brought to the attention of the sheriff's department. It was found at your dump?"

"Yes."

"Those notes were composed and printed on the kitchen computer at the Skedaddle Lake Lodge," she said, watching me closely.

"Both of them?"

"Yes. They'd been erased but our forensic lab found that they were still in the computer's memory cache. They were also both printed on the kitchen printer."

"So, they both had to be written by someone—"

"who had access to that particular computer." She finished my thought.

"Well, Hell," I said.

"I'm told that Mr. Keene and the Bensons are the only ones who had access to that computer."

"So, if Peachy didn't write those notes?" I didn't like what I was thinking.

"Too early to tell yet." She paused. "I also wanted to ask you if you have any thoughts about the other trash in that bag."

"Such as...?"

"Basically, the contents consisted of a mixture of—" She put her coffee down, poked at her phone and read: "A piece of granite gneiss weighing 10.2 ounces, 52 ounces of pine sawdust mixed with dried apple pulp and eleven orange peels, three shredded pieces of glue-backed paper that appeared to be a bottle label, a plastic screw cap and the remains of a red squirrel which had been killed with a common warfarin-based rodent poison."

"That's pretty much what I saw, too," I said. "You said there was a label?"

She nodded. "Shredded pieces of glue-backed paper."

I had a thought. "Any printing on that paper? I didn't see any."

"Only this." She swiped her fingers over the phone's screen and turned it toward me. There were two pictures showing. On one I could faintly see print that appeared to say "New Jers—" On the other was what looked like a smeared "190" and the letter "p."

"Liquor bottle . . . from New Jersey, maybe?"

She nodded. "That's what I think. The bottle cap in the bag was also the size which commonly fits a pint liquor bottle. We're waiting for the lab to tell us what kind."

"I don't see how this could tie into Peachy's death beyond the fact that the note was in the same bag. Do you think the notes are connected?"

"At this point we aren't sure."

I shook my head. "None of this makes any sense to me. None of it fits the Peachy I knew at all. What a mess."

"I've got to agree with you there," she said.

As I watched her pull out of my yard in the rain I had a thought. *Oranges and . . . squirrels?*

#

"Put that damn hard hat—" Fred Gordon yelled over the high-pitched roar of the four seat all-terrain vehicle which held me, Charlie Winchenbach and Floyd Masterman.

"On your damn hard head." finished Floyd, the other half of "Frick and Frack."

Charlie, who was sitting in the back seat with me while Fred and Floyd rode up front, started laughing.

"I told you so, Bobby. Didn't I say you'd get yelled at?" Charlie shouted as we bounced up the dirt road that leads from the maintenance garage to the base of the Buster triple chair lift where I spend my winters in the liftey shack at the top. I had an awful feeling that the day was not going to go well, even though it was glorious weather, without a cloud in the sky. There wasn't a breath of the wind that, in winter, can easily blow you right off your feet and, if you're not careful, give you a wicked case of frostbite in just a few minutes.

"Yeah, Charlie. Thanks for the friggin' warning," I yelled back as I fought to hold the aluminum helmet on my head while clinging to the seat with the other hand as Floyd bounced us over the ruts and potholes that dotted our route up to Buster's base station. Charlie'd recruited me the day before to help Fred, Floyd and him inspect and recondition the lift tower sheave wheels that carry the thick main wire rope that whips the chairs up and down the hill. I know that they're required by the Maine Fire Marshal's Office, who certify the safety of all ski lifts and other rides in Maine, to do a certain number of those wheels every year.

Usually, I don't get involved with The Mountain much in the summer, but Charlie said that the guy that usually helps with this chore had to have an appendectomy and would be out for a couple of weeks. I was free, being retired and "at leisure," and a little extra cash never hurts.

As we pulled up to Buster there was an excavator machine standing next to the base station.

"OK, Bobby," said Floyd. "Since you're new at this—"

"We need to do a little—," Fred said.

"Safety briefing," Floyd finished.

My neck would be sore tonight if I had to keep shifting back and forth between them, I thought. It was like watching a ping pong match.

"First thing to do is—" Fred began.

"Hook up the maintenance basket, there—" Floyd pointed to the thing next to the excavator that looked a lot like a bucket you see on a lineman's truck. It had a metal arm sticking up that had a clamp on top like the ones that hold the chairs to the rope.

"To the uphill rope. Then—" Fred said.

"Charlie and Fred will—" Floyd said.

"Ride in the basket and do the inspections, while Floyd—" Fred said.

"Runs the lift," Floyd said, nodding his head.

I was getting a little dizzy at that point. I was relieved when Floyd hopped into the cab of the excavator and Fred hooked a chain to the basket. In a few minutes they had the basket clamped to the uphill rope.

Charlie had told me on the phone that my job would be simple. I was going to stay on the ground under the basket and act as a safety man in case anything, or anyone, fell out. Thankfully I could follow them up and down in the ATV. My legs aren't what they were twenty years ago.

As we watched Fred and Floyd at work, Charlie said, "Did you meet that hot state police detective yet?"

"Yeah."

"Mister man, I wouldn't kick her out of bed," Charlie said.

I looked at him. "Isn't she a *little* out of your league?"

"Nah." he said. "I can dream, can't I? Besides, if Mitzi Benson has the hots for me, can Miss Maine State Trooper of 2017 be far behind?" He laughed.

You've got to be kidding, I thought. I only knew Charlie from work and I hadn't heard him say this sort of thing before.

"What do you mean Mitzi has the hots for you?"

"Hey," he said with a leer, "Every time she sees me, she tells me to 'come up and see me.' You know what I mean? She's pretty clear about what she wants if you ask me."

Oh, boy, I don't believe this.

"She wanted to know what I thought happened to Peachy," he went on. "The ice queen detective, I mean."

I fought down my first urge to hit him over the head with a wrench.

"So, what did you tell her?" I asked, trying to keep my voice level.

"I told her that I thought that 'Snotzy' there finally had enough of Peachy's BS and did him in," Charlie said with a wink. "I mean, you saw how they always treated each other. Snort was always lording it over Peachy. I think he knew that Peachy wanted to get Mitzi in the prone position, if you know what I mean." He grinned and winked at me, again.

I was getting wicked uncomfortable with this conversation.

"No, Charlie. I don't think—"

"Seriously Bobby, Snort's trying to get everybody to think that Peachy killed himself and he's all busted up about it, but I told that detective that I know better." Charlie winked a third time.

"So," I said, "if Snort is arrested for Peachy's murder, you think that you and Mitzi . . . ?"

"I'll be moving in the very next day. Just you wait and see."

I was *really* starting to get pissed at that point. Looking back on it now, I don't think I should have said, "You know, Charlie, maybe somebody *besides* Snort did it. Maybe even *you.*"

"Daoouh! That's stupid. I wouldn't do anything like that. Besides, who else besides Snort *could* have done it?" His eyes narrowed. "Mitzi couldn't have lifted him far enough to tie the rope to that conduit." He looked over to where Fred was waving us toward the lift. "Come on," he said sharply. "Time to get to work."

Charlie climbed the ladder that Floyd had set up against the base station wall and got into the basket with Fred. We all had portable radios to coordinate our actions, and we started up the mountain side, stopping at each tower we came to.

Everything went smoothly for a couple of hours. After all, everybody but me had been doing this chore for years. Once they'd finished with the wheels on a couple of towers, Charlie and Fred would lower the old ones they'd had to replace to me on a rope and I'd stow them in the back of the ATV. I'd got over my initial mad at Charlie, but I still couldn't bring myself to believe he was serious.

But you know, when you think about what he said—

"Bobby! Watch out!!"

#

An hour later Doc Jeffries was peering at my left eye through one of those bright light things that doctors use to look into your ears and mouth while you say "Ahh." Despite the warm weather outside, I was shivering in a backless hospital johnny sitting on his exam table at the Rangeley Health Center, where he'd just poked, prodded and probed everything of mine there was to poke, prod or probe.

"You know, Bobby. At the risk of using an old cliché, we really should stop meeting like this. If it hadn't been for sheer luck, and that." He pointed to the hard hat which now sat on his desk with an enormous dent in it. "I'd probably be in the morgue at the Farmington hospital marveling at the prodigious size of your liver." He smirked and shook his enormous shaggy head. "You were lucky. That wheel that Charlie dropped just struck a glancing blow. At worst I think you may have a mild concussion and maybe some whiplash in your neck that will probably bother you for a few days," he continued. "You *do* still have that cervical collar I gave you the *last* time you got conked on the head, don't you?"

I closed my eyes and, unfortunately, nodded, which I immediately regretted. "Yeah, it's somewhere. I remember Lummox using it for a cat bed last winter. I'll find it."

Doc grinned and started typing on his computer "Well, good. I want you to put it on as soon as you get home and wear it for at least a week." I groaned. He looked up. "You'll leave here with an appointment to come back next week for a full physical. *And* I want you to lay off the beer until then so I can get an accurate reading on your liver and kidney function."

I grimaced. I had a splitting headache and all I really wanted to do at that point was lie down somewhere and die.

Doc looked at me again. "Seriously, Bobby. You're not getting any younger and you really need to start taking better care of yourself. I'm guessing Peggy Gordon will have a ton of OSHA paperwork for you to fill out, but that can wait a few days."

I grimaced again. "Can I go home now?"

"Yup, in a little bit. You can get dressed and have a seat in the waiting room. I'll have the nurse bring you a large bottle of water. Try to drink all of it." He glanced at the clock on the wall. "In an hour I'll come by and give you another looksee. You should be feeling better by then. If nothing changes, Marti Wallace will be by about then and she'll take you home. I don't advise you to drive until tomorrow at the earliest, so she's taking Bear McGillicuddy up to The Mountain to run The Beast home for you."

After I spent an hour with an ice pack on the back of my neck, trying to drink Poland Spring dry while reading ancient *People* and *Field and Stream* magazines in the waiting room, Doc came by, looked in my eyes and ears again and pronounced me fit to go home.

"Doc," I said. "Can I ask you something while I've got you?"

"Sure, what is it?"

"If somebody spiked your beer with something like vodka, could that make you pass out?"

"Well, *duh*," Doc said sarcastically. "Depending on how high the proof was, a couple of spiked beers could easily push your blood alcohol level to the point where you'd be pretty much comatose." He gave me another look. "Remember what I said about laying off?"

"Yeah, Doc," I said. "Don't worry, it's not for me. I've been thinking about Peachy Keene. It bothered me that his BA was really high. He wasn't a big drinker. Is it possible that someone could have . . . ?"

Doc paused and frowned. "Yeah, that's possible."

Well. Hell.

#

A few minutes later Mitzi Benson walked into the waiting room.

"All your prayers have been answered, Bobby," she said with a smile. "I'm here to take you home." She cocked her head and raised her eyebrows. I felt better seeing her. The things swirling around in my head were rapidly settling back to normal.

"Doc said that Marti was going to . . ."

"She stopped by on her way back to Sally's for an emergency," Mitzi said. "Nadine called her and said that one of the live bait tanks sprung a leak and they'd have to move all the shiners into a spare tank until they fix it. She asked if I'd pick you up. The Beast is home, and I already took Bear back to his wood lot. You ready?"

"More than ready."

Once we were settled in her car she looked at me said, "I have an ulterior motive, Bobby. I wanted to thank you again for the other day."

"No problem. I expect Snort would have done the same for me."

She started the car and put it in gear. "I expect you're right," she said as she pulled out of the parking lot. "He's a lot better now. He's called a professional cleaning service and arranged to have our kitchen completely cleaned out and sanitized. He's throwing out all the food we had in stock. I checked before I left, and he was working in the walk-in. I was worried about that, but he seems like he's coping pretty well now."

"Well, that's good," I said. "Has anybody made any. . . arrangements?"

"For the funeral? Yes. The chaplain from the American Legion post called and said he'd help if we'd like. Once they release Peachy's body he'll be cremated and interred at the Maine Veteran's Cemetery in Augusta. The Maine National Guard has a unit that specializes in veteran's funerals."

"Did he have family?"

"No," she said as she turned into my dooryard. "He was the only child of two only children and they both died years ago. Snort and I were his only family."

She put the car in park and turned to me. "Can I ask you a favor, Bobby?"

"Sure. What is it?"

"I've been having trouble with that Charlie Winchenbach from the campground next door. He's taken to staring at me with a funny look whenever I see him lately and I think he may have been watching me with binoculars when I'm out on the dock. I can see flashes from his cabin window. He's always given me the creeps." She sighed. "I don't know what possessed Peachy to take up with him."

"Peachy?"

"Yes," she said. "One of the biggest fights that Peachy and Snort had recently was when Snort found out the Peachy and Charlie were meeting up in the kitchen to sample that awful beer that Charlie makes."

"Yeah. I ran into Charlie coming out of the kitchen a couple of days before Peachy . . ."

She sighed. "I found out that Peachy gave Charlie a key to the kitchen door so he could borrow Snort's big stock pot at night when he wasn't there."

"So, Charlie has a key to the kitchen?"

"Yes. If I'd known ahead of time I'd have stopped it. That's the favor I'm asking. Can you talk to Charlie and get the key back? I'd rather not have to change all the locks in the Lodge. Cash is going to be tight enough for a while as it is."

"I'll see what I can do," I said.

"Thanks, Bobby," she said. "Is the Little League game still on for tomorrow afternoon?"

I winced. I'd forgotten.

"Far as I know."

"Snort and I will be there," she said. "It'll be good for him to get out . . . and away."

I unclicked my seatbelt and climbed out.

"Thanks, Bobby. You're a good friend." She waved as she drove away.

#

I was sitting in my TV recliner the next evening eating the hot dogs with mustard I'd boiled myself for supper and watching the real Red Sox game. The Little League game had gone really well that afternoon and our own Skedaddle Gore Red Sox had trounced the Coplin Plantation Cardinals fifteen to three before the umpire invoked the runs rule. I felt sorry for the Cardinals coaches because I know what it's like to try to pick up the kids' spirits after a loss like that. I've done it enough times myself.

I'd dumped the team equipment bag on my porch and pulled off that damn cervical collar as soon as I came through the door. Of course, I'd had to tell the sad story of why I was wearing it about ten times at the game, but Angie Gilchrist from the Chicken House had hugged me and volunteered to come over tomorrow and help me straighten up the cabin. Let me tell you, that gave my spirits a boost.

Jerry Remy, the color commentator for the real Dirt Dogs, had just told a funny story from his playing days that I'd heard about three times before when Lummox suddenly jumped up into the front window. I put my plate on the kitchen counter next to the sink and walked over to see what had piqued his attention. Sometimes we'd have a visitor but usually it was just a stray chipmunk on the porch that got this kind of a reaction.

I recognized Charlie Winchenbach's old blue Ford 150 rust bucket as it rolled to a stop in my dooryard and the penny finally dropped.

Well, Hell.

I realized that I was likely going to need some help, and fast. The plan that suddenly popped into my head sounded iffy, but . . .

I grabbed my land line telephone off the table next to my chair, dialed 911 and set it on the floor with the receiver off the hook. Then I took out my cell phone and punched the icon that Sergeant Norton had showed me. I put the phone face down on the side table just as Charlie came to the screen door with a backpack hanging off one shoulder.

"Hey, Bobby," he said. "I'm here to make good on my promise."

"What promise was that, Charlie?" I asked as he let himself in. I stood facing him in the center of the room.

"I told you that I was cooking up a new batch of beer and you said to save you a couple of bottles. Remember?" he said as he dropped his backpack on my kitchen table.

"Yeah," I said, hoping this was getting through to the dispatcher who was listening in Farmington. "I remember. Back when we met at the Lake Lodge. The day before Mitzi found Peachy's body."

"Well, here it is," he said, pulling two unlabeled beer bottles out of his pack. "My new special brew. I call it 'Bobby's Blueberry Bomb.' I think it's one of my best efforts. You're really gonna like it. It's got a wicked punch."

He pulled out a bottle opener, popped the caps off and set them on the table.

"I'm sure it does, Charlie," I said. "But, much as I'd like to try it, I'm sorry to say that I'm under orders from Doc Jeffries to lay off the beer for at least a week. So, I guess I'll have to take a raincheck."

Charlie turned and looked at me. He grinned, but his eyes were hard. "You gotta be kidding me, man. Come on. I've never heard of you turning down a beer before. Give it a try. One little beer won't kill you."

OK, here it comes, I thought. I braced myself mentally and rocked forward onto the balls of my feet.

"It killed Peachy, Charlie," I said. "Didn't it?" Charlie's eyes hardened and he turned away from me toward his backpack resting on my table. "Why, Charlie?" I raised my voice. "What did Peachy ever do to you that would warrant killing him?"

"I didn't kill him, you blockhead," Charlie said over his shoulder. "And you couldn't prove it even if I did."

In for a penny. "I think I can, Charlie. You told me the day you dropped that sheave wheel on me that you want Mitzi for yourself, remember?"

He turned toward me and nodded. "Yeah," he said. "And when this is over *I'll* be living in that big house with her and that miserable *puke* she married'll be rotting in prison."

"So that really *is* why you did it, Charlie. You had a key to the kitchen that you got from Peachy, right?"

He gave me a questioning look.

"Yeah," he said. "How did you—?"

"You let yourself into the kitchen one night and used the Lodge's computer to print a note calling Snort a pervert. I'm guessing you meant to try to implicate him in what you were planning. Maybe you thought it would make Mitzi wonder about his extra-curricular activities. Right?"

His eyes narrowed and I saw his jaw muscles tighten.

"But then," I said. "you thought better of it and threw the note in the trash with the remains of your "Canadian Crapshoot" mash and a dead squirrel you poisoned at Boogie's place. You told me yourself that she was having a rodent problem. Remember?"

"Yeah." Charlie glared at me. "I remember."

"A few nights later you met Peachy in the kitchen after work to share a few of your beers, right?"

"So?"

"So," I said. "Peachy didn't know that you had laced the beer you brought him with 190 proof grain alcohol you got through the internet from a place in New Jersey."

His head jerked in surprise, and I knew my guess was right.

"I looked them up online, Charlie. Grain alcohol has no taste, but about ten times the kick of beer. One laced beer would have put Peachy over the limit. How many did you feed him, Charlie friggin' Winchenbach?" I yelled, hoping the 911 dispatcher could hear me.

"Two, damn you," Charlie turned toward his backpack again. "It only took two. After the first he couldn't see straight and after he drank the second he put his head down on the table and passed out cold."

With that he turned to face me. His right hand held a knife that looked to me like a friggin' bayonet.

I took a deep breath. I hoped it wouldn't be my last. I heard the faint sound of a siren. *Stall*.

"Then you hung him from the electrical conduit in the walk-in and let him strangle, while you watched him twitch his life away. How did that feel, I wonder? Did you feel anything for Peachy at all? Did you hate him that much?"

Charlie's face was beet red.

"Yeah, you friggin' meddling bastard," he screamed. "I killed him. And now I'm going to friggin' do you, *too*."

I braced myself as he took a step forward. A black and white streak flew out from behind me, landed on Charlie's face and, with a primal scream that I'd never heard before, sank tooth and claw smack into his nose. Charlie let out his own scream and swung his hands up to his face, dislodging a spitting Lummox and leaving a drizzle of blood dripping from his chin. He lunged at me with the knife and I stepped back, slipping on the damn cervical collar I'd left lying on the floor. As I fell I heard what sounded just like the clunk of an ax cutting into a pine log as Charlie landed on top of me. I waited for the first sting of the knife piercing my chest as the siren cut off abruptly.

Well, Hell!

#

"You can get up, Bobby," a voice said. "He's out cold."

I looked past Charlie's body, which I realized was lying limp and still on top of me, to see Snort standing behind him holding one of my Little League baseball bats from the bag on the porch. Lummox was pawing worriedly at my shoulder.

"I heard the radio call on my scanner," Snort said, panting. "I thought you might need some help. I think I blew the friggin' motor in my old Chevy."

For some stupid reason I just started to laugh. Snort joined in as Willie Brackett came through the door in a Weaver combat stance with a .45 caliber Glock 21 in her hand. At that moment I thought that she was about the prettiest thing I'd ever seen.

Well, Hell.

#

Snort and Mitzi Benson and I stood on the lawn in front of the Skedaddle Lake Lodge on a glorious sunny afternoon in July, along with most of the population of Skedaddle Gore. I'd managed, with the help of a seamstress from the Community of Satin, to fit, very snugly, into my old Coast Guard Chief Petty Officer's uniform. Snort wore the uniform of a U.S. Army Staff Sergeant and Mitzi looked like a fashion model in a modest black knee length dress, sunglasses and a matching black sun hat.

Snort stood at attention holding the urn containing Peachy's ashes as the sound of Taps sounded out over the lake. As the last bugle notes faded, Snort about-faced smartly and placed the urn, draped with a Silver Star, in the back of the hearse that would take Corporal Martin Luther Keene to his final rest at the Maine Veteran's Cemetery in Augusta. He took one step back and slowly came to the salute as the first volley of shots rang out.

Eight: Sins of the Father

I haven't been called "Junior" since I was nineteen and left my childhood home in Thomaston, Maine, to enlist in the Coast Guard. Technically my dad was Robert Edward Wing, Senior, but he always went by Bob and, since I was about four years old, everybody and his brother has called me Bobby. So, it was kind of a surprise when Marti Wallace, our rural mail carrier, fire chief and the co-owner of Sally's Motel and Bar and Live Bait and Convenience Store, pulled her Jeep into my dooryard one morning last May to personally deliver something instead of stuffing it in my roadside mailbox like she usually does. Most days she doesn't even slow down much on the way by, just blows her horn. She's got delivery down to a science.

I set my coffee cup on the porch railing, hoisted Lummox, my lazy old cat, off my lap and got up to stand by the screen door. We'd been enjoying the warming spring sunshine and Lummox grumbled and growled halfheartedly at being jostled, like he always does; but he likes Marti. As she clambered out onto the last melting crust of snow on my lawn he spotted the treat box she had in her hand. He went on alert, jumped onto the porch railing and started to nuzzle the door handle. It was the most I'd seen him exert himself all week. I groaned a little because I've been trying to wean him off those things since his vet told me what's in them.

"I didn't know you was a 'junior,' Bobby," Marti said with a grin as she stepped onto the porch and handed me a big square brown envelope. It looked like the kind that those big mail order outfits use to send you little tiny stuff in, but it didn't have any advertising logos on it.

"I'm not," I said, puzzled. "Well . . . I guess technically I am, but nobody's called me that since high school, and that was a dog's age and a half ago."

I looked at the address on the envelope and was dumbfounded to read "Junior Wing" with my mailbox number and "Skedaddle Gore, Maine" under it.

"I assume that's you," Marti looked at me with the anticipatory twinkle of a born gossip in her eye. I knew she was about to pounce. *Well, Hell.*

"Now, that's interesting," I said, turning it over. "Any idea where it's from? I don't see a return address."

"Let me look." She grinned as she grabbed it. "Nope," she said, handing it back. "It was cancelled at a regional distribution center, so it could be from pretty much anywhere east of the Mississippi."

She put a handful of kitty treats on the porch railing and you would have thought Lummox had lost ten years and ten pounds by the way he went nuts chowing down on them. Marti grinned and scratched him behind the ears, his favorite spot. He was making ecstatic groaning noises in his throat as he chomped. Marti looked at me expectantly.

"Aren't you gonna. . . ?" she asked.

"I'll open it later, after you're gone," I said, pointedly.

Her face fell.

"Damn you, Bobby Wing. Nobody these days appreciates what I go through. Have you any idea what it's like to wonder every day what's in the stuff I bring to folks?" She peered at me with a scowl. "Aren't you at all curious?"

"Nope."

"Well, you should be," she said, looking hurt. "It could be important, or critical or . . . dangerous."

I sighed. I knew that if I *did* open the package the whole story of what it was and whoever sent it would be all over town by that afternoon. Marti is the main stalk on the local grapevine, you see. But if I *didn't* open it she would start a salacious rumor of some kind about what the contents might be that I'd be hearing, and trying to stop, for days.

"OK," I said, resigned.

I pulled my jackknife out of its pouch on my belt and slit the flap, turning away from Marti as I peeked inside.

"Better be careful," I said. "Might be a bomb."

I know she made a face at me even though I couldn't see it.

"Yeah, right. That thing's been through more metal detectors and sniffer machines than you have to pass by to get into a Walmart these days."

I felt her trying to sneak up and peek over my shoulder. I reached inside and pulled out the only thing in the envelope, a book that was about a half inch thick and the size of a sheet of copier paper. It had a "fine embossed leatherette cover" and a name on the front that I recognized: *Trigon.*

"I'll be damned."

"What is it?" Marti asked, bouncing on her tip toes. I felt the porch floor shake a little.

"It's a yearbook," I said. "My high school yearbook."

With Marti now looking over my shoulder I opened the cover and read my name on the inside liner, written what must have been over a hundred times in a tiny, precise script, with a "Mrs." in front of each line.

Marti burst out laughing.

Well, Hell.

#

It wasn't easy but I finally got Marti, after she stopped laughing, back into her Jeep and on her way to her next stop. Lummox looked at me with disappointment as we watched her wave out the window as she tore off up the road.

"You know I just saved your life, right?" I asked him. "Those treat things'll kill you eventually."

He pointedly glanced over at the plastic bag full of empty beer cans sitting next to the front door that I'd been meaning to take to the bottle return place for a couple of weeks and growled.

"Point taken," I said.

I sat down in my porch chair and stared for a while at the book in my lap. I was almost afraid to open it again. Forty-some years ago I'd been on the Georges Valley High School senior class advertising committee for the yearbook. I volunteered because I liked April McLain, who was the editor and chairman of the yearbook committee. Jimmy Burlingame, who'd finally ditched his old nickname, "Stinky," during our freshman year, when the baseball coach told him he'd have to shower daily or he couldn't play, and I were appointed "solicitors." We were charged with visiting stores, restaurants, gas stations and the like around the town of Thomaston selling ads to help my class pay the publishing company from Boston to print up copies of the yearbook to give as keepsakes to our parents, grandparents, aunts, uncles and anyone else we could think of. In return those businesses got to buy an advertisement on the last few pages to show how generous and civic minded they were.

I turned the book over and opened the back cover first to look at some of the fruits of my ancient labors and spent the next fifteen minutes nostalgically wondering what had ever happened to the likes of Mrs. Dora Beedy, the owner of Ma Beedy's Corner Store, where my old crowd hung out. She had a belly laugh as big as she was and a heart of gold.

I remembered hearing somewhere that nasty old Dr. Middleton ran off with his secretary a couple of years after we graduated, leaving two little kids and a wife with multiple sclerosis and a twenty-year mortgage behind.

Then there was cranky old Luther Mitchell, who'd done nothing during our sales pitch but complain about how the last year's ad had misspelled the name of his business, Mitchell's Ship Chandlery. It was just one letter off, but he threatened to sue us and the publisher for slander, libel and printing vile obscenities. I pointed out to him that it was last year's edition and Stinky and I weren't at all involved with it. That didn't help until I offered him half off on this year's ad with a promise to print an apology for the previous class's spelling mistake. I looked the ad up and chuckled when I saw the apology, which of course had to reprint the error to make sure everyone knew exactly what we were apologizing for. I wondered how the class behind us had done with Mr. Mitchell when their time came.

I flipped to the front and looked at that list again. The handwriting was a little familiar, but I couldn't immediately think of anyone who might have been so smitten with my gawmey teenaged charms that she would do such a thing. Then I noticed a bookmark just peeking out about halfway in the middle of the book. I opened it to the page marked. April McLain's face smiled back at me. There was a note on the bookmark.

"I need to see you. I'll be there next week."

After over forty years I'd completely forgotten what April had looked like. She was . . . beautiful.

Well, Hell.

I stood up slowly, set the book on the chair and moved over to the screen door. Lummox walked toward me along the porch rail until I could resume petting him. As we stood together, watching the shimmer of the morning sun off the surface of Rangeley Lake in the valley below us, I remembered . . .

During my sophomore year in high school my dad got a twenty-year-old Plymouth Valiant station wagon from one of his fellow guard buddies at the old Maine State Prison at the south end of Main Street in Thomaston. After surviving ten Maine winters in the salty coastal air, it had been retired to sit laid up in an old hay barn for another ten. It probably was originally silver colored, but by the time Dad got it, it was a very rusty, dull and mottled dirty grey. Dad's buddy gave it to him for nothing because he needed the room in his barn but didn't want the bother of hauling the thing over to the junk yard in Rockland. We went over to his buddy's house, loaded the thing onto a trailer borrowed from another guard and hauled it home. Mom immediately blew her stack, as Dad had warned me she probably would. After she stomped back into the house we hid the wreck from her sight under a tarp behind the garage. It lived there for the rest of the summer while we tinkered on it.

Once we finally got the Valiant started it smoked like a chimney and wouldn't back up, but Dad had been a Machinist's Mate in the Coast Guard, which meant he knew how to revive dead iron. He taught me a lot about living with grease under your fingernails that summer as the two of us pretty much rebuilt the old girl from the ground up. We forged a lifelong bond as I listened to his stories lying in the oily dirt under her belly. I know that was the main reason I chose the same rate he'd had when I went onto the Coasties myself three months after I graduated, although by then they were calling it "Machinery Technician." I never got a good explanation why.

Anyway, Dad had promised me that if I managed to get my Maine driver's license before I turned seventeen the old Valiant would be mine. With that for incentive I took Driver's Ed the next year and, for the first time in my life, got an A. I passed my road test with flying colors on the first try just after I turned sixteen, which was the youngest you could take it in those days. I'll never forget Dad dropping the keys into my hand as Mom stood behind him gnashing her teeth.

The fact that my car was a dowdy old station wagon did earn me a bit of teasing and a few cat calls from the guys as I cruised past them parked in from of Ma's on Fridays after school. I put those to rest for good when I blew the doors off Butchy Baker's Chevy one night out on the straight stretch of U. S. Route One just outside of town that we called the "Dragway." Dad and I had done a few things to Old Val's bulletproof slant six, as well as her carburetor, timing and exhaust system that may not have been exactly street legal but sure came in handy. I got Johnny Rackliffe, whose dad worked at a local body shop, to paint flames on the hood and front fenders. Dad cracked up laughing when he saw them. Mom wasn't so pleased.

My social life after that pretty much revolved around that car and girls, or *one* girl really. I'd noticed April McLain, who was the daughter of the minister of the Presbyterian Church in town, a few years before when we both hit puberty. She was slim, funny, as tall as me and wicked smart. She also had bright blue eyes, a walk that grabbed *all* your attention and long, thick brunette hair that I spent a lot of time running my fingers through, in my dreams. Once I had Old Val's keys in my pocket, though, *she* finally noticed *me*.

We dated a few times during our senior year while we were both working on the yearbook and, as the chairman, she used to get a big kick out of ordering me around. I didn't mind though, because she showed me two or three things I'd only heard about before at the local drive-in movie theatre. I guess you could say I fell in lust with her at that point.

Old Val really proved her worth at the abandoned granite quarry after the traditional unsanctioned senior class pre-graduation party in Foster's gravel pit got broken up by the cops. April had a bottle of vodka that she'd got somewhere, and she suggested that we fold the rear seat down to get more room. The rest, as they say, is history.

Truth be told my first time wasn't all that great. There was a lot of sweaty fumbling with unfamiliar fasteners and me figuring out what went where, and when. April kept complaining that I was getting her hair caught underneath her. After a couple of embarrassing false starts due to the vodka the deed was finally done, but I thought it turned out to be surprisingly messy. Once I'd dropped April off back at her house, I spent the better part of an hour at the 24-hour coin-op car wash cleaning up, both myself and Val. Mom would have killed me if she'd found out, not to mention April's father.

A week later April got a letter from a fundamentalist religious college in Oklahoma accepting her application. She said there was a whole raft of paperwork to fill out including a solemn pledge to Jesus that she would never smoke, drink or have "sexual intercourse out of wedlock."

"Just a little too late for that," she said, with a giggle.

I promised not to tell if she didn't. Then she really dropped a bomb. It seemed that her dad had accepted a new job at a church in upstate New York and they would be moving there right after graduation. I was pretty busted up at first, but April told me that she thought we needed to "move on." She said she had big plans for her life and was looking forward to the future. At that point I realized that those plans didn't include me. That did hurt some, but I realized that I would probably get over it eventually and, all things considered, it *was* probably for the best. She did promise to write every day. We did it again the night before she moved, and I never saw her again. She never wrote, either.

Lummox gave me a head butt after a bit and looked up at me like he was actually concerned, or maybe he was just hungry. I sighed and gave him a chin scratch. Then I picked up the yearbook and walked back inside. Sitting down in my TV chair I looked around and decided I'd have to finally call Elizabeth, the housekeeper from the Community of Satin, to get the place in some kind of order. I didn't know when or how April was coming, but at least the cabin and I could look decent when she got here. I also realized that I needed a haircut.

#

The next Wednesday morning there was a soft warm breeze blowing up from the valley and I opened all the windows in my cabin to take advantage of the opportunity to air things out. About ten o'clock I heard a burbling rumble coming up the road. I looked out my front window in time to see an immaculate sky-blue Harley Davidson Electra Glide flow majestically into my dooryard. I had to take a moment to catch my breath. I didn't know anyone who owned anything close to such a gorgeous piece of classic machinery. I opened the door with mixed feelings of envy and anxiety as I realized who this must be.

I stood in the doorway and watched as the rider lowered the kickstand, tilted the behemoth onto it with practiced ease and shut the engine off. I felt a little disappointment as that legendary sound died away, leaving just the ticking of a cooling exhaust. The riding gloves came off and were laid across the gas tank, then the chin strap of a shiny blue helmet was unfastened, and I was startled to see a cascade of long brown hair fall to rest on the rider's shoulders as it was pulled off. She hung the helmet over the throttle side mirror and pulled off a set of gold aviator sunglasses, folding them with a snap and hanging them by one bow from the unzipped breast pocket of a tightly-fitting weathered black leather jacket. I remember thinking that it was one of the sexiest moves I'd ever seen and for just a second there I completely forgot to breathe. She shook her head to settle her hair and smiled up at me. Mister man, I have to tell you that in my wildest dreams I could not have imagined that the April I knew would show up looking like that.

She swung her right leg deftly over the rear fender in a dismount and walked to my front stoop.

"I trust that you are Robert Edward Wing, Junior," she said with a hint of a slow southern drawl. "If not, I've ridden this old horse a hell of a long way for nothing. Although," she turned to look down into the valley. "just this here view *would* be worth it."

"April?"

She rounded back on me and stood hipshot like a fashion model, with fisted hands on her hips and her chin thrust forward. I could just see the beginning of crow's feet at the corners of clear eyes that matched the color of her ride.

"Sorry," she said, cocking her head to one side, "I should introduce myself. My name is February McLain. April McLain was my mother. She died in hospice back home a month ago from lung cancer. I think you might be my father."

Well, Hell.

#

"Why would *anyone* name their kid, especially their daughter, 'February'?" I asked as we sat at my kitchen table a few minutes later. "February is the coldest, most miserable month of the year."

She set down my best coffee cup, the Skedaddle Ridge one I use for formal guests, and laughed.

"It's the month I was born. Mom thought it would be cute, given *her* name. February 2. Groundhog Day. My birthday."

I paused, trying to do the math in my head. She saw the wheels turning, picked up her cup again and took a sip.

"It fits. If you guys were doing the nasty right around the time you graduated high school, it was just nine months."

"But it was only *twice,* and both of us had no idea what we were doing." I said, sputtering a little. "Believe me, it wasn't even all that great!"

She shook her head and peered at me with lowered eyebrows.

"You have kids?" she asked.

"Yeah. A daughter. In Oregon."

"A wife?"

"I'm a widower."

"Sorry," she said, with a frown.

We both lifted our coffee cups in silence. She put hers back down without drinking.

"If you have a kid, I'm assuming that by now you know how it works. It only *takes* once."

"Duh," I replied.

She shook her head again and her eyes narrowed.

"And you've got at least two things wrong, Mr. Wing."

"What's that?"

"Maybe it was *your* first time, but it wasn't hers. Not by a long shot. That's why I'm here." She paused and her voice softened. "And . . . she thought you were the best lover she ever had."

Well. Hell.

That took my breath away. I just sat there silent, not knowing what else to do.

Lummox, who had been lying at her feet giving her leathers a thorough sniffing, chose that moment to jump into her lap. She grunted with the impact, then smiled and stroked his back. He curled up and started to purr. She took a breath and looked at me. Her voice dropped and hardened.

"You met the Reverend, my grandfather?"

I nodded.

"Did you like him?"

"No," I said, cautiously. "I didn't. Frankly, I kind of thought he was a sanctimonious dink." I shrugged. "Sorry."

"Don't be," she said. "From what Mom told me you've just nailed his personality in two words."

She shifted in her chair and Lummox gazed up at her. She took another breath and looked down into his eyes.

"I'll just jump right in with both feet. The Reverend Jeremiah McLain began to touch his daughter, my mother, when she was seven years old." February said, watching Lummox lick his paw. "He taught her to touch him, too. He told her it was the way that all fathers and daughters showed their love for each other. He said it was God's will."

She looked back up at me and her eyes were glistening. I was stunned.

"He took her virginity when she was twelve. By then my mom knew it was wrong, but she didn't know what to do about it. She thought nobody would believe her. He was the voice of God to some in his congregation, for pity's sake!" She paused.

"Her mom, my grandmother, never uttered a word, even though Mom was sure she knew. Mom thought her mother was afraid the town would find out and she wouldn't be able to stand the shame, much less the loss of my grandfather's income. She never even talked to my mom about sex or what was happening to her body as she developed."

She sat back in the chair and looked at the ceiling.

"My holier-than-thou grandfather had sex with my mother at least once a week from the age of twelve until she left for college in Oklahoma. Usually on Sunday night after church. He said it was worshipful."

She looked back at me. I was horrified. Her face softened.

"Mom said that you were the only boy she really liked in high school, even well before you two started going together. She thought you were funny, kind and cute." She pulled a tissue out of her jacket pocket and wiped her eyes. "She loved your car."

"Old Val?"

"Yeah, that's what she said you called it." She crumpled the tissue and tossed it at the trash can in the corner, then she laughed. "Mom called it the 'Sin Wagon.'"

"Really?"

"Yup, really. Did you see the front page in the yearbook I sent you? She wrote your name there once a day until I was born."

"Really?" I said again.

She nodded.

"Yeah," I said ruefully. "Thanks to our local RFD driver the whole town knows about that now."

February grinned. "Y'all got one of those, too?" Her drawl was stronger now. "Growin' up in a little West Virginia town everybody knew what I was readin', who I was seein' and what I was doin'. Sometimes even before *I* did!"

"February," I said, looking into her big blue eyes. "What ever happened to your mother? She promised to write me. I never heard a peep."

"Sweet Bobby." She cocked her head. "That's what Mom always called you when she got nostalgic, or drunk. Can I call y'all Bobby?"

"Sure."

"Call me Febs. Everybody down home calls me Febs, except the cops."

"What do *they* call you?

"To my face, 'Your Honor.' Behind my back, most everything you could lay your tongue to." She grinned. "I'm a judge, or I was."

I think I must have looked surprised. I certainly *was*.

"But let me answer your question about my mom before I get into that. OK, Bobby?" She looked down again at Lummox. "Sweet Bobby. I can't believe I'm saying that, or that I'm actually *talking* to you."

"Why?"

"I think I can answer that best by tellin' y'all our story, Mom's and mine. OK?"

"Sure.

What else could I say? She was obviously her mother's daughter and I remembered that April usually did what April was going to do.

"Mom said that next to fallin' for you, the best thing that ever happened to her before I was born was finally gettin' away from the Reverend. After they left Thomaston, Mom did the devout, dutiful and loving daughter act for his new congregation in New York that next summer until he and my grandmother dropped her off at the airport in Albany with a ticket for Tulsa, a hundred bucks in cash money and two suitcases. That was the last time Mom ever saw either of them. 'And good riddance, too,' she used to say."

"Sounds like it," I said.

"When she got to that Bible-thumpin' institution of higher learnin' she just cut loose. She said she got so drunk the first weekend that she almost fell out a fourth-floor dormitory window, but somebody grabbed her by the skirt and hauled her back in." She shrugged. "'Course that was before she knew that I was along for the ride."

We both laughed.

"When Mom realized *that* she was already in deep crap with the Dean of Women. She said she was on academic probation within a month and spent more time in the dean's office getting 'counseling' that first semester than she did in class. When she started to show her prissy roommate turned her in. She was forced to take an internal examination by a handsy old doctor and then she was expelled before you could say Jack Robinson. They even refused to give her back her tuition payment. Said she'd violated her "vow" to Jesus.

We sat in silence for a bit.

"So there she was," Febs said. "Pregnant, single, broke and on the street in 'Jesusland.' She told me she had two choices to put a roof over our heads and, rather than choose the more lucrative option, she got a job."

I spit out the last of my coffee. Febs wiped it off my chest and the table with another tissue, laughing.

"She got a night job behind the counter at a diner outside Tulsa owned by a *truly* righteous woman named Helen Hanlon. The place catered to traveling salesmen and long-haul truckers. Mom said that her belly kept the worst of them away, but she did get a few propositions from time to time. She was surprised to find that she liked the job, and the truckers apparently liked her, because she saved enough from her tips to buy a rusty old VW bug just after I was born. A month later she piled me and everything we owned into it, said a tearful goodbye to Helen and Tulsa and headed east for Thomaston."

I searched my memory. "I wasn't there. I was in bootcamp with the Coast Guard."

"I'm sure she didn't know that, but it didn't matter in the end because that old bug finally blew up on Interstate 79 on the south end of the Allegheny Plateau in West Virginia."

"Which I'm guessing explains your accent," I said.

"Accent? What accent?" She pointed a finger at me and grinned. "Y'all got the accent, not me, Charlie."

I bowed my head in acquiescence.

"Anyway, Plan 'B' went into effect at that point, and she got *another* waitressing job in *another* diner. This one was in the middle of Main Street in a little town just off the Interstate. It did a real good business, mostly with the locals. I pretty much spent most of my first five years either getting cuddled by a whole passel of honorary aunties in a booth in the back of that diner or getting underfoot in the kitchen. Later on I was either running around with a pencil behind my ear dodging wandering hands, reading in the local library or cheerleading for the Eagles, our high school football team. The whole town sort of adopted me and Mom. I grew up right there in the old Main Street Diner."

I started to imagine a road trip down south in the Beast. I wondered how Lummox would take to a cat carrier.

"Speaking of diners," I said. "I'm getting hungry. How about I buy you lunch, and you can finish the story over a beer and a cheeseburger."

Sounds great," she said, pulling a cell phone out of her jacket. "I've got a reservation for the night that I made over the internet.

I should probably check in before lunch." She peered at the screen. "Do y'all know some place called 'Sally's Motel and Bar and Live Bait and Convenience Store?'"

#

"Wow," Febs said, setting down her glass and eyeing the sixteen ounce "pounder" can she'd expertly filled it from. "Y'all make some good beer up here." She picked up the can and nodded at it. "That there's a wild boar on the can. We got plenty of those down home in the southern part of the state. They're nasty, but tasty." She picked the glass back up and took another pull. "Old Thumper," she said, reading from the label. "What kind of a name is that?"

Shipyard Brewing down in Portland makes one of my favorite brews and I'd taken the liberty of ordering one for each of us. The can has a picture on it of a raging wild boar with six-inch-long tusks staring straight at you.

She frowned. "Is it supposed to be that old boy there's name or is it all about the kick the brew's got?" she asked, shaking her head. "'Cause it sho' 'nuf *has* one."

I was happy to note that her glass was now only half full. We were sitting in my regular booth at Sally's. All the windows in the place were open to the breeze, which rustled the curtains and added the scent of wild lupines to the room. Nadine, the bartender and part owner who'd delivered our drink order, slapped four burger patties, sliced onions and a healthy charge of bacon on the grill.

Her eyes had popped wide open as soon as we walked through the door. She'd given Febs an appreciative once over, nodding hello to me like I wasn't even there. Febs had given the room and Nadine, who's not so bad looking herself, the once over right back and nodded to me in approval. She'd followed me down from my place on her bike and made an entrance through the front door of Sally's looking like a cover model for one of those glossy biker magazines.

Bear McGillicuddy at the bar looked like he'd just swallowed his teeth and in the next booth over from mine old Palmer Murphy's eyeballs were ready to roll right out of his face onto the table. It gave me a real nice warm fuzzy feeling.

"Do you know if they ship this stuff? Febs asked, holding up the can.

"Absolutely," Nadine shouted from behind the grill, over the noise of a passing logging truck. "I'll give you the email address of my distributor. Mention my name and he'll give you a good deal. Maybe even throw in the shipping."

"What *is* yo' name, darlin'?" Febs hollered back.

"Nadine Bonaventure," she replied. "What's yours, honey?"

"February McLain. Febs to my friends."

Another pulp truck roared by out front.

"Nice place. Yours?" Febs bellowed.

"Yup," Nadine yelled. "Mine and my partner's. She should be in here in a few minutes."

The truck passed by, and it became relatively quiet in the bar.

"She's usually done with her mail route by now," Nadine said, at a more normal volume. "Unless she's stopped to gossip with somebody."

Febs looked at me and mouthed the word, "Oh."

I nodded. "Yup, that one."

Nadine pointed at me with her spatula.

"What's a girl like you doing hanging out with this old drunk?" she asked. "Girl lookin' like you could do a lot better. He'd better be paying for this up front, sweetheart. His tab's long enough as it is."

"It's my treat," Febs said, raising her voice again. "When I get good service, I don't mind paying the freight." She raised an eyebrow suggestively.

I heard old Palmer choking on his chili dog.

"Ain't *that* the truth," Nadine yelled, laughing over the sound of yet another truck.

Febs looked at me with a grin. "Diners are the same wherever you go. Only the faces change."

I raised my glass to her.

"Ain't *that* the truth," I said.

"I like this place," Febs said, signaling for a refill. "Reminds me of home."

"It might as well be his," Nadine said as she slid plates in front of us. "As much time as he spends here." She nodded at me as she took Feb's offered credit card. "And don't believe a thing he says, darling. It's all BS. Isn't it, Bobby?"

"The truth, the whole truth and nothing but the truth," I said.

This time it was Febs who spit all over herself.

After Nadine had mopped up we just sat for a bit and ate in friendly silence.

"So," I finally said. "You were saying about your mom?"

Febs took a long pull on her fresh beer, gave the glass a fond look and set it back down.

"Well, Mom waitressed for twelve years total. She had a couple of boyfriends along the way, too, but none that ever stuck."

"Did she ever marry?"

"Mom? No, not her." She shook her head and dipped a french fry in catsup before inhaling it. "We talked a lot about men while I was growing up, more like we were girlfriends then mother and daughter. She had good cause, you know, to go off men completely, but that wasn't her. She told me once that *you* were the only reason she had any faith left at all in the male sex."

I think I probably blushed at that.

"Did she always waitress?" I asked.

"Lord, no," Febs said, shaking that mane of hers again. "You, sir, are looking at the proud daughter of a single mother who worked her way through college waiting tables before eventually becoming the first female managing editor of one of the most respected newspapers in the whole State of West Virginia."

I set down my glass and stared at her. "April? April McLain? My . . . *our.* . . April?"

"The very same," she said, raising her glass in salute. "My Mom, bless her. Here's to her."

I raised my glass and we drank a toast to her.

After a few moments of silence I said, "You said something about being a judge."

She waved her hand forward in a bow. "The Honorable February Helen McLain, late of the West Virginia Circuit Court, at your service."

"Pardon me," I said, leaning over and looking pointedly at her legs under the table. "But you don't exactly look the part."

"Thank you. That's what my husband says, too."

Well, Hell

Nadine brought over the receipt for our lunch and gave Febs the room registration form to fill out.

"He's not staying the night here, too. Is he?" She said, looking straight at me.

"Nah," Febs said. "Old fart like him? He'd never last the night. Besides, my husband's a very large and heavily tattooed professional wrestler."

Nadine walked away laughing.

"I hope that's a joke."

She grinned. "Yeah. Actually John's about your size. And only one tattoo. He has my name on his butt."

"His butt?"

"Yup." She laughed. "The result of an unfortunate evening at a builder's convention in Chicago a couple of years ago. I think it's actually kind of sweet, but I told him if he does it again he's cut off for six months. If I find out another woman has seen it, he's a dead man!" She drained her beer and signaled Nadine yet again. "He's the owner of one of the largest construction companies in the state. He could have your place torn down and rebuilt in two weeks, all nice, modern and . . . clean."

"I like my place just fine the way it is, thank you."

"Yeah, so do I," she said.

"So," I said, "much as I appreciate it, I suspect you didn't come all this way just to tell me that story. Was there something else?"

She looked around the room, but it was empty; the lunch crowd, such as it was, having trickled back to work.

"The thing is, Bobby," she said, leaning toward me, her voice barely above a whisper. "I need to be *sure*."

"Sure of what?"

She took a breath.

"I need to be sure that my grandfather was not my *biological* father."

"Oh."

"I've just left the bench and taken a tenure-track teaching position at the University of West Virginia School of Law. It's a big step up for me professionally and personally."

"Congratulations," I said. "Shall I order another round in celebration?"

"Thanks, sure. You're good for it?"

"I've got an extravagant pension from Uncle Sam and a couple of lucrative part-time jobs. I can afford it. Probably."

She laughed.

"Seriously," she said. "My new job comes with a raise and a house in Morgantown rent free."

"Nice."

"You're welcome to visit any time, really." Her face turned serious, and I realized that she could probably be wicked scary looking from up on a judge's bench if she wanted. "But there *is* something else."

"Yes?"

Febs paused and pursed her lips. I realized with a start that she was working up her courage. "I'm thirty-eight years old, Bobby, and, just like Marisa Tomei said in *My Cousin Vinnie*, 'My biological clock is ticking.'" She stomped her foot three times. "Thump, thump, thump."

I laughed. "I thought that scene was hilarious."

"It was, in context, but my situation is a little different. My husband and I would like to have a baby, maybe more than one."

"Great," I said. "But . . . ?"

She sighed. "Mom told me that if you're not my father then the Reverend is. You're the only two candidates."

"Oh."

"And if that's the case I'm worried about genetic problems for the baby. My doctor says that if it turns out it *was* him I should have a lot more tests before John and I start seriously going at it."

"I see . . ."

"I know this is going to be an awful lot to ask and I wouldn't if it wasn't so important to us, but . . ."

"Yes?"

She took a very deep breath.

"Would you be willing to take a DNA test to see if you're my real dad. I know we've only known each other for about four hours, but—"

"Sure," I said. "Piece of cake. What do I have to do?"

Her face lit up and for just a second I could swear I was eighteen again and sitting in Old Val at the drive-in with my arm around April. Her daughter reached across the table, grabbed the front of my shirt and kissed me full on the lips.

Marti cleared her throat loudly behind me. I looked around to see her gawking at us.

"Congratulate me, Marti," I said. "I'm going to be a father."

If there hadn't been a chair behind her she would have landed on her well-padded patoot.

Well, Hell.

#

Febs showed up in my dooryard with the test the next morning. We both put on rubber gloves and, after a few off-color comments about what we might be about to do, she opened the kit and handed me a cotton swab on the end of a long wooden stick. She read the instructions to me as I swabbed the inside of both cheeks and stuck the wet swab head down into a plastic vial from the kit. As instructed I broke off the stick at the end of the vial and placed a seal from the kit over it. Febs filled out the form with me and sealed everything into a mailing envelope. Like I said, piece of cake.

Afterwards we sat on my porch with Lummox looking out over the valley and the lakes below. Febs sighed and told me she was a little homesick. We had a last quiet cup of coffee together and she handed me a sealed envelope with my name written on it in a now familiar tiny, precise script. She said her mother had written it before she died and had made her promise to find me and deliver it. She didn't know what was in it and didn't want to. She also said that she was worse at writing than her mother was, but she would be in touch. Then she climbed onto her Harley and rolled, rumbling, down the hill.

I stared after her for a long time before I picked up the envelope and opened it. I won't tell you what it said. Some things are just too personal. I hope you'll understand.

As promised Febs didn't write, but three months later, on Labor Day no less, I got a phone call telling me that I was going to be a Grampa.

Well, Hell.

Nine: 'Til Death Do Us Part

I slit the edge of the envelope and pulled out the paper inside. There, all signed, sealed and now delivered, was my completed commission from the Maine Secretary of State as a legally qualified and duly appointed Notary Public, authorized to witness and certify the signing of legal documents, real estate transfers, voter petitions and, most importantly at the moment, perform the ceremony and certify the legality of the marriage of two adult human beings.

Well, Hell.

#

Nadine Bonaventure, the bartender and part owner of Sally's Motel and Bar and Live Bait and Convenience Store, answered on the second ring.

"Sally's. This is Nadine. How can I help you?"

"Hi, Nadine. It's me. Is Marti there?"

"Sure. Just a sec—"

"No, Nadine," I said. "it's the both of you I wanted to talk to. Can she pickup?"

"OK," she said, with a questioning tone. "Marti," she bellowed. "Pick up the phone. It's Bobby."

I heard the phone click.

"What the hell does *he* want?" Marti yelled in my ear. I guess she didn't realize yet that she'd already picked up. "Hello?"

"And a gracious good afternoon to you, madam," I said with a chuckle. "Have I reached the party to whom I am speaking?"

"Cut the crap, Bobby. I'm in the middle of something. What do you need?"

"Well," I said. "Since I have spent the better part of the past month studying deep into the night so that I could take a rather

191

difficult online multiple-choice test, which I had to do twice, I might add, *and* after undergoing an extensive and highly invasive background check, I thought you two might be interested in what was in that official-looking envelope you dropped in my mailbox this morning."

"Yeah, I saw that."

Nadine broke in. "Was it what I think it was?" she said, sounding excited. "Really?"

"Yup," I said. "You reprobates have lived in sin for what, ten years?"

"Fifteen," Marti said.

"That long?"

"Tell us, you blockhead," Marti said, with a growl.

"Now is that any way to talk to the man who is about to officiate at your wedding?"

Luckily I had had the presence of mind to take the receiver away from my ear, because Nadine screamed long and loud.

"Hallelujah!"

#

Ever since before I retired to Skedaddle Gore there's been a local landmark called "The Folks in the Barrel" sitting right next to the intersection where the Moxie Hill Road meets the road up to old Sam Parsons' house. Somebody some years ago—nobody has ever owned up to it—stuck two sticks in a rusty barrel and hung a pair of old work pants and a pair of worn-out L.L. Bean boots on them so that it looks like some drunk staggered up to the barrel and decided to do his business into it but was so hammered that he passed out and fell in headfirst. After a couple of years a pair of female mannequin legs joined the old boy. No doubt somebody thought that he needed some feminine companionship to get him through the long winter nights. Sometimes she'd wear high heels and fishnet stockings and sometimes, mostly in the winter, she'd get her own pair of Beanies.

Folks use the couple as a landmark to give people from away directions, since the town still hasn't gotten around to putting up street signs, even though the State of Maine sent them a letter some time ago saying that they had to. Jake Beaverstool, the town's First Assessor, called them up in Augusta and told them that if they wanted those "dumbass" signs put up, they could, "by the Jesus," pay for it themselves. That was a few years ago now and the State sort of dropped the issue somewhere along the way, probably because they didn't think it was really worth pushing it. There aren't that many roads in the Gore and most everybody knows where everybody else in town lives anyway.

One crispy fall day somebody passing by noticed that the lady's legs had somehow disappeared, leaving the gentleman looking a little sad and droopy. They stopped at the Town Office and told Aggie Heikkenen, our town clerk, about it. Having learned her lesson the last time, she called up Jake and asked him if she should get me to go look into the situation. Jake was right out straight in the barn making oxen out of two bull calves and just said, "Whatever."

Marti and Nadine's wedding wasn't scheduled for another three weeks and most of the arrangements had already been made. Nadine is a wiz at that sort of thing, so I didn't have anything pressing when Aggie called. I hopped in The Beast and went to the crime scene to see if I could find the legs in the puckerbrush and stick them back in the barrel. I figured it was probably just some kids from Rangeley, the next town over, having fun with "those hicks from up in the Gore."

There wasn't a whole lot to see. The leaves were starting to fall, and the barrel was collecting its share. I made a mental note that somebody'd have to come by and dump it out or it would overflow before long. Shorty Devereaux, who comprises the entire public works department for the Gore, would probably bitch about the extra work, but that's not my department.

Whoever had riled Aggie up was right. The shapely mannequin legs were definitely missing. I hopped out of The Beast and walked around the space, poking into the woods a few feet without finding a trace of anything except a little roadside litter and a pile of dog poop. I shrugged and started to climb back into my truck when I heard a dog bark, just once. I thought that was odd because most dogs I know will keep barking until somebody yells or throws something at them. I looked around again but still didn't see anything. I shrugged and put my hand on the door handle again when I heard another single bark and a rustle from behind me. I turned and saw a face in the brush that I recognized.

The first time I met George, the wolfdog who lives with Squatch, the Gore's hermit, I thought he was about to have me for lunch, but he proved real handy dealing with the Regan brothers when Starr Phavogue ran away and right into their arms. Despite that, I still felt my butt hole pucker a bit as he cocked his head and showed me his teeth.

I felt an odd sensation, as if I was being pulled forward. George cocked his head and I suddenly knew that he wanted me to come with him. He turned away and the feeling died off.

"What is it, George?"

He rounded toward me, and the feeling came back, stronger than before. I felt an urgency this time, a feeling that I was needed.

George wheeled again and looked over his shoulder at me. I grabbed a water bottle and my sheath knife from under the seat and punched the lock button on The Beast's key fob.

I followed George nearly fifty yards into the woods, pushing aside the thick brush, until we came to a very faint narrow path. George picked up speed but kept looking back to see if I was keeping up as we climbed a hill that got steeper the farther we went. I was puffing a bit and thinking about pulling up for a water break when George disappeared into a thicket by a sheer rock face. I stopped in front of the thicket and looked up. The cliff above us was probably fifty feet or more high and I couldn't see any possible way to climb it.

George poked his head out and I felt that feeling again. I pushed the bushes aside and walked forward until I came to him sitting in a small clearing next to a rock that probably had fallen from the cliff.

"What now, George? I can't climb tha—"

He put a paw the size of a small snowshoe on the rock and pushed. There was a hum of machinery and a section of the cliff slid toward us on a hinge, revealing what looked very much like a ship's watertight door.

Well, Hell . . .

#

"Hello, Bobby," an oddly mechanical voice said as George led me into something that I can only describe as looking as if it belonged in a scene out of a science fiction movie involving the launch of a rocket ship. I was in a room the size of one of the audience seating rooms in the multiplex movie theatre down in Farmington. The entire wall opposite the door that George had just led me through appeared to be a gigantic electronic display screen. It was showing a picture of the view over the Rangeley Lakes Valley that was the same one I see almost every summer's day out my front window. In the very center of the screen was a section about four feet by six feet in size which showed some scrolling text that matched what the disembodied voice was saying. There were smaller screens arranged in three semi-circular rows around the room that were blank. About three quarters of the way to the back wall where I was standing was an elevated platform with a chair that looked remarkably like Captain Kirk's command chair from *Star Trek*. The chair was occupied by someone with longish brown hair who made no move to turn toward us.

George bounded forward and stopped next to the chair, raising his paw to touch its occupant. I followed him farther into the room until I saw Squatch sitting, slightly slumped, behind a large keyboard with his right hand on a computer mouse.

"I apologize for doing this," the voice droned. "But it appears that I have no choice and little time. I know that during your military service you were granted a confidential information clearance level of "secret." In order to explain everything you may see and hear while you are here would require a much higher level than that, but I was pleased and reassured to learn that the agent who conducted your investigation noted that you would probably qualify for a much higher level."

"How in the world did you—?"

"In any event your experience should tell you the importance of keeping anything you learn here in this room to yourself. I'm sorry to put you in such a position but this is an emergency far more serious than it may first appear."

Squatch's head slowly turned toward me, and I was shocked to see that his face was thin and grey. He looked as if he'd aged ten years.

"I appear to have contracted a medical condition which is causing me to lose voluntary control of my body," the voice continued. It seemed to come from the ceiling, but Squatch sat stone faced. "Yesterday I lost the ability to move my legs and today I am rapidly losing my speech. I am typing this while I still have the ability, but that too is fading. I have set my non-internet connected computer to read this to you when you get here with George. I have used the various resources available to me to research my symptoms and I have concluded that I am likely to very shortly lose all control of my bodily functions, including the ability to breathe. It is possible that this is the result of outside action, but I cannot say more than that.

"I have downloaded my medical history and my conclusions about my condition to that memory stick." He looked down toward the desk in front of him. "Hopefully it will enable a doctor to help me, but I require your assistance to move me quickly away from here and into care. Bringing a doctor here is out of the question. George will guide you to a means for transport. Please hurry. I have not yet completed my mission. Thank you, Bobby. You've been a good friend." The voice stopped and the room was silent.

Well, Hell.

#

"What the hell have you brought me, Bobby?" Doc Jeffries asked as he walked out the door of the Rangeley Health Center. Squatch lay in the bed of The Beast staring wide eyed at the sky with a blanket over him.

"He's a friend of mine, Doc. He lives in the woods. He says he's paralyzed and losing the ability to breathe."

Doc climbed into the bed of The Beast, pulled his stethoscope from around his neck and reached under the blanket.

"Oh, this is not good," he said. "His heartbeat is fading, and his breathing is reedy and labored. Help me get him inside."

Doc, who's the size of an Olympic heavyweight wrestler, reached down and picked Squatch up like you'd pick up a small child. I lowered the tailgate and he jumped to the ground and sprinted toward the clinic's entrance.

"Call 911 and grab a gurney," He shouted as he ran through the door. "We have a patient in respiratory distress who may be going into cardiac arrest!"

The receptionist grabbed the phone as Doc's nurse came around the corner pulling a gurney behind her. Doc laid Squatch on it and began to bark instructions. "Bobby," he said. "You'd better stay here. Tell Dolores everything you know about this guy."

I handed Doc the memory stick. "He left this. He said everything you need to know is on it plus his idea of what's wrong."

"I hope it helps," Doc said as ran up the corridor. "He's going to need it."

I heard a howl from the woods across the street.

#

"Your Mr. Noone has been an interesting case," Doc said over my home landline the next day.

"How is he?" I asked.

"Once we got him stabilized he was flown in an air ambulance from the Rangeley Airport directly down to Maine Medical Center in Portland, where he's on a ventilator. They read through the information on the memory stick you gave me and found that his self-diagnosis was correct. He must have some kind of medical training. He's suffering from Guillian-Barre Syndrome, which causes the symptoms you saw and definitely could have killed him if you hadn't gotten him to us in time."

"Is he going to be OK?"

"The good news is that Guillain-Barre is treatable and he's responding well so far. People with his condition respond differently to treatment, but Mr. Noone is doing better every day. They anticipate removing the ventilator tomorrow and he might be recovered enough to release in two or three weeks."

"That's great," I said.

"Did you know that he named you as his next of kin? He also designated you as his guardian if it came to the point where life or death decisions had to be made. On the memory stick he says that he has no other living relatives.

Well, Hell.

My cell phone made a noise I'd never heard before. It sounded like a bugle fanfare of some kind. I said goodbye and thanks to Doc and hung up. I pulled the cell out of the plastic holster on my belt. The screen told me I'd received a text from "Chick." I didn't know a "Chick" and couldn't remember if I ever had. I also had never received a text from anyone before. Not knowing what else to do I tapped on the notice and a little thing popped up that said "open."

What the hell. Why not?

A new screen popped up. "We need to talk. Vitally important."

Now what do I do? I wondered.

There was a box at the bottom of the screen that said, "iMessage." I typed "Who is this?" and tapped the little blue arrow. I know that's how you send emails off a cell phone, so I gave it a shot. I waited nearly thirty seconds and was about to give up when a grey blob popped up on the edge of the screen.

"Chad."

Well, Hell.

Chad Fairchild was the only Chad I knew. He was the state trooper that Willie Brackett, our local deputy sheriff, had a crush on six months before. After a couple of dates he dropped out of sight and Willie finally gave up on him, figuring he wasn't interested in her anymore. As far as I knew she hadn't dated anyone else since, though.

"What it ip?" I typed. I kept hitting the wrong tiny little keys. *I hate this friggin' thing,* I thought as I gave up and tapped the send arrow again.

Almost immediately another grey blob popped onto the screen

"Can't say on text," it read. "Must talk. Much danger. Meet at MacIntire's in Auburn?"

I thought a minute. "Mini gilf place in lake?" I typed.

"Right. 10 AM. I'll find you. OK?

I remembered the last time I'd seen Chad last winter at the Chicken House when Paul Freeman tried to jump off the roof. I'd liked the kid and I admit I was getting intrigued by this whole thing. I couldn't do anything about Squatch right now but wait and nothing else was on my agenda. I shrugged.

"OK. See yo rhen."

"Tell no one. Life or death. Delete this."

Well, Hell . . .

#

It takes an hour and a half to drive from Skedaddle Gore to Auburn, which is roughly southwest of us in the Androscoggin River Valley. The area down there is much more urban and heavily populated. Auburn and its twin city Lewiston on the other side of the river used to be a big manufacturing hub, with a whole raft of big red brick factories built in the eighteen fifties which housed shoe making and weaving mills and the industries that go with them. Those businesses started moving overseas in the nineteen fifties and sixties, leaving those massive antique buildings to weather and deteriorate until some of them literally fell or burned down. There have been periodic spurts of economic optimism when some "entrepreneur" type from away decides he's going to borrow a mess of money from out-of-state banks who ought to know better and turn some of the remaining factory buildings into upscale apartments or trendy spa hotels for other people from away who want to share in the "Maine Mystique," or whatever they call it these days. Usually those projects get started with a lot of hype and fanfare but fizzle out in a year or two, creating lots of business for lawyers and bankruptcy judges.

MacIntire's is basically an old-fashioned roadside burger and ice cream joint with a mini golf course and a big driving range. It sits next to Lake Auburn, which is the water supply for the whole surrounding area. Logically swimming isn't allowed in the lake because, even though they say they wouldn't dream of it, most people *do* "pee in the pool" if they get the chance. I hear the fishing is decent though, if you're into that sort of thing. Just don't fall out of the boat.

I parked The Beast in the field across the road from the one-story cement block building that holds the takeout kitchen and the putter rental shop. After World War II, old Farmer MacIntire's surviving boys built the place in a roadside hayfield of their father's when they realized that dairy farming wouldn't pay well enough to keep their family farm going. They started catering to local families who wanted to escape from the "city" atmosphere in the summer and eat red snapper hot dogs, french fries and burgers while making believe that looking like a damn fool while using a rusty old putter to knock a golf ball through the mouth of a scary-faced clown was fun. They put a bunch of wooden picnic tables around the property where people could drink milkshakes and eat deep fried onion rings while enjoying the relaxing "country" atmosphere. The MacIntire's have done pretty well with the place for decades now and almost everybody in the state has been there at one time or another.

I sat waiting in the parking lot but didn't see hide nor hair of Chad. I was about to give the whole thing up as a waste when a character right out of a Mad Max movie pulled in. He was riding a big, loud jet-black Sportster with hanger handlebars that looked as if they'd been made for the orangutan in that old Clint Eastwood movie. The guy was tall, rangy and dressed all in black. Black leathers, black boots and even black tassels hanging from his handlebars. He had a shaggy black Fu Manchu mustache and longish black hair held down by a black leather strap that looked as if it was attached to his forehead with chrome plated tacks. He rolled through the parking lot like a death angel messenger from Hell, pulled in right next to The Beast, killed his engine and glanced over at me.

"Hey, Bobby," he said, looking down at the gas cap on his bike. "Long time no see."

Well, Hell.

I did a double take and tried to imagine this ghost rider type without the leather and the hair.

"Chad?"

"Chick, man. Everybody calls me Chick these days," Chad Fairchild said with a scowl. "Look around, slowly. If you see anybody watching us, tell me."

"Do you know what you look like, Ch . . . ick?" I asked. "*Everybody* here is watching you."

"Yeah," he said softly, looking straight ahead as he slowly unzipped his jacket. "I get that a lot. Don't look at me. The heat'll die off in a few minutes. I'm going across and order a burger. If the cops don't arrive within ten minutes we'll assume that these good citizens have decided I'm not here to rape their daughters at knifepoint. Then I'll sit here and eat my lunch while we talk, OK? And . . . thanks for coming." There was a hint of a smile as the corner of his mustache lifted a bit. "Just play along. These days I never know who's watching me." He reached inside his jacket, pulled out a pack of cigarettes and lit one with a match he scratched to life on the sleeve zipper of his jacket. Throwing the match on the ground he dismounted and walked slowly across the street like he owned it.

Well, that's new, I thought.

"Act as if you're reading something off your cell phone," Chad/ Chick said when he got back with his food. He slung his leg over his ride and sat, balancing a chocolate frappe on the gas tank.

"Only look at me if you can look scared on cue."

"No problem. What the —"

"Hell's going on?" Chad mumbled. He stared off into the woods as if he was casually savoring his food. I realized that I was hungry.

"Yeah, I know," he said, between bites. "The *Reader's Digest* version is that I'm undercover, embedded in a really nasty cartel of thugs who are running guns from Maine to Connecticut, where they're sold under the table to whoever can pay the most."

As instructed I pretended to be reading off my phone. "Terrorists?"

"Some of them, but mostly homegrown thugs who shouldn't have them, for very good reasons. I'm working with the ATF and the Violent Crime Task Force to try to take them out of circulation permanently. We're very close now. You should read something in the papers about it in a week or two."

"Why'd you call me?"

"I'm under strict orders not to contact anyone, not even my superiors in the state police. My lieutenant is the only one who knows where I am."

He took a drink off his frappe. I could just taste it.

"Something's come up that involves the Gore and I'm in so deep that I can't even afford to contact my handlers at this point. I need your help."

"OK?" I said, a little hesitantly.

"You know that fundamentalist cult up in Hogan's Goat?"

"The Love of God Church? Those nut cases who preach at the top of their lungs on the sidewalks in Farmington and drive that white van that says, 'God Hates Queers?'"

"That's them. They're being used as "straw men" by this cartel I'm embedded in. They're being paid to buy guns all over the state with stolen identities and fake ID's. The money they make keeps them afloat. Last year it's estimated they put almost a thousand guns into criminal hands in New England alone."

"Wow," I said.

"I've worked my way up to being their link with the cartel and I've gotten pretty close to one of the younger members of the cult. She doesn't like what they're doing but she can't get away because her parents hardly ever let her out of their sight. She told me that their leader, Reverend Castonguay, got wind that the two women who run Sally's are getting married."

I had all I could do to stay calm and sit still. "I'm presiding at the wedding."

"My source says the church is planning to kidnap one of them and try to convert them through prayer. My contact thinks that they'll kill her if she won't turn."

I fought the urge to turn to look at him. "Do you know which one or when?"

"No, but it'll be before the wedding."

"That's in three weeks!"

Chad finished his burger, crumpled up the cardboard container and threw it over his shoulder. I put that down to maintaining his anti-authority, in-your-face image.

"I know," he said. "My handler at ATF says they may have indictments and arrest warrants soon but that's still iffy. I don't want anybody in the Gore to get hurt but I can't break cover. Can you do something?"

"I guess I'll have to. Can you let me know if you find out when the arrests are going to happen?"

"I'll try but like I said, I'm being watched too. This bunch doesn't trust anybody. They killed one of their own the year before last because they only suspected he was a nark." He tilted his head back and finished his frappe, throwing the cup on the ground as well. "If you get a text saying 'now' it means the warrants have been issued and the whole operation, here and in Connecticut, is about to be raided."

"OK," I said. "Be careful. Can I tell Willie?"

He picked up his gloves and started to put them on. "Not yet. We have to maintain absolute secrecy. If the cartel finds out what I am I'll just disappear without a trace. If my handlers find out I've told you this much, it'll be the end of my career." He stopped and looked into the woods again. "How is she?"

"She thinks you found someone else and have forgotten her."

"I think about her every day, Bobby," he said, shaking his head. "I'll be really glad when this is over."

He started the bike, flipped up the kick stand and gunned the throttle, spraying rocks toward the other cars in the lot as he left

Well. Hell.

#

I spent the whole drive back to the Gore trying to figure out what to do. If I told Marti and Nadine that they were in danger they'd probably just laugh at me and think I was joking. The Love of God Church can be obnoxious and exasperating, but until now nobody has ever considered them as anything more than a bunch of crazy blowhards. On the other hand, if I didn't warn them, it sounded as if there was every possibility that somebody I like very much would suffer, maybe even die.

As I was coming north on Route Four in Phillips, the sound system in the Beast let out a blat that sounded like a ship's whistle. It startled the crap out of me like it always does, and I reminded myself again to look up the instructions on how to stop it doing that. The fancy little screen on my dashboard showed the picture of a red phone and a green one. Under it was the caption "Martha Wallace."

I poked the green phone.

"Hey, Marti. What's up?"

"Hi, Bobby. Is Nadine with you?" she asked, sounding wicked anxious, which isn't like her.

"No, I haven't seen her since yesterday afternoon at the bar. What's the matter?"

She started to cry, which is *really* unlike her. "She didn't show up to open the bar this morning. I can't find her anywhere. She's disappeared!"

Well, Hell.

#

By the time I got to Sally's at three o'clock nearly everybody in town was standing in the parking lot. Mike Hawkins, our game warden, was next to his truck with a topographical map of the area spread out on the hood. He was organizing a grid search of the woods within a mile of us and assigning sectors and people to search them. Willie Brackett recruited me to ride with her patrolling the roads. Everybody was on edge.

I ran up the stairs to Marti's apartment over the bar and spent a few minutes talking to Marti while Mitzi Benson and Boogie Mann fed her tea with gin and tried to keep her from climbing the walls. She told me that it looked like Nadine had gone for an early morning run. When she finished her RFD route around noon Nadine still wasn't back. Nothing was missing except her running gear, her cell phone and the key to the front door that she tucks unto her pocket when she goes out. The phone wasn't responding to Marti's locator app, and she said, sounding panicky, that Nadine *never* shuts it off. I told her we'd find Nadine come hell or high water. She gave me a sad smile, but I don't think my reassurance helped much.

I climbed into the passenger seat of Willie's cruiser, and we started out to patrol the roads, stopping to check anything that looked out of place or suspicious. Marti said that Nadine jogs all over town and doesn't have any habitual route, so Willie decided we should hit as many of the roads as possible before dark. It was early fall, so we had a few hours left.

Mostly we rode in silence, pointing out things to each other along the way that should be investigated. I noted that the folks in the barrel had been reunited. I got really excited when I saw a single sneaker sitting upside down in a ditch but when Willie and I examined it close up it was obvious that it had been there for a long while. I was itching to tell Willie about meeting with Chad.

By five o'clock we had covered every road close to town and had moved over the more outlying roads.

"You know," I said. "I've been thinking. What if somebody *took* Nadine. Kidnapped her?"

"I've been thinking about that too, since I first got the call," Willie said. "I hate to say it, but she *is* very nice looking and there *are* people out there . . ." Her voice trailed off.

"I wonder," I said.

Here goes.

"We know she's gay."

"Yeah," Willie said, giving me a questioning look.

"What if somebody took her because of *that*?"

"What do you mean?"

"That Love of God Church up in Hogan's Goat."

"The wackos? What about them?"

"You know their van. The one that says, 'God Hates Queers' on the side?"

Willie snorted. "That old wreck? Dog Berry gave them a ticket last month for bald tires and no taillights. He said they tried to put a curse on him. They damned him to the lowest reaches of hell. They're a joke." Her voice changed. "But . . ."

She turned the cruiser around and headed north, at which point my cell phone played that bugle call again. I pulled it out of its holster and read "now" on the screen. *That was quick,* I thought.

Well, Hell . . .

"Willie, pull over," I said. "I've got something to tell you."

#

We made a very noisy skidding right turn at the intersection on Main Street in the middle of Rangeley and went flying up the road to Hogan's Goat, which is twenty miles north. "Up in the williwacks," as we say.

"The boss is gonna to hear about that one," Willie said as she steadied the fishtailing cruiser and floored the accelerator again.

Once she had regained her composure after hearing what I had to say, she'd hit the blue lights and siren and called for backup. At several points during the next few minutes I noted that we *were* actually flying, as the road was full of bumps and several "whoop-de-dos" that took us airborne. My stomach was queasy and I was glad I'd tightened my seatbelt. Willie's jaw was set, and her lips were drawn back in a fighting grin as she gripped the wheel. It was a sight to see, let me tell *you*, mister.

Franklin County dispatch advised us that backup was enroute, but the nearest available unit was Willie's father, the chief deputy, who had just been called out from his home in Phillips.

Willie acknowledged through clenched teeth and looked at me.

"I hope you know how to defend yourself."

Just then we met a big white van on a sharp curve. As we passed it I saw "God Hates Queers" painted crudely on the side.

"Willie?"

"I see it," she said as she hit the brakes. *Where'd she ever learn the bootlegger's turn?* I wondered as we spun.

The van was sitting by the side of the road just ahead of us as the cruiser came to a stop behind it.

"You take the passenger side," Willie said as she unclicked her seatbelt. "Holler if you see a weapon."

A weapon?

She picked up the second microphone hanging on the dash and announced on the cruiser's PA. "This is the sheriff's office. Shut off your vehicle and throw the keys out the window." She drew her Glock and stepped onto the pavement, taking cover behind the driver's door. I mimicked her movement on my side.

"Throw the friggin' keys out the friggin' window," she bellowed. I heard a jingle, which I hoped was the keys hitting the ground.

"Driver," Willie shouted. "Open the door and show me your hands."

I heard the door open.

"What the hell?" Willie said.

Nadine stepped out onto the pavement with her hands in the air and smiled at us.

"Looking for me?"

Well, Hell!

Bowing toward us Nadine turned and waved her hand toward the members of the Love of God Church, who were sitting inside the van covered in mud, grass and pine needles. Several sported multiple cuts and bruises. The man in the shotgun seat, whom I recognized as the Reverend Castonguay, leaned over and shouted at Willie, "This woman is the devil incarnate. You must save us from her!"

Nadine, who was clean and tidy, looked at us, grinned and shrugged.

"OK, sir" said Willie. "I will. You're all under arrest."

#

"Since you have entered into this honorable estate of matrimony by mutual promises, by virtue of the authority vested in me by the State of Maine, I now pronounce you legally married."

I turned to Marti, resplendent in the full-dress uniform of the Fire Chief of Skedaddle Gore, Maine, and went off script, "And may God have mercy on your soul." The crowd before me roared with laughter.

Nadine, equally resplendent in her great grandmother's lace-trimmed wedding gown, which, according to her, had been worn by every bride in the Bonaventure family since 1918, slapped the back of my head, which hurt.

I looked at her reproachfully.

"Ouch."

She beamed as any bride should. "Serves you right," she said, with an emphatic nod.

I turned to Marti and said, "You may now, *finally*, kiss your bride."

As the overflow crowd gathered in the parking lot of Sally's Motel and Bar and Live Bait and Convenience Store cheered and threw cardboard bar coasters and confetti in the air, Marti took Nadine's hand, swung her in a circle and bent her backward in a deep dip while planting one square where it belonged. I looked up as the crowd cheered again to see Willie and Chad standing in the back row in their dress uniforms and holding hands.

Well, Hell!

Once Nadine had caught her breath, she and Marti joined hands and walked together beneath an archway of shiny chrome ceremonial fire axes held by members of the Skedaddle Gore Volunteer Fire Department alternating with the members of Nadine's ten-year-old beginners' karate class, wearing immaculate white gis and bowing to their sensei in the wushu salute. Reaching the end of the honor guard, the newlyweds turned to the crowd and Nadine, brushing confetti out of her hair, shouted "Party time!" to another appreciative roar.

As I watched all this foolishness from the platform erected for the ceremony in front of Engine Five, which had been waxed and buffed to within an inch of her life, I caught a slight movement from the edge of the woods. Looking closer I could just see two dark shapes in the shadows. The taller of them raised a hand and waved, before they faded into the forest.

Well, Hell.

Ten: Humbug

Now, I'm about to tell you a story and I want you to just sit there, shut up and listen. I haven't ever told this to anybody else and I guarantee that at some point in the next few minutes you're going to look at me with a raised eyebrow and say something along the lines of "You are as full of crap as a Christmas goose," if I don't tell you not to in advance. Tell you what. *If* you still feel that way when I'm done, you can say whatever you want. Just hold onto your tongue for a bit, OK?

OK. You know that old movie where this sweet little girl and her father are looking at the Christmas tree there at the end and she says: "Every time a bell rings, an angel gets his wings?" Well, that's *bull*. How do I know that? Because an angel told me so.

Don't say it! Just bear with me, OK?

OK. I really used to love Christmas as a kid. Grampy and Grammy Mac used to have us up for the day in Bangor. They'd stuff me with cookies and pie and candy until I could pop. And all those presents . . .

Twenty years ago, on Christmas Eve, my wife Pam got hit broadside by a drunk driver on the way to pick up our daughter C.J. after her Girl Scout Christmas Party. She died instantly. The ship's chaplain broke the news to me while we were sitting in the Persian Gulf doing anti-aircraft radar picket duty in the build up to Operation Desert Fox. Ever since then I almost always get grumpier than hell around Christmas time.

Around Thanksgiving I start pushing people away and spend most of my days in December sulking in front of the TV with a twelve pack of beer when I'm not freezing my tail off working up at the summit on The Mountain. Can you blame me? Hell, I'm a retired old fart widower with greying hair, an aching back and a daughter who lives almost a whole continent away. She calls me twice a year to complain about how bad her husband—or fiancé of the moment—treats her. It's been years since anything female has really given me the look—and don't think I haven't *tried,* mister. I live in a ratty old hunting camp halfway up the side of a mountain in western Maine. Hell, the winter wind around here blows a gale almost every day and it's so cold that the birds who forgot to fly south in the fall try to commit suicide by knocking at my cabin door and throwing themselves down in front of Lummox, my ancient Maine Coon cat. That fat old hair bag is so lazy that he just looks at them and yawns. Then I have to scoop them up and put them in the old birdcage that Filthy Phillips, my old Coast Guard buddy who left me the place in his will, left up in the rafters. I set the cage next to the stove and give them a little water and birdseed. Usually within an hour or so they think better of the idea, and I take them back outside and let them go. It's a friggin' miserable lonely way to live.

Anyway, late last Christmas Eve, in a wicked snowstorm, I was out in The Beast plowing out a bunch of my neighbors' dooryards. I was feeling like crap as usual and not paying a lot of attention when I came up behind an old woman walking, or actually staggering, down the middle of the Ridge Road. I jammed on the brakes, swore under my breath and got out of the truck to check on her. I figured she was probably just drunk, which was something I could relate to. I thought that maybe I could take her home to her family, or wherever, because it was colder than a well digger's patoot that night.

When I got close enough to get a good look at her, though, I wasn't so sure that if I *did* take her to wherever it was that she belonged, they'd even let her in. She was, without a doubt, the filthiest, ugliest female I've ever seen, and in my life I've seen more than my share, let me tell you. Her face was blue, she smelled like a pigsty, even out there in the wind, and she looked to be a hundred years old if she was a day. She was dressed in an old-timey-looking long black dress that didn't look like it would keep anybody warm in mid-summer, least of all that night. She had an old black bonnet covering her hair, which was white and looked like she probably hadn't washed it since last spring. That was all she was wearing, I swear. No coat and no boots. Not even shoes that I could see under that dress with the hem dragging through the snow.

"OK, mister," she peered at me and croaked. "How 'bout you just tell me your whole damn miserable life story so we can get this over with before midnight. I'll probably turn into a damn pumpkin this time around, or maybe, the way my luck's been going lately, a friggin' sasquatch."

"What?" I said, dumbfounded.

"You heard me, numbskull." She gestured back toward The Beast. "At least you've got something decent looking to do this in. Come on. Let's get you out of this weather."

She clumped back to my truck, yanked open the door, hiked up her skirt and hopped easily into the passenger seat. Her feet were bare. Judas!

I stood there like I was frozen, the snow collecting on the brim of my old Red Sox ball cap, until my ears began to sting in the cold.

"Come on, dumbass," she hollered from inside. "Get us out of the middle of the friggin' road! Shorty Devereaux's back around the corner headed this way in the town plow. If you don't move out of the way, he'll wing the both of us off into the puckerbrush. Then where will you be? I can do a lot of stuff, but I can't save you from the likes of that. Close your mouth and get in."

I was honestly at a total loss for words, which, as you likely know by now, doesn't happen very often. Closing my mouth, which was indeed hanging open like a barn door, I did what she said. Staring at her from the driver's seat, I hit the button to raise my plow, pulled the transmission into drive and eased out into the worsening storm.

"Pull over up ahead there in the Nixons' driveway until Shorty gets by," she said in a voice that sounded like she knew what she was doing. Then she snorted. "You know, I got assigned a guy named Nixon one year back along." I looked at her. "Yeah, that one. Let me tell you it was really hard to come up with a reason for him to go on living, but I did. Did you know that he was a sucker for puppy dogs? I just plunked a Cocker Spaniel in his lap, and he climbed down off the White House roof just like that. Died in his bed some years later, he did."

"Who *are* you?" I managed to say.

"I'm Sarah. Sarah Good. I'm an angel. Actually, a Seraph, First Class."

"*A WHAT*?" I jerked the wheel in surprise and we skidded a bit.

"An angel," she repeated. "A snow-white-winged, bugle-blaring friggin' messenger from the heavens; sent by the Almighty to save your body and soul, set your mind on the right path and help you find eternal redemption. Or at least that's what it says in the recruiting brochure that idiot King Jamie published a few centuries back."

"Well. Hell." I said, very slowly and softly, to myself.

She snorted. "Not even close."

I pulled into Percy Nixon's driveway, put the transmission in park and just sat there. It took a minute to sink in. I must have fallen asleep at the wheel, I reasoned.

Maybe I'm dead, I thought. *Sweet Jesus, I hope I didn't kill anybody else.*

"No, you're not," she said, with a cackle that I hoped was an excuse for a laugh.

"Not what?"

"Asleep, or dead, you useless fool," she said. "And you haven't killed anybody. Except for Jose Hernandez, that guy you machine gunned, of course. You really never needed to lose any sleep over that, you know. He deserved it. He was diddling his eight-year-old daughter when he wasn't running dope. He went . . . elsewhere, shall we say, when you were done with him."

As I watched her talking, her face seemed to fill in and soften somehow. I realized that she looked a little younger and healthier. Her skin wasn't blue anymore, either.

I shook my head and stared. "How did you know that?" I choked out. "I didn't even tell Pam about that."

"Pam? Your wife? Oh, she knows . . . now. We play Mahjongg together on Wednesdays. She's doing very well, you know. She speaks highly of you. Working on her second-class stripes, she is. In another hundred or so of your years, she'll be a first class, like me."

She looked at me then and smiled for the first time. Suddenly the inside of my truck smelled a lot better, sort of like the butterscotch pudding Grammie Mac used to make us for dessert at Christmas. Somehow, the lump I carry around in my chest felt a little lighter too. Weird.

"Sooo, you're dead?"

"Oh, yeah," she said, laughing. I swear I could faintly hear little bells ringing in the background. "A bit over three hundred years dead, actually. You remember the witch trials down in Salem, Massachusetts around 1692?"

"They taught us about that in school."

"Yeah, I've read those stories. Most of them are complete B.S.," she said. "They say the winners write the history books, right? Well, those so-called upstanding Puritan elders won the day back then, but most of them need asbestos overshoes now." She giggled. "They accused me of bewitching some little girls in town, causing them to pitch fits and the like. I mean . . . really?

"Truth be told, they didn't like me because I was poor and plain and couldn't afford to dress up and give buckets of money to their friggin' church. That idiot husband I had wouldn't stand up for me at the trial either, so, after my baby died while I was waiting for the hangman, I finally just let 'em have it. Right there under the friggin' tree at the end of July. I told them all exactly what I thought of the whole business, and them. They hung me then, and four others."

"Wow," I said. I didn't know what else to say.

She looked out the window at the snow, which was letting up a bit. "If I'd known then what I was in for I'd have just pled guilty and gone straight to Hell. I was (she actually made those air quote things with her fingers) 'saved,' though. At least that was what those 'men of God' thought they were doing. They put a noose around my neck while I was telling them off. When I stopped for breath they dragged me up on a rope thrown over a branch of that crooked old tree and watched me strangle." She snorted again and turned toward me. "Do you know what happens to the 'saved?'"

"No, I guess not. I don't go to church much."

"Doesn't matter. Most of them churches don't have a clue. The 'saved' go to a place that looks like a big-assed corporate headquarters, get assigned a cubicle and get stuck in it, just like me," she said, ruefully. "Stuck in a rut, spinning your wheels for all eternity. Time goes by so fast there you hardly notice it after a while. Every Christmas Eve that comes along though, we, the 'good guys,' get plunked down somewhere random, usually on Earth because that's the place with the biggest proportion of idiots per capita in the universe, and we have to talk some poor bastard out of committing suicide. I remember one time I wound up on top of a bridge dressed like a little old man. I did the best I could, but the idiot jumped anyway after talking to me for only five minutes. Sometimes, despite all your good intentions, it just *doesn't* work out."

"But I'm not even thinking about . . . I don't believe . . ."

She hitched around in the seat and looked me right in the eye. "Just because you don't believe something doesn't always mean it isn't true."

"OK. listen." I said. "I'll admit I *can* be grumpy. I *do* drink a bit and I have a few PTSD problems and I *do* get down in the mouth when it starts getting dark early, but I have never—"

"Oh, for Christ's sake, Bobby Wing! Who the hell do you think you're talking to?" She pointed a gnarly looking finger and glared at me. "Wake up and smell the B.S. you're slinging around. Look at yourself. You spend your days drinking beer and moping around feeling sorry for yourself. All because you think you haven't done anything 'good' with your life.

"I got news for you, Bud. Compared to most of the people *I* meet, you got nothing to bitch about." Her voice and her eyes softened. "You're a *good* guy, Bobby. Believe me, I know." Her voice dropped off and she smiled. "*And* you're actually one of the lucky ones. You've got a good roof over your head, plenty to eat, a clean place to sleep and a bunch of mostly good people who love you, when you let them. Dammit, you've even got a jeezley cat who loves the crap out of you, despite thinking you're too stupid to live." She paused and sighed. "I wish I still did." She shook her head.

"Listen, I will give you a big, fat, cast-iron, lifetime guarantee that *that* is all you really need to be happy." She shifted around to look out the windshield, where the snow had almost stopped falling. "*That* . . . and Angie Gilchrist."

"What?" I think my heart stopped for an instant. "Are you sure?"

"Hey, remember? I'm an angel. I'm ethereal, omniscient and omnipotent . . . well, almost." She shrugged, then slapped her hand down hard on the Beast's dashboard and pointed that finger at me again. "I will bet you a whole set of *free* harp lessons when the time comes that if you show up later this morning at the Chicken House, you'll get dinner and a kiss. OK?"

"Yeah, but—" I stammered.

"And tell Doc Jeffries the *whole* story for once. He can help you."

"But—"

"And call your daughter in Oregon, she *really* needs to talk to her dad right now."

My eyesight dimmed and I started to tear up. "But—"

"No more buts. Just *do* it!"

I caved. "OK. I will."

I felt a tear run down my cheek. I hadn't cried since April McLain went off and left me in high school. Hell, I hadn't even cried on the C130 transport back from Desert Fox on compassionate leave.

I looked over again, but the passenger seat was empty. I sat there alone in The Beast in the Nixons' dooryard and cried for twenty solid minutes. Bawled my eyes out. I'm not ashamed to admit it. I felt better afterward, happier than I had in years.

#

I had the best chicken and dumplings I ever tasted for Christmas dinner. Then the whole Community of Satin and I stood around the tree and sang carols, in perfect four-part harmony. I loved it. Afterward we watched some football and laughed a lot at how badly the Christmas Day game is always played. You have to sympathize with the players though. I mean, who really wants to work on Christmas?

At halftime I begged off because the west coast is three hours behind us, and I had a phone call that I wanted to make before it got dark. Angie took my hand in hers and squeezed it, then said she'd walk me out to The Beast. When we got there she pulled me to her without a word and kissed me like she *really* meant it.

OK. *Now* you can tell me I'm full of it.

No?

Well, Hell . . .

#

I woke up slowly, realizing groggily that something was different, but I couldn't quite put my finger on it. I opened my eyes a bit reluctantly to see that the sun was already shining into my bedroom through the picture window out in the living room. It was spring, I remembered, my favorite time of the year. The trees were just starting to bud out and I'd have to break out the lawn mower soon. I was relaxed and happy about that.

That must be what's different, I thought. *I feel happy.*

Lummox jumped off the foot of the bed as I reached to pull the covers away. I realized that I was hanging half off the side of the bed, which struck me as odd. Then something shifted in the bed next to me that was a lot bigger than Lummox. I turned my head to the left and found myself looking into a pair of gorgeous gold-flecked hazel eyes set below a tousled crown of curly light brown hair.

"Hey, sleepyhead," Angie said with a big, beautiful smile. "I was wondering when you'd finally come to." She cocked her head. "You'd better not fall asleep on me again, eh? That would make me wonder if I've forgotten *all* my skills."

"Hey, yourself," I said as she reached for me under the covers.

Well, Hell, I thought. *I'm going to need a bigger bed.*

Local Reaction

"I want it known that I voted against signing that damned blanket release." – Rhonda "Pinky" Pickens, Third Assessor, Skedaddle Gore, ME

"Don't read this, it's fake news!" – Norman Wrinklestat, Franklin County (ME) Commissioner

"He was such a nice, smart boy in school. It's sad that he never lived up to his potential." – Margaret Applebee, Thomaston, ME (Retired junior high school teacher)

"Total Horses**t! Don't waste your (expletive deleted) money!"- Anonymous threat (edited)

"I laughed myself sick! Really!!" – Eimon "Doc" Jeffries, MD, Rangeley, ME

"Where does he come up with this stuff?" - Aloysius Tiberius "Snort" Benson, Skedaddle Gore, ME

"Huh? Bobby wrote a *book*?" – Stewart "Fly" Fleance, Skedaddle Gore, ME

Glossary

It has occurred to me that there may be some who choose to read this *work of fiction* who are from away and/or not familiar with the vernacular often used in the beautiful mountainous region of northwestern Maine. The following is a list of word definitions and common expressions compiled to assist in following Bobby's ramblings. It is presented in no particular order.

Note – any grammatical errors, especially parts of speech, are attributable to the fact that I was unable to pay complete attention to Ms. Blanche Applebee in seventh grade because I was distracted by puberty and the cute girl assigned to sit in front of me. (By the way, whatever happened to you, Janet?)

Legend:

Frequency of use – {vc}=very common {c}=common {unc}=uncommon {r}= rare

Social consideration – [p]=polite [v]=vulgar

Smartass – (noun){c}[v] an intelligent person with an ass

Dumbass – (noun){c}[v] a stupid person with an ass

Wiseass – (noun){c}[v] (even a dumbass could figure *this* one out)

Numb – (adj){vc}[p] stupid, example: a driver who leaves his right blinker flashing for five miles without turning

Numbskull – (noun){c}{p] add five miles to the above

Blockhead – (noun){c}[p] numbskull who then turns left in front of a school bus

Blinker(ah) – (noun){vc}[p] turn signal

Some – (adj){c}[p] indicates intensification, as in "That pie was *some* good."

Mister – (adj){c}[p] supplemental intensification, as in "That pie was *some* good, mister.

Mister man – (adj){c}[p] supreme intensification, as in "That pie was *some* good, mister man."

Mister manny – (adj){unc}[p] (Excuse me, I need some of that pie, *right now!!*)

Chummy (adj){unc}[p] see "mister," more commonly used by flatlanders

Frig – (verb){vc}[v] semi-polite substitution for the vulgar and archaic Anglo-Saxon verb naming an action between two individuals which sometimes induces procreation, either intentional or accidental, often used to get away with swearing in front of Mother

Frig it – expression meaning, well, you know . . .

Friggin' – (adj){c}[p] slightly more intense than "some" but less than "mister" as in, "You friggin' numbskull!"

Frickin' – (adj){c}[p] milder, more socially acceptable form of "friggin'" Acceptable form of swearing in front of Grandma

Blat – (noun){c}[p] loud noise, shout or scream

Dooryard – (noun){vc}[p] the space between your front door and your mailbox where you leave your junk.

Junk – (noun){vc}[p] anything not currently in use, broken down or for sale. May not actually belong to you, also – {vc}[p] chunk, as in "a junk of firewood," also – {c}[v] the body parts used to frig, which are *not* normally left in your dooryard

Backyard – (noun){vc}[p] the space behind your house where you leave the junk you don't want anymore

Dump – (noun){vc}[p] the place where you take your junk when you run out of room in the backyard, may or may not be officially run by a municipality

Dump Guy – (noun){vc}[p] archaic name for a Solid Waste/ Recycling Technician, may be female these days

Hard tellin' not knowin' - {c}[p] expression meaning "I don't know," usually accompanied by a shrug – see also "damfino"

Damfino – {c}[v] expression meaning "Damned if I know."

Dite – (adj){c}[p] tiny amount; as in "Unfortunately he turned out a dite numb, like his father."

Culcha – (noun){c}[p] culture, habitual way of doing things

Frappe – (noun){c}[p] (pronounced "frap") a cold drink usually made in a high-speed mixer comprising milk, flavored sweet syrup and ice cream. Primary usage limited to New England.

Milkshake – (noun){unc}[p] same as frappe without ice cream, also – what a frappe is called outside New England.

Out straight – {c}[p] expression meaning "I'm busy"

Right out straight – {c}[p] expression meaning "I'm very busy. Go away."

Old Timer(ah) – (noun){c}[p] senior citizen

Old Fart – (noun){c}[p] bad tempered senior citizen

Stove up – (adj){c}[p] broken, possibly destroyed; as in "He stove up his cah."

For fair – (adv){unc}[p] completely or totally; as in "He stove up his cah for fair."

Cah – (noun){vc}[p] automobile or {c} pickup truck

Greasy – (adj){c}[p] slippery

Crispy – (adj){c}[p] outside temperature below 0 degrees Celsius

Frosty – (adj){c}[p] outside temperature below 0 degrees Fahrenheit

Honkin' – (adj){c}[p] indicates intensive augmentation, similar to "friggin'" above, as in "That's a big honkin' patoot."

Patoot – (noun){c}[p] set of buttocks

Butt – (noun){c}[v] see "patoot"

Gawmey – (adj){unc}[p] clumsy

Feather(ah) white – pale faced, usually as the result of surprise or fear

Down sullah – (noun){c}[p] (if so equipped) the floor of a house or cabin which is in contact with the earth under it, often actually *is* the earth

Story – (noun){c}[p] floor in a house, as in "He built an indoor bathroom on his second story."

Shack – (noun){c}[p] crudely built structure intended as emergency shelter from the elements if banned from home by Mother. May also house family dog.

Cabin – (noun){c}[p] small one-story dwelling

House – (noun){c}[p] the place where you live, may be a cabin and may or may not be home.

Home – (noun){c}[p] the place where Mother lives

Camp – (noun){c}[p] the place used to live in when away hunting, fishing or tending one's trapline

Trapline – (noun){c}[v] string of girlfriends' cabins

Mother(ah) – (noun){vc}[p] the woman who gave birth to you, or – {c}[p] the woman you live with

Finest kind – (adj){r}[p] expression meaning "the best" (note) – controversial, primarily used by people from away when they want to sound like a stern man, i.e., nobody northwest of Belfast actually says this

Stern man – (noun){r}[p] employee who does all the work on a lobstah boat

Lobstah boat – (noun) {r}[p] extremely smelly coastal vessel normally engaged in fishing for overgrown nautical cockroaches

Bookin' it – (verb){c}[p] proceeding very rapidly, often without direction

Pisser(ah) – (adj){c}[v] very good

Cunnin' – (adj){c}[p] pretty or cute, normally used to politely describe somebody else's baby or significant other, even if they're not

Flatlander(ah) – (noun){c}[p] anyone born, or currently residing, less than 150 feet above sea level, also – (noun){c}[p] most people living east of Augusta or south of Auburn

Masshole – (noun){c}[v] resident of the State of Massachusetts

Away – (noun){vc}[p] not here

From away – (noun){c}[p] not born in the municipality in which you are currently standing

Native – (noun){c}[p] born in the municipality in which you are currently standing

Ayuh –{r}[v] expression of agreement, (note) – controversial, rarely actually used by Maine mountain people unless one is trying to impress a piece from away, generally considered really numb by natives

A piece – (noun){c}[p] a short distance, or {c}[v] an attractive female not related to you

BMW – (noun){c}[p] large native female, stands for "Big Maine Woman," also – (noun){r}[p] a pretentious foreign automobile not normally driven by a native unless it's stolen

Beater(ah) – (noun){vc}[p] older vehicle used primarily for casual or winter driving, often unregistered and uninspectable, occasionally stolen

By the Jesus – {c}[v] expression meaning "I am *seriously* serious about this."

Chaage – (noun){c}[p] a fairly good-sized amount, usually referring to firewood, or – {c}[v] expression used upon seeing a piece for the first time

Yessah – {c}[p] expression meaning "I agree"

Christly – (adj){c}[v] very disagreeable, as in "My christly boss ordered me to stay after work."

Jeezley – (adj){vc}[v] same as above, only more so.

Daoouh – {vc}[p] expression used to emphatically express the negative, roughly translated as: "*No*, gosh darn it!"

Huffy – (adv){c}[p] angry, as in "Don't get huffy with *me*, chummy."

Wrathy – (adv){r}[p] see "huffy"

Whatever(ah) – {vc}[p] expression of ambivalence or indifference, often used when a person you have lived with for longer than six months requests "a little"

A little – (noun){vc}[v] (use your imagination)

Williwacks – (noun){c}[p] puckerbrush beside the road, or {c}[p] *waay* out in the woods

Williwags – alternate spelling of above

Puckerbrush – (noun){c}[p] (Hey, numbskull, do I have to explain *everything* to you?)

Wicked – (adj){c}[p] very, see also "some," (note) – controversial, has been co-opted by hoity toity writers from away to imply that the speaker is a "hick from the sticks." Nevertheless the word has persisted in the vernacular

Hoity Toity – (adj){c}[p] stupidly self-important or self-righteous, snobbish or pretentious

About the Author

Sanford Emerson is a native Maine-iac and "boomer" who came of age in the 1960s and still remembers most of it. He is a graduate of Bates College in Lewiston, Maine, mostly through the efforts of his college sweetheart, who he credits with inducing him to actually study by using subtle hints and tempting promises. Two weeks after graduation they were married, even though she *was* "from away." Returning to the real world, Sandy did a stretch in the Navy followed by a thirty-five-year law enforcement career in the mountains of western Maine, during which he wrote mostly non-fiction in the form of police reports, pre-sentence investigations and proposals to his superiors for improvements to the profession which went mostly nowhere. During this period he was privileged to gain some insight into the process, frustration and angst of professional fiction writing through osmosis by watching his sweetheart, Kathy Lynn Emerson, write over sixty books in several genres and under several names.

These days Sandy lives in Wilton, Maine on a former Christmas tree farm with his lovely and talented wife and a slightly psychotic cat who thinks he is a real numbskull. Oh, and he also runs a woodworking business in his spare time, but then nearly every retiree in Maine does that.

sanfordemerson@roadrunner.com

If you have enjoyed this book, please consider leaving a short review at the website where you first found it. As Sanford Emerson does not actively market or promote his writing, it stands or falls entirely by the readers' opinions of it. Thank you.

Lightning Source UK Ltd.
Milton Keynes UK
UKHW041542250223
417655UK00001B/60